POUL ANDERSON

"The shock at the end, after the action, when you suddenly realize that you've been cheering the wrong side, or the weaklings aren't, or some basic law has been ignored ... the color, smell, taste of an alien world, a nonhuman society, a globular cluster or the universe seen from the very edge of lightspeed ... these things Poul shows better than anyone."

—Larry Niven

"Everybody 'knows' that Poul Anderson is one of the best: they're wrong—<u>he's better</u>!"

—J.E. Pournelle

Other Poul Anderson titles published or soon to be published by TOR:

THE PSYCHOTECHNIC LEAGUE
   Volume 1 of the first book publication of the other major
   series by the author of Dominic Flandry and the
   Polesotechnic League

FANTASY
   It begins with the introduction of Leonardo to Einstein—and
   goes on from there!

THE GUARDIANS OF TIME
   The classic Time Patrol story—an example *par excellence*.

COLD VICTORY
   Book II of the Psychotechnic League.

STARSHIP
   Book III of the Psychotechnic League.

CONFLICT
   After First Contact came—CONFLICT!

MAURI AND KITH
   After Armageddon the Sea People reconstruct a more hu-
   mane and organic kind of high-tech civilization . . . or is it?

POUL ANDERSON

Starship

With a Foreward and
interstitial material by
Sandra Miesel

TOR

A TOM DOHERTY ASSOCIATES BOOK

Copyright © 1982 by Poul Anderson

A TOR Book

First printing, June 1982

ISBN: 523-48533-6

Cover art by: Vincent DiFate

Acknowledgements: The stories contained herein were first published and copyrighted as follows: "The Pirate," *Analog*, © 1968 by Conde Nast Corporation "Virgin Planet," *Venture*, © 1957 by Mercury Press, Inc. "Teucan," *Cosmos Science Fiction and Fantasy*, © 1954 by Star Publications, Inc. "The Chapter Ends," *Dynamic Science Fiction*, © 1953 by Columbia Publications, Inc. "Star Ship," *Planet Stories*, © 1950 by Love Romances Publishing Co. "Gypsy," Astounding, © 1950 by Street and Smith, Inc.

Printed in the United States of America
Distributed by Pinnacle Books, Inc.

Pinnacle Books, Inc.
1430 Broadway
New York, New York 10018

Starship

POUL ANDERSON

CONTENTS

Foreward

With the development of a faster-than-light hyperdrive in 2784, the eight century-long saga of Earthlings in space entered a bold new phase. Previously, slower-than-light craft had crept from star to star, each journey requiring decades, even generations, of travel to complete. But now at last, the whole galaxy lay open to our kind.

Yamatsu's classic history *Starward!* may be consulted for details but let us pause here to commend those twentieth century pioneers who first pierced our homeworld's sky. Achieving spaceflight has been called "a tragic era's proudest boast." That our remote ancestors, crushed by three world wars, could still spare enough energy from vital reclamation projects to launch spaceships demonstrates the resilience of the human spirit.

Moreover, space research was the one great twentieth century innovation that kept its initial promise. Neither the preliminary form of global government established in 1965 nor any succeeding regime was able to guarantee peace and justice. Psychodynamics, the ambitious science by which humanity sought to remake itself, not only failed to attain this goal, its techniques were grossly misused by the Psychotechnic Institute. From age to age, our species has remained indomitable but imperfectible.

Naturally, the pace of extraterrestrial expansion slowed or quickened in response to overall social trends. As our previous volumes, *The Psychotechnic League* and *Cold Victory*, have shown, that first idealistic surge of colonization gave way to frustration and then to conflict. In the twenty-second century, anti-scientific Humanism challenged the pro-scientific Values of the New Enlightenment, only to be supressed in its turn following the bloody Revolt of 2170. Afterwards, a precarious balance among factions was maintained well into the twenty-third century.

Given the chronic material and spiritual malaise afflicting the Solar Union, is it any wonder that the stars came to have the same frontier significance that the New World once had for the weary peoples of the Old. Both visionaries and malcontents sought an absolutely fresh start under some other sun. Indeed, the launch of the first Centauri-bound craft in 2126 was as much an experiment in sociodynamics as in astronautics.

Although starflight could not avert that systemwide plunge into ruin known as the Second Dark Ages, it gave the forces of renewal a potent rallying symbol. Just as in the aftermath of World War III, dire sacrifices were made to get Earthlings spaceborne again.

By the twenty-seventh century, improved STL ships ranged the stars once more. Stellar colonies again took root and seeded other colonies in their turn. Some of the communities thus planted grew in curious patterns far removed from the original norm of Solar civilization. The hyperdrive breakthrough meant an end to colonial isolation as well as quicker dispersal of new settlers.

Enthusiastic emigrants did not immediately recognize that transit time and distance scales made their cherished transatlantic analogy imperfect. Whether achieved slower or faster than lightspeed, the very process of interstellar travel itself would change the travellers.

GYPSY

From afar, I caught a glimpse of the *Traveler* as my boat swung toward the planet. The great spaceship looked like a toy at that distance, a frail bubble of metal and air and energy against the enormous background of space. I thought of the machines within her, humming and whirring and clicking very faintly as they pursued their unending round of services, making that long hull into a living world—the hull that was now empty of life—and I had a sudden odd feeling of sympathy. As if she were alive, I felt that the *Traveler* was lonely.

The planet swelled before me, a shining blue shield blazoned with clouds and continents, rolling against a limitless dark and the bitterly burning stars. Harbor, we had named that world, the harbor at the end of our long journey, and there were few lovelier names. Harbor, haven, rest and peace and a sky overhead as roof against the naked blaze of space. It was good to get home.

I searched the heavens for another glimpse of the *Traveler*, but I couldn't find her tiny form in that thronging wilderness of stars. No matter, she was still on her orbit about Harbor, moored to the planet, perhaps forever. I concentrated on bringing the spaceboat down.

Atmosphere whistled about the hull. After a month in the gloom and poisonous cold of the fifth planet, alone among utterly unhuman natives, I was usually on fire to get home and brought my craft down with a recklessness that overloaded the gravity beams. But this time I went a little more carefully, telling myself that I'd rather be late for supper than never arrive at all. Or perhaps it was that brief chance vision of the *Traveler* which made me suddenly thoughtful. After all, we had had some good times aboard her.

I sent the boat slanting toward the peninsula in the north temperate zone on which most of us were settled. The outraged air screamed behind me as I slammed down on the hard-packed earth that served us for a landing field. There were a few warehouses and service shops around it, long low buildings of the heavy timbers used by most of the colonists, and a couple of private homes a kilometer or so away. But otherwise only long grass rustled in the wind, gardens and wild groves, sunlight streaming out of a high blue sky. When I stepped from the boat, the fresh vivid scent of the land fairly leaped to meet me. I could hear the sea growling beyond the horizon.

Tokogama was on duty at the field. He was sitting on the porch of the office, smoking his pipe and watching the clouds sail by overhead, but he greeted me with the undemonstrative cordiality of old friends who know each other too well to need many words.

"So that's the portmaster," I said. "Soft touch. All you have to do is puff that vile-smelling thing and say hello to me."

"That's all," he admitted cheerfully. "I am retained only for my uncommonly high ornamental value."

It was, approximately, true. Our aircraft used the field with no formality, and we only kept this one space vessel in operation. The portmaster was on hand simply to oversee servicing and in the unlikely case of some emergency or dispute. But none of the colony's few public posts—captain, communications officer, and the rest—required much effort in as simple a society as ours, and they were filled as spare-time occupations by anyone who wanted them. There was no compensation except getting first turn at using the machinery for farming or heavy construction which we owned in common.

"How was the trip?" asked Tokogama.

"Pretty good," I said. "I gave them our machines and they filled my holds with their ores and alloys. And I managed to take a few more notes on their habits, and establish a few more code symbols for communication."

"Which is a very notable brick added to the walls of science, but in view of the fact that you're the only one who ever goes there it really makes no odds." Tokogama's dark eyes regarded me curiously. "Why do you keep on making those trips out there, Erling? Quite a few of the other boys wouldn't mind visiting Five once in a while. Will and Ivan both mentioned it to me last week."

"I'm no hog," I said. "If either of them, or anyone else, wants a turn at the trading job, let 'em learn space piloting and they can go. But meanwhile—I like the work. You know that. I was one of those who voted to continue the search for Earth."

Tokogama nodded. "So you were. But that was

three years ago. Even you must have grown some roots here."

"Oh, I have," I laughed. "Which reminds me I'm hungry, and judging by the sun it's the local dinner time. So I'll get on home, if Alanna knows I'm back."

"She can't help it," he smiled. "The whole continent knows when you're back, the way you rip the atmosphere coming in. That home cooking must have a powerful magnetic attraction."

"A steak aroma of about fifty thousand gauss—" I turned to go, calling over my shoulder: "Why don't you come to dinner tomorrow evening? I'll invite the other boys and we'll have an old-fashioned hot air session."

"I was sort of hinting in that direction," said Tokogama.

I got my carplane out of the hangar and took off with a whisper of air and a hum of grav-beam generators. But I flew low over the woods and meadows, dawdling along at fifty kilometers an hour and looking across the landscape. It lay quietly in the evening, almost empty of man, a green fair breadth of land veined with bright rivers. The westering sun touched each leaf and grass blade with molten gold, an aureate glow which seemed to fill the cool air like a tangible presence, and I could hear the chirp and chatter of the great bird flocks as they settled down in the trees. Yes—it was good to get home.

My own house stood at the very edge of the sea, on a sandy bluff sloping down to the water. The windy trees which grew about it almost hid the little stone and timber structure, but its lawns and gardens reached far, and beyond them were the fields from which we got our food. Down by the beach stood the boathouse and the little dock I had made, and I knew our sailboat lay waiting there for me to take her out. I felt an almost physical hunger for the sea again, the mighty surge of waves out to the wild horizon, the keen salt wind and the crying white birds. After a month in the sterile tanked air of the spaceboat, it was like being born again.

I set the plane down before the house and got out. Two small bodies fairly exploded against me—Einar and Mike. I walked into the house with my sons riding my shoulders.

Alanna stood in the doorway waiting for me. She was tall, almost as tall as I, and slim and red-haired and the most beautiful woman in the universe. We didn't say much—it was unnecessary, and we were otherwise occupied for the next few minutes.

And afterward I sat before a leaping fire where the little flames danced and chuckled and cast a wavering ruddy glow over the room, and the wind whistled outside and rattled the door, and the sea roared on the nighted beach, and I told them of my fabulous space voyage, which had been hard and monotonous and lonely but was a glamorous adventure at home. The boys' eyes never stirred from my face as I talked, I could feel the eagerness that blazed from them. The gaunt sun-seared crags of One, the misty jungles of Two, the mountains and deserts of Four, the great civilization of Five, the bitter desolation of the outer worlds—and beyond those the stars. But we were home now, we sat in a warm dry house and heard the wind singing outside.

I was happy, in a quiet way that had somehow lost the exuberance of my earlier returns. Content, maybe.

Oh, well, I thought. These trips to the fifth world

were becoming routine, just as life on Harbor, now that our colony was established and our automatic and semiautomatic machines running smoothly, had quieted down from the first great riot of work and danger and work again. That was progress, that was what we had striven for, to remove want and woe and the knife-edged uncertainty which had haunted our days. We had arrived, we had graduated into a solid assurance and a comfort which still held enough unsureness and challenge to keep us from getting sluggish. Grown men don't risk their necks climbing the uppermost branches of trees, the way children do; they walk on the ground, and when they have to rise they do so safely and comfortably, in a carplane.

"What's the matter, Erling?" asked Alanna.

"Why—nothing." I started out of my reverie, suddenly aware that the children were in bed and the night near its middle. "Nothing at all. I was just sitting thinking. A little tired, I guess. Let's turn in."

"You're a poor liar, Erling," she said softly. "What were you really thinking about?"

"Nothing," I insisted. "That is, well, I saw the old *Traveler* as I was coming down today. It just put me in mind of old times."

"It would," she said. And suddenly she sighed. I looked at her in some alarm, but she was smiling again. "You're right, it is late, and we'd better go to bed."

I took the boys out in the sailboat the next day. Alanna stayed home on the excuse that she had to prepare dinner, though I knew of her theory that the proper psychodevelopment of children required a balance of paternal and maternal influence. Since I was away so much of the time, out in

space or with one of the exploring parties which
were slowly mapping our planet, she made me oc-
cupy the center of the screen whenever I was
home.

Einar, who was nine years old and getting interested in the microbooks we had from the
Traveler—and so, ultimately, from Earth—looked
at her and said: "Back at Sol you wouldn't have
to make food, Mother. You'd just set the au . . .
autochef, and come out with us."

"I like to cook," she smiled. "I suppose we could
make autochefs, now that the more important
semirobot machinery has been produced, but it'd
take a lot of fun out of life for me."

Her eyes went past the house, down to the beach
and out over the restless sun-sparked water. The
sea breeze ruffled her red hair, it was like a flame
in the cool shade of the trees. "I think they must
miss a lot in the Solar System," she said. "They
have so much there that, somehow, they can't have
what we've got—room to move about, lands that
never saw a man before, the fun of making something ourselves."

"You might like it if you went there," I said.
"After all, sweetheart, however wisely we may talk
about Sol we know it only by hearsay."

"I know I like what we have here," she answered. I thought there was a faint note of defi-
ance in her voice. "If Sol is just a legend, I can't be
sure I'd like the reality. Certainly it could be no
better than Harbor."

"All redheads are chauvinists," I laughed, turning down toward the beach.

"All Swedes make unfounded generalizations,"
she replied cheerfully. "I should'a known better
than to marry a Thorkild."

"Fortunately, Mrs. Thorkild, you didn't," I bowed.

The boys and I got out the sailboat. There was a spanking breeze, and in minutes we were scudding northward, along the woods and fields and tumbling surf of the coast.

"We should put a motor on the *Naughty Nancy*, Dad," said Einar. "Suppose this wind don't hold."

"I like to sail," I said. "The chance of having to man the sweeps is part of the fun."

"Me too," said Mike, a little ambiguously.

"Do they have sailboats on Earth?" asked Einar.

"They must," I said, "since I designed the *Nancy* after a book about them. But I don't think it'd ever be quite the same, Einar. The sea must always be full of boats, most of them powered, and there'd be aircraft overhead and some sort of building wherever you made landfall. You wouldn't have the sea to yourself."

"Then why'd you want to keep looking for Earth when ever'body else wanted to stay here?" he challenged.

A nine-year-old can ask some remarkably disconcerting questions. I said slowly: "I wasn't the only one who voted to keep on searching. And—well, I admitted it at the time, it wasn't Earth but the search itself that I wanted. I liked to find new planets. But we've got a good home now, Einar, here on Harbor."

"I still don't understand how they ever lost Earth," he said.

"Nobody does," I said. "The *Traveler* was carrying a load of colonists to Alpha Centauri—that was a star close to Sol—and men had found the hyperdrive only a few years before and reached the nearer stars. Anyway, *something* happened.

There was a great explosion in the engines, and we found ourselves somewhere else in the Galaxy, thousands of light-years from home. We don't know how far from home, since we've never been able to find Sol again. But after repairing the ship, we spent more than twenty years looking. We never found home." I added quickly, "Until we decided to settle on Harbor. That was our home."

"I mean, how'd the ship get thrown so far off?"

I shrugged. The principles of the hyperdrive are difficult enough, involving as they do the concept of multiple dimensions and of discontinuous psi functions. No one on the ship—and everyone with a knowledge of physics had twisted his brains over the problem—had been able to figure out what catastrophe it was that had annihilated space-time for her. Speculation had involved space warps —whatever that term means, points of infinite discontinuity, undimensional fields, and Cosmos knows what else. Could we find what had happened, and purposefully control the phenomenon which had seized us by some blind accident, the Galaxy would be ours. Meanwhile, we were limited to pseudovelocities of a couple of hundred lights, and interstellar space mocked us with vastness.

But how explain that to a nine-year-old? I said only: "If I knew that, I'd be wiser than anyone else, Einar. Which I'm not."

"I wanna go swimming," said Mike.

"Sure," I said. "That was our idea, wasn't it? We'll drop anchor in the next bay—"

"I wanna go swimming in Spacecamp Cove."

I tried to hedge, but Einar was all over me, too. It was only a few kilometers farther up the coast, and its broad sheltered expanse, its wide sandy beach and the forest immediately behind, made it ideal for such an expedition. And after all, I had nothing against it.

Nothing—except the lure of the place.

I sighed and surrendered. Spacecamp Cove it was.

We had a good time there, swimming and picnicking, playing ball and loafing in the sand and swimming some more. It was good to lie in the sun again, with a cool wet wind blowing in from the sea and talking in the trees. And to the boys, the glamour of it was a sort of crown on the day.

But I had to fight the romance. I wasn't a child any more, playing at spacemen and aliens, I was the grown man with some responsibilities. The community of the *Traveler* had voted by an overwhelming majority to settle on Harbor, and that was that.

And here, half hidden by long grass, half buried in the blowing sand, were the unmistakable signs of what we had left.

There wasn't much. A few plasticontainers for food, a couple of broken tools of curious shape, some scattered engine parts. Just enough to indicate that a while ago—ten years ago, perhaps—a party of spacemen had landed here, camped for a while, made some repairs, and resumed their journey.

They weren't from the fifth planet. Those natives had never left their world, and even with the technological impetus we were giving them in exchange for their metals they weren't ever likely to, the pressures they needed to live were too great. They weren't from Sol, or even some colony world—not only were the remains totally unlike our equipment, but the news of a planet like Harbor, almost a duplicate of Earth but without a native intelligent race, would have brought settlers here in swarms. So—somewhere in the Galaxy, someone else had mastered the hyperdrive and was exploring space.

As we had been doing—

I did my best to be cheerful all the way home, and think I succeeded on the surface. And that in spite of Einar's wildly romantic gabble about the unknown campers. But I couldn't help remembering—

In twenty years of spacing, you can see a lot of worlds, and you can have a lot of experience. We had been gods of a sort, flitting from star to star, exploring, trading, learning, now and again mixing into the destinies of the natives. We had fought and striven, suffered and laughed and stood silent in wonder. For most of us, the dreadful hunger for home, the weariness of the hopeless quest, had shadowed that panorama of worlds which reeled through my mind. But—before Cosmos, I had loved every minute of it!

I fell into unrelieved moodiness as soon as we had stowed the *Naughty Nancy* in our boathouse. The boys ran ahead of me toward the house, but I followed slowly. Alanna met me at the door.

"Better wash up right away," she said. "The company will be here any minute."

"Uh-huh."

She looked at me, for a very long moment, and laid her hand on my arm. In the long dazzling rays of the westering sun, her eyes were brighter than I had seen them before. I wondered if tears were not wavering just behind them.

"You were at Spacecamp Cove," she said quietly.

"The boys wanted to go there," I answered. "It's a good place."

"Erling—" She paused. I stood looking at her, thinking how beautiful she was. I remembered the way she had looked on Hralfar, the first time I kissed her. We had wandered a ways from the camp of the detail exploring that frosty little world and negotiating with its natives for supplies. The sky had been dark overhead, with a shrunken sun casting its thin pale light on the blue-shadowed snow. It was quiet, breathlessly quiet, the air was like sharp fire in our nostrils and her hair, the only color in that white horizon, seemed to crackle with frost. That was quite a long time ago, but nothing had changed between us since.

"Yes?" I prompted her. "Yes, what is it?"

Her voice came quickly, very low so the boys wouldn't hear: "Erling, are you really happy here?"

"Why"—I felt an almost physical shock of surprise—"Of course I am, dear. That's a silly question."

"Or a silly answer?" She smiled, with closed lips. "We did have some good times on the *Traveler.* Even those who grumbled loudest at the time admit that, now when they've got a little perspective on the voyage and have forgotten something of the overcrowding and danger and weariness. But you—I sometimes think the *Traveler* was your life, Erling."

"I liked the ship, of course." I had a somewhat desperate sense of defending myself. "After all, I was born and raised on her. I never really knew anything else. Our planetary visits were so short, and most of the words so unterrestrial. You liked it, too."

"Oh, sure, it was fun to go batting around the Galaxy, never knowing what might wait at the next sun. But a woman wants a home. And—Erling, plenty of others your age, who also had never known anything else, hated it."

"I was lucky. As an officer, I had better quarters, more privacy. And, well, that 'something hid behind the ranges' maybe meant more to me than to most others. But—good Cosmos, Alanna! you don't think that now—"

"I don't think anything, Erling. But on the ship you weren't so absent-minded, so apt to fall into daydreams. You didn't sit around the place all day, you were always working on something—" She bit her lip. "Don't misunderstand, Erling. I have no doubt you keep telling yourself how happy you are. You could go to your cremation, here on Harbor, thinking you'd had a rather good life. But—I sometimes wonder!"

"Now look—" I began.

"No, no, nothing more out of you. Get inside and wash up, the company'll be coming in half a minute."

I went, with my head in a whirl. Mechanically, I scrubbed myself and changed into evening blouse and slacks. When I came out of the bedroom, the first of the guests were already waiting.

MacTeague Angus was there, the old first mate of the *Traveler* and captain in the short time between Kane's death and our settling on Harbor. So was my brother Gustav Thorkild, with whom I had little in common except a mutual liking. Tokogama Hideyoshi, Petroff Ivan, Ortega Manuel, and a couple of others showed up a few minutes later. Alanna took charge of their wives and children, and I mixed drinks all around.

For a while the talk was of local matters. We were scattered over quite a wide area, and had as yet not produced enough telescreens for every house, so that communication was limited to direct personal travel by plane. A hailstorm on Gustav's farm, a minor breakdown in the vehicle factory superintended by Ortega, Petroff's project of a fleet of semirobot fishing boats—small gossip. Presently dinner was served.

Gustav was rapturous over the steak. "What is it?" he asked.

"Some local animal I shot the other day," I said. "Ungulate, reddish-brown, broad flat horns."

"Oh, yes. Hm-m-m—I'll have to try domesticating some. I've had pretty good luck with those glug-gugs."

"Huh?" Petroff stared at him.

"Another local species," laughed Gustav. "I had to call them something, and they made that kind of noise."

"The *Traveler* was never like this," said Ortega, helping himself to another piece of meat.

"I never thought the food was bad," I said.

"No, we had the hydroponic vegetables and fruits, and the synthetic meats, as well as what we picked up on different planets," admitted Ortega. "But it wasn't this good, ever. Hydroponics somehow don't have the flavor of Earth-grown stuff."

"That's your imagination," said Petroff. "I can prove—"

"I don't care what you can prove, the facts remain." Ortega glanced at me. "But there were compensations."

"Not enough," muttered Gustav. "I've got room to move, here on Harbor."

"You're being unjust to the *Traveler*," I said. "She was only meant to carry about fifty people, for a short voyage at that. When she lost her way for twenty years, and a whole new generation got jammed in with their parents, it's no wonder she grew crowded. Actually, her minimum crew is ten or so. Thirty people—fifteen couples, say, plus their kids—could travel in her in ease and comfort, with private apartments for all."

"And still . . . still, for over twenty years, we fought and suffered and stood the monotony and the hopelessness—to find Earth." Tokogama's voice was musing, a little awed. "When all the time, on any of a hundred uninhabited terrestroid planets, we could have had—this."

"For at least half that time," pointed out MacTeague, "we were simply looking for the right part of the Galaxy. We knew Sol wasn't anywhere near, so we had no hopes to be crushed, but we thought as soon as the constellations began to look fairly familiar we'd be quickly able to find home." He shrugged. "But space is simply too big, and our astrogational tables have so little information. Star travel was still in its infancy when we left Sol.

"An error of, say, one percent could throw us lightyears off in the course of several hundred parsecs. And the Galaxy is lousy with GO-type suns, which are statistically almost certain to have neighbors sufficiently like Sol's to fool an unsure observer. If our tables had given positions relative to, say, S Doradus, we could have found home easily enough. But they used Sirius for their bright-star point—and we couldn't find Sirius in that swarm of stars! We just had to hop from star to star which *might* be Sol—and find it wasn't, and go on, with the sickening fear that maybe we were getting farther away all the time, maybe Sol lay just off the bows, obscured by a dark nebula. In the end—we gave it up as a bad job."

"There's more to it than that," said Tokogama. "We realized all that, you know. But there was Captain Kane and his tremendous personality, his driving will to success, and we'd all come to rely more or less blindly on him. As long as he lived, nobody quite believed in the possibility of failure. When he died, everything seemed to collapse at once."

I nodded grimly, remembering those terrible days that followed—Seymour's mutinous attempt to seize power, bringing home to us just how sick and weary we all were; the arrival at this star which might have solved it all, might have given us a happy ending, if it had been Sol; the rest on Harbor, a rest which became a permanent stay—

"Something else kept us going all those years, too," said Ortega quietly. "There was an element among the younger generation which liked to wander. The vote to stay here wasn't unanimous."

"I know," said MacTeague. His level gaze rested thoughtfully on me. "I often wonder, Erling, why some of you don't borrow the ship and visit the nearer stars, just to see what's there."

"Wouldn't do any good," I said tonelessly. "It'd just make our feet itch worse than ever—and there'd always be stars beyond those."

"But why—" Gustav fumbled for words. "Why would anyone *want* to go—stargazing that way? I . . . well, I've got my feet on ground now, my own ground, my own home . . . it's growing, I'm building and planting and seeing it come to reality before my own eyes, and it'll be there for my children and their children. There's air and wind and rain, sunlight, the sea, the woods and mountains —Cosmos! Who wants more? Who wants to trade it for sitting in a sterile metal tank, riding from star to star, homeless, hopeless?"

"Nobody," I said hastily. "I was just trying—"

"The most pointless existence—simply to be a . . . a spectator in the universe!"

"Not exactly," said Tokogama. "There was plenty we did, if you insist that somebody must do something. We brought some benefits of human civilization to quite a number of places. We did some extensive star-mapping, if we ever see Earthmen again they'll find our tables useful, and our observations within different systems. We . . . well, we were wanderers, but so what? Do you blame a bird for not having hoofs?"

"The birds have hoofs now," I said. "They're walking on the ground. And"—I flashed a glance at Alanna—"they like it."

The conversation was getting a little too hot. I steered it into safer channels until we adjourned to the living room. Over coffee and tobacco it came back.

We began reminiscing about the old days, planets we had seen, deeds we had done. Worlds and suns and moons, whirling through a raw dark emptiness afire with stars, were in our talk—strange races, foreign cities, lonely magnificence of mountains and plains and seas, the giant universe opening before us. Oh, by all the gods, we had fared far!

We had seen the blue hell—flames leaping over the naked peaks of a planet whose great sun almost filled its sky. We had sailed with a gang of happy pirates over a sea red as new-spilled blood toward the grotesque towers of a fortress older than their history. We had seen the rich color and flashing metal of a tournament on Drangor and the steely immensity of the continental cities on Alkan. We had talked philosophy with a gross wallowing cephalopod on one world and been shot at by the inhumanly beautiful natives of another. We had come as gods to a planet to lift its barbaric natives from the grip of a plague that scythed them down and we had come as humble students to the ancient laboratories and libraries of the next. We had come near perishing in a methane storm on a planet far from its sun and felt then how dear life is. We had lain on the beaches of the paradise world Luanha and let the sea sing us to sleep. We had ridden centauroids who conversed with us as they went to the aerial city of their winged enemies—

More than the wildly romantic adventures —which, after all, had been pretty dirty and bloody affairs at the time—we loved to remember the worlds themselves: a fiery sunset on the snowfields of Hralfar; a great brown river flowing through the rain forest which covered Atlang; a painted desert on Thyvari; the mighty disk of New Jupiter swelling before our bows; the cold and vastness and cruelty and emptiness and awe and wonder of open space itself. And, in our small clique of frank tramps, there had been the comradeship of the road, the calm unspoken knowledge of having friends who would stand firm—a feeling of *belonging*, such as men like Gustav had achieved only since coming here, and which we seemed to have lost.

Lost—yes, why not admit it? We didn't see each other very often any more, we were too scattered, too busy. And the talk of the others was just a little bit boring.

Well, it couldn't be helped—

It was late that night when the party broke up. Alanna and I saw the guests out to their planes. When the last vehicle had whispered into the sky, we stood for a while looking around us. The night was very still and cool, with a high starry sky in which the moon of Harbor was rising. Its light glittered on the dew under our feet, danced restlessly

on the sea, threw a dim silver veil on the dreaming
land—our land.

I looked down at Alanna. She was staring over
the darkened view, staring as if she had never seen
it before—or never would again. The moonlight
was tangled like frost in her hair. *What if I never
see open space again? What if I sit here till I die?
This is worth it.*

She spoke at last, very slowly, as if she had to
shape each word separately: "I'm beginning to realize it. Yes, I'm quite sure."

"Sure of what?" I asked.

"Don't play dumb. You know what I mean. You
and Manuel and Ivan and Hideyoshi and the others
who were here—except Angus and Gus, of course.
And quite a few more. You don't belong here. None
of you."

"How—so?"

"Look, a man who had been born and raised in a
city, and had a successful life in it, couldn't be expected to take to the country all of a sudden.
Maybe never. Put him among peasants, and he'd go
around all the rest of his life wondering vaguely
why he wasn't honestly happy."

"We— Now don't start that again, sweetheart," I
begged.

"Why not? Somebody's got to. After all, Erling,
this is a peasantry we've got, growing up on Harbor. More or less mechanized, to be sure, but still
rooted to the soil, close to it, with the peasant
strength and solidity and the peasant's provincial
outlook. Why, if a ship from Earth landed tomorrow, I don't think twenty people would leave with
it.

"But you, Erling, you and your friends—you
grew up in the ship, and you made a successful
adaptation to it. You spent your formative years

wandering. By now—you're cosmopolites. For you, a mountain range will always be more than it really is, because of what's behind it. One horizon isn't enough, you've got to have many, as many as there are in the universe.

"Find Earth? Why, you yourself admitted you don't care whether Earth is ever found. You only want the search.

"You're a gypsy, Erling. And no gypsy could ever be tied to one place."

I stood for a long while, alone with her in the cold calm moonlight, and said nothing. When I looked down at her, finally, she was trying not to cry, but her lip was trembling and the tears were bright in her eyes. Every word was wrenched out of me:

"You may be right, Alanna, I'm beginning to be horribly afraid you are. But what's to be done about it?"

"Done?" She laughed, a strangely desolate laugh. "Why, it's a very simple problem. The answer is circling right there up in the sky. Get a crew who feel the way you do, and take the *Traveler*. Go roaming—forever!"

"But . . . you? You, the kids, the place here . . . you—"

"Don't you see?" Her laughter rang louder now, echoing faintly in the light night. "Don't you see? I want to go, too!" She almost fell into my arms. "I want to go, too!"

There is no reason to record the long arguments, grudging acceptances, slow preparations. In the end we won. Sixteen men and their wives, with half a dozen children, were wild to leave.

That summer blazed up into fall, winter came, spring, and summer again, while we made ready.

Our last year on Harbor. And I had never realized how much I loved the planet. Almost, I gave up.

But space, free space, the open universe and the ship come alive again—!

We left the colony a complete set of plans, in the unlikely event that they should ever want to build a starship of their own, and a couple of spaceboats and duplicates of all the important automatic machinery carried by the *Traveler*. We would make astrogating tables, as our official purpose, and theoretically we might some day come back.

But we knew we never would. We would go traveling, and our children would carry the journey on after us, and their children after them, a whole new civilization growing up between the stars, rootless but tremendously alive. Those who wearied of it could always colonize a planet, we would be spreading mankind over the Galaxy. When our descendants were many, they would build other ships until there was a fleet, a mobile city hurtling from sun to sun. It would be a culture to itself, drawing on the best which all races had to offer and spreading it over the worlds. It would be the bloodstream of the interstellar civilization which was slowly gestating in the universe.

As the days and months went by, my boys grew even more impatient to be off. I smiled a little. Right now, they only thought of the adventure of it, romantic planets and great deeds to be done. Well, there were such, they would have eventful lives, but they would soon learn that patience and steadfastness were needed, that there was toil and suffering and danger—and life!

Alanna—I was a little puzzled. She was very gay when I was around, merrier than I had ever seen her before. But she often went out for long walks, alone on the beach or in the sun-dappled woods, and she started a garden which she would never harvest. Well—so it went, and I was too busy with preparations to think much about it.

The end came, and we embarked on the long voyage, the voyage which has not ceased yet and, I hope, will never end. The night before, we had Angus and Gustav in for a farewell party, and it was a strange feeling to be saying good-by knowing that we would never see them again, or hear from them. It was like dying.

But we were alone in the morning. We went out to our carplane, to fly to the landing field where the gypsies would meet. From there, a boat would take us to the *Traveler*. I still could not fully realize that I was captain—I, captain of the great ship which had been my world, it didn't seem real. I walked slowly, my head full of the sudden universe of responsibility.

Alanna touched my arm. "Look around, Erling," she whispered. "Look around at our land. You'll never see it again."

I shook myself out of my reverie and let my eyes sweep the horizon. It was early, the grass was still wet, flashing in the new sun. The sea danced and glittered beyond the rustling trees, crying its old song to the fair green land, and the wind that blew from it was keen and cold and pungent with life. The fields were stirring in the wind, a long ripple of grass, and high overhead a bird was singing.

"It's—very beautiful," I said.

"Yes." I could hardly hear her voice. "Yes, it is. Let's go, Erling."

We got into the carplane and slanted skyward. The boys crowded forward with me, staring ahead for the first glimpse of the landing field, not seeing the forests and meadows and shining rivers that slipped away beneath us.

Alanna sat behind me, looking down over the land. Her bright head was bent away so I couldn't see her face. I wondered what she was thinking, but somehow I didn't want to ask her.

Thus the Traveler *became the first Nomad ship. Sixteen restless families had blithely founded a whole new culture in which wandering was to be a way of life. As one of their own songs later put it, "No Eden seen however green/ Could hold you from your faring." These colorful and cunning star gypsies did much to enliven the annals of the following centuries.*

But if voluntary settlement made the Nomads uncomfortable, enforced confinement planetside could be just as hard on other star-roving humans.

STAR SHIP

With sunset, there was rain. When Dougald Anson brought his boat in to Krakenau harbor, there was only a vast wet darkness around him.

He swore in a sulfurous mixture of Krakenaui, Volgazani, and half a dozen other languages, including some spaceman's Terrestrial, and let down the sail. The canvas was heavy and awkward in the drenching rain; it was all he could do to lash it around the boom. Then he picked up the long wooden sweep and began sculling his boat in toward the dock.

Lightning flared bluely through the rain, and he saw the great bay in one livid flash, filled with galleys at anchor and the little schooners of the fishing fleet. Beyond the wharfs, the land climbed steeply toward the sky, and he saw the dark mass of the town reaching up to the citadel on the hilltop. Dark—dark! Hardly a light showed in the gloom.

What in the name of Shantuzik was up? The waterfront, at least, should have been alive with torches and music and bawdy merriment. And the newly installed street lights should have been twinkling along the main avenues leading up to the castle. Instead Krakenau lay crouched in night, and—

He scowled, and drove the light vessel shoreward with rhythmic sweeps of the long oar. Uneasiness prickled along his spine. It wasn't right. He'd only been gone a few days. What had happened in the meantime?

When he reached the pier, he made fast with a quietness unusual to him. Maybe he was being overcautious. Maybe it was only that the king had died or some other reason for restrained conduct had arisen. But a man didn't spend years warring among the pirates of the outer islands and the neighboring kingdoms around Krakenau without learning to be careful.

He ducked under the awning in the bows which was the boat's only shelter, and got a towel from the sea chest and rubbed his rain-wet body dry. He'd only been wearing a tattered pair of breeches, and the water ran along his ribs and down his flanks. Then he shrugged on a tunic, and a coat of ring-mail over that. A flat-bladed sword at his side and a helmet over his long yellow hair completed his outfit. He felt secure now, and jumped up to the pier.

For a moment he stood in thought. The steady rain washed down over his leather cape, blurring vision a few meters away, and only the intermittent flicker of lightning broke the darkness. Where to go? His father's house was the logical place, perhaps. But the Masefield dwelling was a little closer to here, and Ellen—

He grinned and set out at a long stride. Masefield's be it.

The street onto which he turned opened before him like a tunnel of night. The high steep-roofed houses lay dark on either side, walling it in, and the fluoroglobes were unlit. When the lightning blinked, the wet cobblestones gleamed; otherwise there was only darkness and rain.

He passed one of the twisting alleys, and glanced at it with automatic caution. The next instant he had thrown himself to the ground, and the javelin whipped through the place where his belly had been.

He rolled over and bounded to his feet, crouched low, the sword whining out of its scabbard into his hand. Four Khazaki sprang from the alley and darted at him.

Dougald Anson grunted, backed up against a wall. The natives were armed and mailed, they were warriors, and they had all the unhuman swiftness of their species. Four of them—!

The leading attacker met his sword in a clang of steel. Dougald let him come lunging in, took the cut on his mailed ribs, and swept his own weapon murderously out. Faster than a man could think, the Khazaki had his own blade up to parry the sweeping blow. But he wasn't quite fast enough; he met it at an awkward angle and the Terrestrial's sheer power sent the sword spinning from his hand. The hand went too, a fractional second later, and he screamed and fell back and away.

The others were upon Anson. For moments it was parry and slash, three against one, with no time to feel afraid or notice the cuts in his arms and legs. A remote part of his brain told him bleakly: *This is all. You're finished. No lone Earthling ever stood up long to more than two Khazaki.* But he hardly noticed.

Suddenly there were only two in front of him. He

darted forth from the wall, his sword crashing down with all the power of his huge body behind it. The warrior tried to skip aside—too late. The tremendous blow smashed his own parry down and sang in his skullbones.

And the last of the attackers died. He tumbled over beside the second, and each of them had a feathered shaft between his ribs.

The bowman came loping through the rain. He paused, in typical Khazak fashion, to slit the throat of the wounded being, and then came up to where Dougald Anson stood panting.

The human strained through the rainy dark. Lightning glimmered in the sky, and he recognized the newcomer. "Janazik!"

"And Anson," nodded the Khazaki. His sharp white teeth gleamed in his shadowed face. "You seem to have met a warm welcome."

"Too warm. But—thanks!" Anson bent over the nearest of the corpses, and only now did the realization penetrate his brain. They all wore black mail of a certain pattern, spiked helmets, red cloaks—Gods of Gorzak! They were all royal guardsmen!

He looked up to the dark form of Janazik, and his lean face was suddenly tight. "What is this?" he asked slowly. "I thought maybe bandits or some enemy state had managed to enter the city—"

"That would be hard to do, now that we have the guns," said Janazik. "No, these are within our own walls. If you'll look closely, you'll see they wear a gold-colored brassard."

"Prince Volakech—but he—"

"There's more to this than Volakech, and more than a question of the throne," said Janazik. Then suddenly, urgently: "But we can't stay here to talk.

They're patrolling the streets, it's dangerous to be abroad. Let's get to shelter."

"What's happened?" Anson got up, towering over the native by a good quarter meter, his voice suddenly rough. "What happened? How is everyone?"

"Not well. Come on, now."

"Ellen? Masefield Ellen?"

"I don't know. Nobody knows. Now come on!"

They slipped into the alley. Anson was blind in the gloom, and Janazik's slim six-fingered hand took his to guide him. The Khazaki were smaller than Terrestrials and lacked the sheer strength and endurance which Earth's higher gravity gave; but they could move like the wind, they had an utter grace and balance beside which humans were clumsy cattle, and they saw in the dark.

Dougald Anson's mind whirred in desperate speculation. If Volakech had gotten enough guardsmen and soldiers on his side to swing a palace revolution, it was bad. But matters looked worse than that. Why should Volakech's men have assaulted a human? Why should Janazik have to sneak him into a hiding place? How had the revolutionists gotten control in the first place, against King Aligan's new weapons? What powers did they have now?

What had become of the human community in Krakenau? What of his father, his brother and sisters, his friends? What of Masefield Ellen? What of Ellen?

He grew aware that Janazik had halted. They were in an evil-smelling, refuse-littered courtyard, surrounded by tumbledown structures, dark and silent as the rest of the city. Anson realized that all Krakenau was blacked out. In such times of danger, the old Khazaki clandom reasserted itself.

Families barricaded themselves in their dwellings, prepared to fight all comers till the danger was past. The city was awake, yes—it was crouched in breathless tension all around him—but not a light showed, not a hand stirred, not a voice spoke. They were all waiting.

Janazik crouched at the base of one of the old buildings and lifted a trapdoor. Light gleamed dimly up from a cellar. He dropped lightly down and Anson followed, closing the door behind him.

There was only one smoky lamp in the dank gloom. Shadows were thick and huge around the guttering wick. The red flame picked out faces, shimmered off cold steel, and lost itself in darkness.

Anson's eyes scanned the faces. Half a dozen humans: Chiang Chung-Chen, Du-Frere Marie, Gonzales Alonzo and his wife Nora who was Anson's sister, Dougald Joan, Masefield Philip— No sign of Ellen.

"Anse! Anse!" The voices almost sobbed out of the dim-lit hollowness. Joan and Nora sprang forward as if to touch their brother, make sure he was alive and no vision of the night, but Janazik waved them back with his sword.

"No noise," hissed the Khazaki's fierce whisper. "No noise, by all the thirteen hells! Volakech's *burats* are all over the city. If a patrol finds us—"

"Ellen!" Anson's blue eyes searched for Masefield Philip, crouched near the lamp. "Where's your sister, Phil?"

"I don't know," whispered the boy. "We're all who seem to've escaped. They may have caught her—I don't know—"

"Father." Joan's voice caught with a dry sob. "Anse, Father and Jamie are dead. The rebels killed them."

For a moment, Anson couldn't grasp the reality of that. It just wasn't possible that his big laughing father and young Jamie-the-brat should be killed—*no!*

But—

He looked up, and then looked away. When he turned back to face them, his visage had gone hard and expressionless, and only the white-knuckled grip on his sword showed he was not a stranger.

"All right," he said slowly, very slowly and steadily. "All right. Give me the story. What is it? What's happened in Krakenau?"

Janazik padded around to stand before him. He was not the only Khazaki in the cellar; there were a good dozen others. Mostly they were young males, and Anse recognized them. Bolazan, Pragakech, Slavatozik—he'd played with them as a child, he'd fared out with them as a youth and a man to the wars, to storm the high citadel of Zarganau and smite the warriors of Volgazan and pirate the commerce of the outer islands. They were good comrades, yes. But Father and Jamie were dead. Ellen, Ellen was vanished. Only a fragment of the human community remained; his world had suddenly come down in ruin about him.

Well—his old bleak resolution came back to him, and he met the yellow slit-pupilled gaze of Janazik with a challenging stare.

They were a strange contrast, these two, for all that they had fought shoulder to shoulder halfway round the planet, had sung and played and roistered from Krakenau to Gorgazan. Comrades in arms, blood brothers maybe, but neither was human from the viewpoint of the other.

Dougald Anson was big even for a Terrestrial; his tawny head rode at full two meters and his wide shoulders strained the chain mail he wore. He was young, but his face had had the youth burned out of it by strange suns and wild winds around the world, was lean and brown and marked with an old scar across the forehead. His eyes were almost intolerably bright and direct in their blue stare, the eyes of a bird of prey.

The Khazaki was humanoid, to be sure—shorter than the Terrestrial average, but slim and lithe. Soft golden fur covered his sinewy body, and a slender tail switched restlessly against his legs. His head was the least human part of him, with its sloping forehead, narrow chin, and blunt-muzzled face. The long whiskers around his mouth and above the amber cat-eyes twitched continuously, sensitive to minute shifts in air currents and temperature. Along the top of his skull, the fur grew up in a cockatoo plume that swept back down his neck, a secondary sexual characteristic that females lacked.

Janazik was something of a dandy, and even now he wore the baggy silk-like trousers, long red sash, and elaborately embroidered blouse and vest of a Krakenaui noble. It was woefully muddy, but he managed to retain an air of fastidious elegance. The bow and quiver across his back, the sword and dirk at his side, somehow looked purely ornamental when he wore them.

He was almost dwarfed by Anse's huge-thewed height. But old Chiang Chung-Chen noticed, not for the first time, that the human wore clothing and carried weapons of Khazaki pattern, and that the harsh syllables of Krakenaui came more easily to his lips than the Terrestrial of his fathers. And the old man nodded, gravely and a little wearily.

Janazik spoke rapidly: "Volakech must have been plotting his return from exile a long time. He managed to raise a small army of pirates, mercenaries, and outlawed Krakenaui, and he made bargains with groups within the city. Two day ago, certain of the guards seized the new guns and let Volakech and his men in. Others revolted within the town. I think King Aligan was killed; at least I've seen or heard nothing of him since. There's been some fighting between rebels and loyalists but the rebels got all the Earth-weapons when they captured the royal arsenal and since then they've just about crushed resistance. Loyalists who could, fled the city. The rest are in hiding. Volakech is king."

"But—why us? The Terrestrials—what have we to do with—"

Janazik's yellow eyes blazed at him. "You aren't stupid, blood-brother. Think!"

After a moment Anse nodded bleakly. "The *Star Ship*—"

"Of course! Volakech has seized the rocket boat. No Terrestrial in his right mind would show him how to use it, so he had to capture someone who understood its operation and force them to take him out to the Star Ship. Old Masefield Henry was killed resisting arrest—you know how bloody guardsmen are, in spite of orders to take someone alive. Volakech ordered the arrest of all Terrestrials then. A few surrendered to him, a few were killed resisting, most were captured by force. As far as we know, this group is all which escaped."

"Then Ellen—?"

"That's the weird thing. I don't believe she has been caught. Volakech's men are still scouring the city for 'an Earthling woman' as the orders read. And who could it be but Ellen? No other woman represents any danger or any desirable capture to Volakech."

"Ellen understands astrogation," said Anse slowly. "She learned it from her grandfather."

"Yes. And now that he is dead, she is the only human—the only being on this planet—who can get that rocket up to the Star Ship. And Masefield Carson knows it."

"Carson? Ellen's older brother? What—"

Janazik's voice was cold as Winter: "Masefield Carson was with Volakech. He led the rebels inside the city. Now he's the new king's lieutenant."

"Carson! No!"

"Carson—yes!" Janazik's smile was without mirth or pity. His eyes sought out Philip, huddled miserably beside the lamp. "Isn't that the truth?"

The boy nodded, too choked with his own unhappiness to cry. "Carse always was a friend of Volakech, before King Aligan outlawed him," he mumbled. "And he always said how it was a shame, and how Volakech would know better what to do with the Star Ship than anyone now. Then—that night—" His voice trailed off, he sat dumbly staring into the flame.

"Carson led the rebel guardsmen in their seizure of the city guns," said Janazik. "He also rode to the Masefield house at the head of a troop of them and called on his people to surrender on promise of good treatment. Joe and the mother did, and I suppose they're held somewhere in the citadel now. Phil and Ellen happened to be out at the time. When Phil heard of the uprising, he was afraid to give himself up, in spite of the heralds that went about promising safety to those who did. He heard how the rebels had been killing his friends. He went to Slavatozik here, whom he could trust, and later they got in touch with me. I'd used this hiding place before, and gathered all the fugitives I could find here." Janazik shrugged, a sinuous unhuman gesture. "Since then I've seen Carse, at a distance, riding around like a prince of the blood, with a troop of his own personal guardsmen. I suspect he really runs things now. Volakech wants power, but only Carse can show him how to get it."

"And Ellen—?"

"No sign of her. But as I said, I think she's in hiding somewhere, or the guards wouldn't be out looking for a woman. She wouldn't give herself up."

"Not Ellen." A grim pride lifted Anse's head.

"Remains the problem of finding her before they do," said Gonzales Alonzo. "If they catch her and make her plot an orbit for the rocket, they'll have the Star Ship—which means power over the whole planet."

"Not that I care who's king," growled Pragakech. "But you know that Masefield Carson never did want to use the ship to get out to the stars. And I want to see those other worlds before I die."

"To the thirteenth hell with the other worlds," snarled Bolazan. "Aligan was my king, and it's for me to avenge him and put his rightful heir on the throne."

"We all have our motives for wanting the blood of Volakech and Carson," said Janazik. "Never mind that now; the important thing is how to get at their livers. We're few, Anse. Here are all the free humans we know of, except Masefield Ellen. There can't be more than two or three at large, or perhaps ten dead. That means the enemy holds almost a hundred humans captive. Discounting children and others who are ignorant of Terrestrial science, it still means they'll be able to operate the guns, the steel mill, the atomic-power plant—all the new machines except the rocket boat, and they only need Ellen for that."

Anse nodded, slowly. "What is our strength?" he asked.

"I don't know. Not much. I know where about a hundred Khazaki warriors are hiding, ready to follow us whenever we call on them, and there will be many more sitting at home now who'll rise if someone else takes the lead. But the enemy has all the guns. It would be suicide."

"What about the Khazaki who fled?" Usually, in one of the planet's violent changes of governments, the refugees were powerful nobles who would be slain as a safety measure if they stayed at home but who could, in exile, raise strong forces for a comeback. Such a one had Volakech himself been, barely escaping with his life after his disastrous attempt to seize the throne a few years back.

"Don't be more stupid than you can help," snorted Janazik. "By the time they can have rallied enough to do any good, Volakech and Carson will have the Star Ship, one way or another, and then the whole world is at their mercy."

"That means we have to strike back somehow—quickly!" Anse stood for a moment in thought.

The habits of his warring, wandering years were coming back to him. He had faced death and despair before, and with strength and cunning and bluff and sheer luck had come through alive. This was another problem, more desperate and more urgent, but still another problem.

No—there was more to it than that.

* * *

His face grew bleak, and it was as if a coldness touched his heart. Carson was Ellen's older brother, and even if they had quarreled from time to time he knew she had always felt deeply bound to him. *Carse is everything I never was. He stayed in Krakenau and studied and became an educated man and a skilled engineer while I went hallooing over the world. He's brave and a good fighter—so am I—but he's so much more than that. I imagine it was his example that made Ellen learn the astrogation only her grandfather knew.*

And now I'm back from roaming and roving with Janazik, and I'm trying hard to settle down and learn something so that I won't be just a barbarian, a wild Khazaki in human skin, when we go out to the civilization of the stars. So that I won't be too utterly ashamed to ask Ellen to marry me. And it was all going pretty well until now.

But now—I'm fighting her brother—

Well—he pushed the thought out of his brain. After all, apparently she was in opposition to Carse's plans too.

"I wonder why they tried to kill me?" he asked aloud, more to fill in the time while he thought than out of curiosity.

"You'd be of no use to Carson, having no technical education," said Janazik, "while your knowledge of fighting and your connections with warlike groups make you dangerous to him. Also, I don't think he ever liked your paying attention to Ellen."

"No—he always said I was a waster. Called me a—an absorbed Khazaki. I'd've split his skull if he hadn't been Ellen's brother—No matter now. We've more important things to talk over."

Have we, now? he thought sickly. *Carson must*

*know Ellen well, better than I do. If he thinks he
can have me killed without making her hate him,
then—maybe I never had any chance with her
then—*

"How'd you happen by?" he asked tonelessly.

"I've been out from time to time, looking for
Ellen and killing guardsmen whenever I could
catch them alone." Janazik's white fangs gleamed
in a carnivore's smile. "And, of course, I expected
you back from your fishing trip about this time,
and watched for you lest you blunder into their
hands."

Anse began to pace the floor, back and forth, his
head bent to avoid the basement rafters. If Carson
was in control, and out to kill him . . . There was
more to it than that, of course. The whole future of
the planet Khazak, perhaps of the fabulous Galactic civilization itself, was balanced on the edge of a
sword. If Volakech or a descendant of his took the
warlike race out among the stars, with a high level
of industry to back a scheme of conquest—

But it didn't matter. All the universe didn't matter. There was only Ellen, and his own dead kin,
and himself.

A man's heart can only hold so much.

Janazik stood quietly back, watching his friend's
restless prowling. He had seen that pacing before,
and he knew that some scheme would come out of
it, crazy and reckless and desperate, with his own
cool unhuman intelligence to temper it and make it
workable. He and Anse made a good team. They
made the best damned fighting team Khazak had
ever seen.

Presently the human lifted his head. There was
silence in the hiding place, thick and taut, so that
they could hear their own breathing and the steady

drum of rain on the trapdoor.

"I have an idea," said Anse.

The long night wore on. Janazik had sent most of his Khazaki out to alert the other loyalists in their hiding places, but only they had a chance of slipping unobserved past the enemy patrols. Humans, obviously alien, slowfooted and clumsy beside the flitting shadows of Khazak, would never get free. They had to wait.

Anse was glad of the opportunity for conference with Janazik, planning the assault on the citadel. Neither of them was very familiar with the layout, but Alonzo, as an engineer on the rocket building project, and old Chiang had been there often enough to know it intimately.

It was impossible that a few hundred warriors armed with the primitive weapons of Khazak could take the stronghold. Its walls were manned by more fighters than that, and there were the terrible Earth-type guns as well. Alonzo had a blaster with a couple of charges, but otherwise there was nothing modern in the loyalist force.

But still that futile assault was necessary—

"It's taking a desperate chance," said Dougald Joan. She was young yet, hardly out of girlhood, but her voice had an indomitable ring. The true warriors among the five Earthling families were all Dougalds thought Janazik. "Suppose Ellen doesn't come out of hiding? Suppose she's dead or—or captured already, in spite of what we think."

"We'll just have to try and destroy the rocket then," said Alonzo. "Certainly we can't let Volakech get to the Star Ship." He sighed, heavily. "And the labor of another generation will be gone."

"It wouldn't take us long to build another boat," said his wife. "We know how, now, and we have the industry to do it."

"There are only a few who really know how to handle and build the Terrestrial machines, and most of them are in the enemy's hands," reminded old Chiang. "I'm sure I couldn't tell you much about atomic engines, even though I was on the Star Ship herself once. If those few are killed, we may never be able to duplicate our efforts. What Terrestrials survive will sink back into barbarism, become simply another part of Khazaki culture."

"I don't know—" said Nora.

"I know, because I've seen it happen," insisted Chiang. "In the fifty years since we were marooned here, two generations have been born on Khazak. They've grown up among Khazaki, played with native children, worked and fought with Khazaki natives, adopted the dress and speech and whole outlook of Krakenau. Only a few in this third generation have consciously tried to remain—Terrestrial. I must admit that Masefield Carson is one such. Ellen is another. But few others."

"Would you have us wall ourselves out from the world?" asked Anse with a bridling anger.

"No. I don't see how the situation could be helped. We are a minority in an alien culture with which we've had to cooperate. It's only natural that we'd be more assimilated than assimilating. Even at that, we've wrought immense changes."

* * *

Janazik nodded. The stranded Terrestrials had found themselves in an early Iron Age civilization of city-states, among a race naturally violent and predatory. For their own survival, they had had to league forces with the state in which they found themselves—Krakenau, as it happened. Before they could build the industry they needed, they had to have some security—which meant that they must teach the Krakenaui military principles and means of making new weapons which would make them superior to their neighbors. After that—well, it took an immense technology to build even a small spaceship. The superalloys which could stand the combustion of rocket fuel required unheard-of elements such as manganese and chromium, which required means of mining and refining them, which required a considerable chemical plant, which required—How far down do you have to start? And there were a hundred or a thousand other requirements of equal importance and difficulty.

Besides, the Terrestrials had had to learn much from scratch themselves. None of them had ever built a rocketship, had ever seen one in action even. It was centuries obsolete in Galactic civilization. But gravity drives were out of the question. So—they'd had to design the ship from the ground up. Which meant years of painstaking research . . . and only a few interested humans and Khazaki to do it. The rest were too busy with their own affairs in the brawling barbaric culture.

Ten years ago, the first spaceboat had blasted off toward the Star Ship—and exploded in mid-acceleration. More designing, more testing, more slow building—and now the second one lay ready.

Perhaps it could reach the Star Ship.

The Star Ship—faster than light, weightless when it chose to be for all its enormous mass, armed with atomic guns that could blast a city to superheated vapor. Whoever controlled that ship could get to Galactic stars in a matter of weeks. Or could rule all Khazaki if he chose.

No wonder Carson and Volakech had struck now, before the rocket boat was launched. When *they* had the ship—

But only Ellen knew the figures of its orbit and the complicated calculations by which the boat would plot a course to get there. A bold warrior might make a try at reaching the ship by seat-of-the-pants piloting, but he wouldn't have much chance of making it. So Ellen, and the rocket boat, were the fulcrum of the future.

"Strange," mused Chiang. "Strange that we should have had that accident . . ."

They had heard the story a hundred times before, but they gathered around to listen; there was nothing else to do while the slow hours dragged on.

"We were ten, all told, five men and their wives. Exploratory expeditions are often out for years at a time, so the Service makes it a policy to man the ships with married couples. It's hard for a Khazaki to appreciate the absolute equality between the sexes which human civilization has achieved. It's due to the advanced technology, of course, and we're losing it as we go back to barbarism—"

Anse felt a small hand laid on his arm. He looked down into the dark eyes of Du-Frere Marie. She was a pretty girl, a little younger than he, and until he'd really noticed Ellen he'd been paying her some attention.

"I don't care about equality," she whispered. "A woman shouldn't try to be a man. I'd want only to cook and keep house for my man, and bear his children."

It was, Anse realized, a typical Khazaki attitude. But—he remembered with a sudden pity that Carson had been courting Marie. "This is pretty tough on you," he muttered. "I'll try to see that Carse is saved . . . If we win," he added wryly.

"Him? I don't care about that Masefield. Let them hang him. But Anse—be careful—"

He looked away, his face hot in the gloom, realizing suddenly why Masefield Carson hated him. Briefly, he wished he hadn't had such consistent luck with women. But the accident that there was a preponderance of females in the second and third generations of Khazaki humans had made it more or less inevitable, and he—well, he was only human. There'd been Earthling girls; and not a few Khazaki women had been intrigued by the big Terrestrial. *Yes, I was lucky,* he thought bitterly. *Lucky in all except the one that mattered.*

"—we'd been a few weeks out of Avandar—it was an obscure outpost then, though I imagine it's grown since—when we detected this Sol-type sun. Seeing that there was an Earth-like planet, we decided to investigate. And since we were all tired of being cooped in the ship, and telescopes showed that any natives which might exist would be too primitive to endanger us, we all went down in the lifeboat.

"And the one-in-a-billion chance happened . . . the atomic converters went out of control and we barely escaped from the boat before it was utterly consumed. We were stranded on an alien planet, with nothing but our clothes and a few hand weapons—and with our ship that would go faster than light circling in its orbit not ten thousand kilometers above us!

"No chance of rescue. There are just too many suns for the Galactic Coordinators to hope to find a ship that doesn't come back. Expansion into this region of space wasn't scheduled for another two centuries. So there we were, and until we could build a boat which would take us back to our ship—there we stayed!

"And it's taken us fifty years so far . . ."

Pregakech came in with the rain glistening on his fur and running in small puddles about his padding feet. "We're ready," he said. "Every warrior whose hiding place we knew has been contacted."

"Then we might as well go." Janazik got up and stretched luxuriously. His eyes were like molten gold in the murky light.

"So soon?" Marie held Anse back with anxious hands. "This same night?"

"The sooner the better," Anse said grimly. "Every day that goes by, more of our friends will be found out and killed, more places will be searched for Ellen, Volakech's grip on the city will grow stronger." He put the spiked helmet back on his head, and buckled the sword about his mailed waist. "Come on, Janazik. The rest stay here and wait for word. If we're utterly defeated, such of us as survive will manage to get back and lead you out of Krakenau—somehow."

Marie started to say something, then shook her head as if the words hurt her throat and drew Anse's face down to hers. "Goodbye, then," she whispered. "Goodbye, and the gods be with you."

He kissed her more awkwardly than was his

wont, feeling himself a thorough scoundrel. Then
he followed Pragakech and Janazik out the trapdoor.

The courtyard was filled with Khazaki warriors,
standing silently in the slow heavy rain. It was the
darkness of early morning, and only an occasional
wan lightning flash, gleaming on spears and axes,
broke the chill gloom. Anse was aware of softly-
moving supple bodies pressing around him, of
night-seeing eyes watching him with an impassive
stare. It was he and Janazik who had the plan and
who had the most experience in warfare, and the
rest looked to them for leadership. It was not easy
to stand under that cool, judging scrutiny, and
Anse strode forth into the street with a feeling of
relief at the prospect of action.

As they moved toward the castle, along the
narrow cobbled lanes winding up the hills, their
army grew. Warriors came loping from alleys,
came slipping out of the dark barricaded houses,
seemed to rise out of the rainy night around them.
All Krakenau was abroad, it seemed, but quietly,
quietly.

And throughout the town other such forces were
on the move, gathering under the lead of anyone
who could be trusted, converging on the citadel
and the rocket ship it guarded.

*Tonight—victory, or destruction of the boat and
a drawn battle . . . or repulsion and ultimate shat-
tering defeat. The gods are abroad tonight.*

Somewhere, faint and far through the dull wash-
ing of rain, a trumpet blew a harsh challenge, once

and again. After it came a distance-muted shouting of voices and a clattering of swords.

"One of our bands has come across a patrol," said Janazik unnecessarily. "Now all hell will be loose in Krakenau. Come on!"

They broke into a trot up the hill. Rounding a sharp turn in the street, they saw a close-ranked mass of warriors with spears aloft.

Guardsmen!

The two forces let out a simultaneous yell and charged at each other in the disorderly Khazaki fashion. It was beginning to lighten just a little; Anse could make out enough for purposes of battle. Hai-ah—here we go!

He smashed into a leading guard, who stabbed at him with his long pike. The edge grazed off Anse's heavy chain mail as the Earthling chopped out with his sword. He knocked the shaft aside and thrust in, hewing at the Khazaki's neck. The guard intercepted the blow with his shield, and suddenly rammed it forward. The murderous spike on its boss thudded against the Terrestrial's broad chest and the linked rings gave under that blow—just a little, just enough to draw blood. Anse roared and chopped down across the other's right arm. The Khazaki howled his pain and stumbled back.

Another was on the Earthling like a spitting cat. Swords hummed ad clashed together. Leaping and dodging, the Khazaki lashed out with a blade like a flickering flame, and none of Anse's blows could land on him.

The Khazaki leaped in suddenly, his edge reaching for the human's unprotected throat. Anse parried with his sword, while his left fist shot out like an iron cannon-ball. It hit the native full in the face, with a crunch of splintering bones. The guard's head snapped back and he fell to the blood-running street.

Janazik was fighting two at once, his sword never resting. He leaped and danced like the shadow of a flame in the wind, and he was laughing—laughing! Anse hewed out, and one of the foemen's heads sprang from its neck. Janazik darted in, there was a blur of steel, and the other guardsman toppled.

Axe and sword! Spear and dagger and flying arrows! The fight rolled back and forth between the darkling walls of houses. it grew with time; Volakech's patrols were drawn by the noise, loyalists crouched in hiding heard of the attack and sped to join it. Anse and Janazik fought side by side, human brawn and Khazaki swiftness, and the corpses were heaped where they went.

A pike raked Anse's hand. He dropped his sword and the enemy leaped in with drawn knife. Anse did not reach for his own dirk—no human had a chance in a knife fight with a Khazaki—but his arms snaked out, his hands closed on the native's waist, and he lifted the enemy up and hurled him against another. They both went down in a crash of denting armor and snapping bones. Anse roared his war-cry and picked up his sword again.

Janazik leaped and darted and fenced, grinning as he fought, demon-lights in his yellow eyes. A spear was hurled at him. He picked it out of the air, one-handed, and threw it back, even as he fought another guardsman. The rebel took advantage of it to get it under Janazik's guard. Swifter than thought, the warrior's dagger was in his left hand—and into the rebel's throat.

Back and forth the battle swayed, roaring, trampling, and the rain mingled with blood between the cobblestones. Thunder of weapons,

shrieking of wounded, shouting of challenges—lightning dancing overhead!

Suddenly it was over.

Anse looked up from his last victim and saw that
the confusion no longer snarled around him. The
street was heaped with dead and wounded, and except for a few individual battles that were still
going on, the surviving guardsmen were in full
flight, and the victorious warriors were shouting
their triumph.

"That was a fight!" panted Janazik. He quivered
with feral eagerness. "Now on to the castle!"

"I think," said Slavatozik thoughtfully, "that
this was the decisive struggle as far as the city is
concerned. Look at how many were involved. Almost all the patrols must have come here—and
now they're beaten. We hold the city!"

"Not much good to us while Volakech is in the
castle," said Anse. "He need only sally forth with
the Earth-weapons—" He leaned on his sword,
gasping great lungfuls of the cool wet air into him.
"But where's Ellen?"

"We've had heralds out shouting for her, as you
suggested," said Slavatozik. "Now that the city is
in our control, she should come out. If not—"

"—then I know how to blow up the boat," said
Gonzales Alonzo bleakly. "If we can get inside the
citadel to it."

The loyalists were reassembling their forces.
Warriors moved over the scene of battle, plundering dead guardsmen, cutting the throats of
wounded enemies and badly mutilated friends. It
was a small army that was crowding around
Anse's tall form.

His worried eyes probed into the dull gray light
of the rainy dawn. Of a sudden, he stiffened and
peered more closely. Someone was coming down

the street, thrusting through the assembled warriors. Someone—someone—he knew that bright bronze hair . . .

Ellen.

He stood waiting, letting her come up to him, and his eyes were hungry. She was tall and full-bodied and supple, graceful almost as a Khazaki, and her wide-set eyes were calm and gray under a broad clear forehead and there was a dusting of freckles over her straight nose and her mouth was wide and strong and generous and—

"Ellen," he said wonderingly. "Ellen."

"What are you doing?" she asked. "What have you planned?"

No question of how he was, no look at the blood trickling along his sides and splashed over his face and arms—well—"Where were you?" he asked, and cursed himself for not being able to think of a better greeting.

"I hid with the family of Azakhagar," she said. "I lay in their loft when the patrolmen came searching for me. Then I heard your heralds going through the streets, calling on me to come out in your name. So I came."

"How did you know it wasn't a trick of Volakech's?" asked someone.

"I told the heralds to use my name and add after it—well—something that only she and I knew," said Anse uncomfortably.

Janazik remained impassive, but he recalled that the phrase had been "Dougald Anson, who once told you something on a sunny day down by Zamanaui River." He could guess what the something had been. Well, it seemed to happen to all Earthmen sooner or later, and it meant the end of the old unregenerate days. He sighed, a little wistfully.

"But what did you want me for?" asked Ellen. She stood before Anse in her short, close-fitting tunic, the raindrops glittering in her heavy coppery hair, and he thought wryly that the question was in one sense superfluous. But in another sense, and with time so desperately short—

"You're the only one of us who can plot a course for the rocket," he said. "Alonzo here, or almost anyone, should be able to pilot it, but you're the only one who can take it to the Star Ship. So that, of course, is why Carson and Volakech were after you, and why we had to have you too. If we can get into the citadel, capture the rocket and get up to the Star Ship, it'll be easy to overthrow Volakech. But if he gets there first, all Khazak couldn't win against him."

She nodded, slowly and wearily. Her gray eyes were haunted. "I wonder if it matters who gets there," she said. "I was wonder why we're fighting and killing each other. Over who shall sit on the throne of an obscure city-state on an insignificant planet? Over the exact disposition to be made of one little spaceship? It isn't worth it." She looked around at the sprawled corpses, lying on the bloody cobblestones with rain falling in their gaping mouths, and shuddered. "It isn't worth that."

"There's more to it than that," said Janazik bleakly. "Masefield Carson and his friend—his puppet, I think—Volakech would use the ship to bring all the world under their rule. Then they would mold it into a pattern suited for conquering a small empire among the neighboring stars."

"Volakech always talked that way; before his

first revolution," said Ellen. "And Carse use to say—but that can't be right! He can't have meant it. And even if he did—what of it? Is it worth enough for brothers to slay each other over?"

"Yes." Janazik's voice was pitiless. "Shall the freemen of Khazak become the regimented hordes of a tyrant? Let all this world be blown asunder first!"

"Shall the innocent folk of the other stars become victims?" urged Alonzo. "Shall Khazak become a menace to the Galaxy, one which must be destroyed—or must itself destroy? Shall there be war with—Earth herself?"

"To Shantuzik with that," growled Anse. "These are our enemies, to be fought and beaten. Out there is the great civilization of the Galaxy, and they would keep us from it for generations yet, and make it in the end our foe. And Volakech is a murderer with no right to the throne of Krakenau. I say let's get at his liver!"

"Well—" Ellen looked away. When she turned back, there was torment in her eyes, but her voice was low and steady: "I'm with you in whatever you plan. But on one condition. Carse is not to be harmed."

"Not harmed!" exploded Janazik. "Why, that dirty traitor deserves—"

"He is still my brother," said Ellen. "When Volakech is beaten, he will not be able to do any more harm, and he will see that he was wrong." Her eyes flashed coldly. "Whoever hurts Carse will have me for blood-enemy!"

"As you will," shrugged Anse, trying to hide the pain in his heart. "But now . . . Our plan is to storm the citadel. We can't hope to take it, but we'll keep the garrison busy. Meanwhile a few of us break in, get the rocket, and take it back out here, where you will have an orbit plotted—"

"I can't make one that quickly. And who can pilot it well enough to land it here without cracking it up?"

They looked at each other, and then eyes turned to Gonzales Alonzo. He smiled mirthlessly. "I can try," he said. "But I'm only an engineer; I never imagined I'd have to fly the thing. Chiang Ching-Wei was supposed to be the pilot, but he's a prisoner now."

"If we smash the rocket—well, then we smash it," said Anse heavily. "It'll mean a long and hard war against Volakech from outside, and he'll have all the advantages of the new weapons. We may never overthrow him before he gets another boat built. Still—we'll just have to try."

Ellen said quietly: "I can pilot it."

"You!"

"Of course. I've been working on the second boat from the beginning. I know it as well as anyone, every seam and rivet and wiring diagram. I was aboard when Chiang took her on a practice run only a few days ago. I'll fly it for you!"

"You can't—we have to fight our way into the castle itself, the very heart of Volakech's power—you'd be killed!"

"It's the best chance. If you think we can get in at all, I stand as good a chance of living through it as anyone else."

"She's right," said Janazik. "And while we waste time here arguing, the citadel is getting ready. Come on!"

Automatically, Anse broke into movement, trotting along beside Janazik, and the army formed its ranks and followed them.

He had time for a few hurried words with Ellen,

whispered as they went up the hill: "Stay close by me. There'll be a small group of us getting in, picked fighters, and we'll make a ring about you."

"Of course," she nodded. Her gray eyes shone, and she was breathing quickly. "I begin to see why you were a rover all those years, Anse. It's mad and desperate and terrible—but before Cosmos, we're alive!"

"Most recruits are frightened green before their first battle," he said. "You have a warrior's heart, Ellen—" He broke off, hearing the banality of his own words.

"Listen, my dearest," he said then, quickly. "We may not come alive through all this. But remember what I did say, down by the river that day. I love you."

She was silent. He went on, fumbling for words: "You wouldn't answer me then—"

"I thought it was just your usual talk to women."

"It may have been—then," he admitted. "But it hasn't been since, and it isn't now." His sword-calloused hand found hers. "Don't forget, Ellen. I love you. I will always love you."

"Anse—" She turned toward him, and he saw her eyes alight. "Anse—"

A bugle shrilled through the rain, high and harsh ahead of them. Dimly, they made out the monstrous bulk of the castle, looming through the misty gray light, its towers lost in the vague sky. Janazik's sword flashed from its sheath.

"The battle begins," said a voice out of the blurring rain.

Anse drew Ellen over against a wall and kissed her. Her lips were cool and firm under his, wet with rain; he would never forget that kiss while life was in him.

They looked at each other for a moment of wonder, and then broke apart and followed Janazik.

The loyalists charged in a living wave that roared
as it surfed against the castle walls and spattered a
foam of blood and steel. From three sides they
came, weaving in and out of the hailing arrows,
lifting shields above them, leaving their dead behind them.

The blaster cannon mounted on the walls
spouted flame and thunder. Warriors were mowed
down before that whirling white fury, armor
melted when the lightning-like discharges played
over it, but still the assault went on with all the
grim bitter courage of the Khazaki race.

Old siege engines were appearing, dragged out
of storehouses and hiding places where they had
been kept against such a day of need. Now the
great catapults and ballistae were mounted;
stones and fireballs and iron-headed bolts were
raking the walls. A testudo moved awkwardly
forth up the steep hill toward the gates. It was
blasted to flaming molten ruin, but another got underneath the walls and the crash of a battering
ram came from under its roof.

Shadowlike in the blinding rain, the warriors
flitted up toward the walls. No spot of cover was
too small for one of those ghostly shapes; they
seemed to carry their own invisibility with them.
Under the walls—scaling ladders appearing as if
out of nowhere—up the walls and into the castle!

The ladders were hurled down. The warriors
who gained the walls were blasted by cannon, cut
down by superior numbers, lost in a swirl of battle

and death. Boiling water rained down over the walls on those below, spears and arrows and the roaring blaster bolts. But still they came. Still the howling, screeching demons of Krakenau came, and died, and came again.

Anse cursed, softly, luridly, pain croaking in his voice: "We can't be with them. They're being slaughtered and we can't be with them."

"We're needed worse here," said Janazik curtly. "If only Pragakech can maintain the assault for an hour—"

He and Anse loped in the forefront. Behind them came Gonzales, Ellen, and a dozen picked young Khazaki. They wove through a maze of alleys and streets and deserted market squares, working around behind the castle. The roar of battle came to them out of the gray mist of rain; otherwise there was only the padding and splashing of their own feet, the breath rasping harsh in their lungs, the faint clank and jingle of their harness. All Krakenau not at the storming of the citadel had withdrawn into the mysterious shells of the houses, lay watching and waiting and whetting knives in the dark.

The paths dipped steeply downward, until, when they came around behind the citadel and stood peering out of a tunnel-like alley, there was a sheer cliff-face before them. On this side the castle was impregnable. The only approach was a knife-edged trail winding up the cliff, barely wide enough for one man at a time. At its top, flush with the precipice edge, the wall was built. Against this wall, commanding the trail, there had in the old days been an archer post, but lately a cannon had been mounted there.

Yet that very security, thought Anse, might be a weakness. Except for that gun, the approach wouldn't be watched, epecially with the fight going on elsewhere. So—

"Give me your weapon, Alonzo," said Janazik.

"Here." Gonzales handed him the blaster pistol. "But it only has two charges left in it."

"That may be enough." Janazik slipped it under his cloak. Then he wound a gold brassard about his arm and started up the trail. A couple of his Khazaki came behind them, then Anse, Ellen and Alonzo, and finally the rest of the warriors.

The trail was steep and slippery, water swirling down it, loose rocks moving uneasily beneath the feet—and it was a dizzying drop off the sheer edge to the ground below. They wound upward slowly, panting, cursing, wondering how much of a chance their desperate scheme really had.

Ellen slipped a little. Anse reached back and caught her hand. He smiled lop-sidedly. "Now I don't want to let go," he said.

"I wonder—" Ellen looked away, then back to him, and her eyes were wide and puzzled. "I wonder if I want you to, Anse."

His heart seemed to jump up into his throat, but he let her go and said wryly: "I'm afraid I have to right now. But wait till later."

Up and up—*Later! Will there ever be a later?*

And if there is, what then? I'm still more than half a Khazaki. Can we live together in the great civilization I hardly comprehend?

It was simpler when Janazik and I were warring over the planet . . . Janazik! I wonder if two beings of the same race could ever know as close a friendship as that between us two aliens. We've fought and laughed and sung together, we've saved each other's lives, sweated and suffered and been afraid, together. We know each other as we will never know any other being.

Well, it passes. We'll always remain close friends, I suppose. But the old comradeship—I'll have to give that up.

But Ellen—

Up and up—

Janazik whistled, long and loud, and called: "Hail Volakech! Friends!"

He could dimly see the looming bulk of the blaster cannon, crouched behind its iron shield. Above it the walls of the castle were high and dark and—empty.

The voice came from ahead of him, taut with nervousness: "Who goes there?"

"A friend. I have a message for His Highness." Janazik moved forward almost casually. His eyes gleamed with mirth. It tickled his heart, this dicing with death. Someday he'd overreach himself and that would be the end, but until then he was having fun.

"Advance . . . No, no one else. Just you alone."

Janazik sauntered forward until he stood only a meter from the blunt ugly muzzle. He had his left arm out of his cloak, so that the golden brassard shone in plain view. Underneath, his right hand thumbed the catch of Alonzo's pistol.

"Who are you?" challenged the voice from behind the shield.

"A messenger for His Highness from his allies in Volgazan," said Janazik. "Seeing that there was still fighting going on, I and my men decided to come in the back way."

"Well—I suppose I can let you in, under guard. But your men will have to stay out here."

"Very well." Janazik strolled over behind the shield.

There were three warriors crouched there, in

front of a small door in the wall. One of them was about to blow his trumpet for a guard detail. The other two poised their spears near Janazik's throat. None of them thought that anyone outside the citadel might possess an Earth-weapon.

Janazik shot right through his cloak. In that narrow space, the ravenous discharge blinded and blistered him, stung his face with flying particles of molten iron. The hammer-blow of concussion sent him reeling back against the wall. His cloak caught afire; he ripped it off and flung it down on the three blackened corpses before him.

Vision returned to his dazzled eyes. These Earth-weapons were hideous things, he thought; they made nothing of courage or strength or even cunning. He wondered what changes Galactic civilization would bring to old Khazak, and didn't think he'd like most of them. Maybe Volakech was right.

But Anse was his comrade and Aligan had been his king. He whistled, and the others came running up.

"Quick," rasped Janazik. "The noise may draw somebody—quick, inside!"

"Can't we swing this lightning thrower around and blast them?" wondered a Khazaki.

"No, it's fixed in place." Anse threw his brawny shoulders against the solid mass of the door. It swung ponderously back and they dashed through the tunnel in the thick wall—out into the open courtyard of the castle!

The noises of the fight rose high from here, but there were only a few warriors in sight, scurrying back and forth on their errands without noticing the newcomers—a fact which did not surprise Anse or Janazik, who knew what vast confusion a battle was. The human remembered the layout now—the rocket would be over by the machine shops, near the donjon keep—"This way!"

They trotted across the court, around the gray stone bulk of the citadel's buildings and towers, toward the long wooden shed which housed the new machine shop. The rain was beginning to slacken now, and the sun was up behind its gray veil, so that there was light shining through slanting silver. Against the dark walls, the lean torpedo shape of the rocket boat gleamed like a polished spearhead.

"Now—ahead!" Janazik broke into a run toward the boat, and they followed him in a close ring about Ellen.

A band of fighters came around the corner of the machine shop, in front of the rocket. The wet light shone off their brassards. Janazik swore bitterly, and his hand dropped to his sword.

One of the enemy warriors let out a yell. "Earthlings—two—three of them! Not ours—"

The blaster crashed in Janazik's hand, and five dropped their charred bodies on the ground. With a spine-shivering yell, Janazik bounded forward, and after him came Anse, Alonze, and a round dozen of the fiercest fighters in Krakenan. The blaster was exhausted now—but they had their swords.

The leader of the enemy band was huge for a Khazaki, dark-furred and green-eyed. His men were scattering in panic, but he roared a bull-voiced command and they rallied about him and stood before the rocket.

Volakech. By all the thirteen hells, Volakech!

He must have been leading reinforcements to a threatened point on the wall, thought Anse in a fleeting moment, and his sharp mind had instantly deduced that the invaders were after the rocket—and that they could have no more blaster charges, or they would be using them. And Volakech's band was still larger than theirs, and he had all the forces of the citadel behind him if he could summon them!

The two bands crashed together and steel began to fly. Anse stood before Ellen and lashed out at a spitting Khazaki who reached for his belly with a sword. The enemy dodged past his guard, drilled in close. Ellen shouted and kicked at the native's ankles. He stumbled, dropping his defense, and Anse clove his skull.

Volakech roared. He swung a huge battle axe, and its shock and thunder rose high over the swaying tide of battle. Two of Janazik's men leaped at him. He swept the axe in a terrible arc and the spike cracked one pate and the edge split the other's face open. Alonzo sprang at him with furious courage, wielding a sword. Volakech knocked it spinning from his hand, but, before he could kill the engineer, Anse was on him.

They traded blows in a clamor of steel. Axe and sword clashed together, sheared along chain mail and rang on helmets. It was a blur of rake and slash and parry with Volakech grinning at him behind a network of whirling steel.

Anse gathered his strength and pressed forward with reckless fury. His sword hummed and whistled and roared against Volakech's hard-held guard. He laid open arms, legs, cheek; he probed and lunged for the rebel king' trunk. Volakech snarled, but step by step he was driven back.

Warriors fell, but it was on the bodies of foemen, and even dying they stabbed upward at the enemy. Bitter, bloody, utterly ruthless, the struggle swayed about the rocketship. It was old Khazak that fought, the planet of warriors, and, even as he hewed and danced and slew, Janazik thought bleakly that he was trying to end the gory magnificence of that age; he was bringing civilization and with it the doom of his own kind. Khazak of the future would not be the same world.

If they won—if they won!

"To me!" he yelled. "To me, men of Aligan! Hai, Aligan! Krakenau! Dougald!"

They heard and rallied round him, the last grasping survivors of his band. But there were few of Volakech's men left, few.

"Volakech! Aid the king! To me, men of Volakech!" The rebel shouted at the top of his lungs. And Anse lunged in at him, beating against the swift armor of the axe.

"Anse!" Janazik's urgent shout cut through the clangor of battle. "Anse, here! We're blasting free!"

The human hardly heard him. He forced his way closer in against Volakech, his sword whistling about the usurper's helmeted head.

"Anse!" shouted Janazik. "Anse—Ellen needs you—"

With a tiger snarl, Anse broke free from his opponent and whirled about. A rebel stood before him. There was an instant of violence too swift to be followed, and Anse leaped over the ripped body and up to Janazik.

The Khazaki stood by the airlock. There was a ring of corpses before him; his sword ran blood.

"Ellen?" gasped Anse. "Ellen?"

"Inside," rasped Janazik. "She's inside. We have to get out of here—only way to get your attention—*Come on!*"

Anse saw the armed band swarming at them from one of the outer towers, defenders who had finally noticed the battle at the rocket and were coming to aid their king. Not a chance against them—except the boat!

Man and Khazaki stepped back into the airlock. A storm of arrows and javelins broke loose. Anse saw two of his men fall—then Janazik had slammed the heavy outer valve and dogged it shut.

"Ellen!" he gasped. "Ellen—take the boat up before they dynamite it!"

The girl nodded. She was strapping herself into the pilot's seat before the gleaming control panel. Only Alonzo was there with her, bleeding but still on his feet. Four of them survived—only four—but they had the boat!

Through the viewport, Anse saw the attackers surging around the hull. They'd use ballistae to crush it, dynamite to blow it up, blaster cannon to fry them alive inside the metal shell—unless they got it into the sky first.

"Take the engines, Alonzo," said Ellen.

Gonzales Alonzo nodded. "You help me, Janazik," he said. "I'm sure I—can stay conscious—"

The pilot room was in the bows.

Behind it, bulkheaded off, lay the air plant and the other mechanisms for mantaining life aboard—not very extensive, for the boat wouldn't be in space long. Amidships were the control gyros, and behind still another bulkhead the engine controls. Rather than install an elaborate automatic feed system, the builders had relied on manual controls acting on light signals flashed by the pilot. It wa less efficient, but it had shortened the labor of constructing the vessel and was good enough for the mere hop it had to make.

"I don't know anything about it," said Janazik doubtfully.

"I'll tell you what to do—Help me—" Leaning on the Khazaki's arm, Alonzo stumbled toward the stern.

Anse strapped his big body into the chair beside Ellen's. "I can't help much, I'm afraid," he said.

"No—except by being here," she smiled.

Looking out, he saw that the assault on the castle was almost over—beaten off. It had provided the diversion they needed—but at what cost, at what cost?

"We might as well take off for the Star Ship right away," he said.

"Of course. And that will end the war. Volakech can either surrender or sit in the castle till he rots."

"Or we can use the ship to blast the citadel."

"Oh—oh, Cosmos, no!" Her eyes were filled with sudden horror.

"Why not?" he argued angrily. "Only way we can rescue our people if he won't give them up of his own will."

"We might kill Carse," she whispered.

It was on his tongue to snap good riddance, but he choked down the impulse. "Why do you care for him that much?"

"He's my brother," she said simply, and he realized that in spite of her civilized protestations Ellen was sufficiently Khazaki to feel the primitive unreasoning clan loyalty of the planet. She added slowly: "And when Father died, years ago, Carse took his place, he's been both father and big brother to me. He may have some wrong ideas, but he's always been so—good—"

A child's worship of the talented, handsome, genial elder brother, and she had never really outgrown it. Well—it didn't matter. Once they had the Star Ship, Carse didn't matter. "He'll be as safe as anyone can be in these days," said Anse. "I—I'll protect him myself if need be."

Her hand slid into his, and she kissed him, there in the little boat while it rocked and roared under the furious assaults from without. "Anyone who hurts Carse is my blood foe," she breathed. "But anyone who helps him helps me, and—and—"

Anse smiled, dreamily. The engines began to stutter, warming up, and Volakech's men scattered in dismay. They had seen the fire that spurted from the rocket tubes.

And in the engine room, Masefield Carson held his blaster leveled on Alonzo and Janazik. "Go ahead," he smiled. "Go ahead—take the ship up."

The Khazaki swore lividly. His sword seemed almost to leap halfway out of the scabbard. Carse swung the blaster warningly, and he clashed the weapon back. Useless, useless, when white flame could destroy him before he got moving.

"How did you get here?" he snarled.

The tall, bronze-haired man smiled again. "I wasn't in the fight," he said. "Volakech wanted to save my knowledge and told me to stay out of the battle. I wasn't really needed. But it occurred to me that your assault was obviously a futile gesture unless you hoped in some way to capture the boat. So I hid in here to guard it—just in case. And now—we'll take her up. We may just as well do so. Once I have the Star Ship—" He gestured at Alonzo. "Start the engines. And no tricks. I understand them as well as you do."

Gonzales strapped himself in place and stood swaying with weakness while he manipulated the controls. "I can't—reach that wheel—" he gasped.

"Turn it, Janazik," said Carse. "About a quarter turn—that's enough."

The impassive faces of meters wavered and blurred before Alonzo's swimming eyes. He had been pretty badly hurt. But the engines were warming up.

"Strap yourself in, Janazik," said Carse.

The Khazaki obeyed, sickly. He didn't really need the anti-acceleration webbing—Carse himself was content to hang on to a stanchion with one hand—but it would hamper his movements, he would have no way of making a sudden leap. Between them, he and Alonzo could handle the engines readily enough, Carse giving them their orders. Then once they were at the Star Ship he could blast them down, go out to capture Anse and Ellen—and the old books said one man could handle the ship if necessary—

How to warn the two in the pilot room? How to get help? The warrior's brain began to turn over, cool and steady now, swift as chilled lightning.

The boat spouted flame, stood on its tail and climbed for the sky. Acceleration dragged at Carse, but it wasn't too great for a strong man to resist. Carse tightened his grip on the stanchion. His blaster was steady on them.

Ellen's signal lights blinked and blinked on the control panels. More on the No.3 jet, ease to port, full ahead, cut No.2 . . . Alonzo handled most of it, occasionally gasping a command to Janazik. the bellow of the rockets filled the engine room.

And in the bows, Dougald Anson saw the world reel and fall behind, saw the rainy sky open up in a sudden magnificence of sun, saw it slowly darken and the stars come awesomely out. Gods, gods, was this space? Open space? No wonder the old people had longed to get away!

How to get help, how to warn Anse—Janazik's mind spun like an unloaded engine, spewing forth plan after unusable plan. Quickly, now, by Shantuzik's hells!

No way out—and the minutes were fleeing, the rocket was reaching for the sky, He knew they were nearing the Star Ship and still he lay in his harness like a sheep and obeyed Carse's gun-point orders!

The disgrace of it! He snarled his anger, and at Alonzo's gasped command turning the wheel with unnecessary savagery. The ship lurched as a rocket tube misfired. Carse nearly lost his hold, and in an instant Janazik's hands were at the acceleration webbing, ready to fling it off and leap at him.

The man recovered, and his blaster came to the ready again. He had to shout to be heard above the thundering jets: "Don't try that—either of you! I can shoot you both and handle it myself if I must!"

He laughed then, a tall and splendid figure standing strained against the brutal, tearing acceleration. Ellen's brother—aye! And one could see why she wanted him saved. Janazik's lips curled back from his teeth in a snarl of hate.

The rocket must be very near escape velocity now. Presently Ellen would signal for the jets to be turned off and they would rush weightless through space while she took her readings and plotted the orbit that would get them to the Star Ship. And if then Carse emerged with his blaster—

Anse had only a sword.

But—*Anse is Anse,* thought Janazik. *If there is any faintest glimmer of a chance he will find it. And if not, we're really no worse off than now. I'll have to warn him and leave the rest up to him.*

The Khazaki nodded bleakly to himself. It would probably mean his own death under Carse's blaster flame—and damn it, damn it, he liked living. Even if the old world he knew were doomed, there had been many new worlds of the Galactic cluster. He and Anse had often dreamed of flying over them—

However—

A red light blinked on the panel. Ellen's signal to cut the rockets. They were at escape velocity.

Wearily, his hand shaking, Alonzo threw the master switch. The sudden silence was like a thunderclap.

And Janazik screeched the old Krakenaui danger call from his fullest lungs.

Carse turned around with a curse, awkward in the sickening zero-gravity of free fall. "It won't do you any good," he yelled thickly. "I'll kill him too—"

Alonzo threw the master switch up! With a coughing roar, the rockets burst back into life. No longer holding the stanchion, Carse was hurled to the floor.

Janazik clawed at his webbing to get free. Carse leveled his blaster on Alonzo. The engineer threw another switch at random, and the direction of acceleration shifted with sudden violence, slamming Carse against the farther wall.

His blaster raved, and Alonzo had no time to scream before the flame licked about him.

And in the control sroom, Anse heard Janazik's high ululating yell. The reflexes of the wandering years came back to galvanize him. His sword seemed to leap into his hand, he flung himself out of his chair webbing with a shout . . .

"Anse!" Ellen's voice came dimly to his ears, hardly noticed. "Anse—what is it—"

He drifted weightless in midair, cursing, trying to swim. And then the rockets woke up again and threw him against the floor. He twisted with Khazaki agility, landed crouched, and bounded for the stern.

Ellen looked after him, gasping, for an instant yet unaware of the catastrophe, thinking how little she knew that yellow-maned savage after all, and how she would like to learn, and—

The rocket veered, crazily. Anse caught himself as he fell, adjusted to the new direction of gravity, and continued his plunging run. The crash of a blaster came from ahead of him.

He burst into the control room and saw it in one blinding instant. Alonzo's charred body sagging in its harness, Janazik half out of his, Carse staggering to his feet—the blaster turned on Janazik, Janazik, the finger tightening—

Tiger-like, Anse sprang. Carse glimpsed him, turned, the blaster half swung about . . . and the murderous fighting machine which was Dougald Anson had reached him. Carse saw the sword shrieking against his face; it was the last thing he ever saw . . .

Anse lurched back against the control panel. "Turn it off!" yelled Janazik. "Throw that big switch there!"

Mechanically, the human obeyed, and there was silence again, a deep ringing silence in which they floated free. It felt like an endless falling.

Falling, falling—Anse looked numbly down at his bloody sword. Falling, falling, falling—but that couldn't be right, he thought dully. He had already fallen. He had killed Ellen's brother.

"And I love her," he whispered.

Janazik drifted over, slowly in the silent room. His eyes were a deep gold, searching now. *If Ellen won't have him, he and I will go out together, out to the stars and the great new frontier. But if she will, I'll have to go alone, I'll always be alone—*

Unless she would come too. She's a good kid . . . I'd like to have her along. Maybe take a mate of my own too . . . But that can never be, now. She won't come near her brother's slayer.

"You might not have had to kill him," said Janazik. "Maybe you could have disarmed him."

"Not before he got one of us—probably you," said Anse tonelessly. "Anyway, he needed killing. He shot Alonzo."

He added, after a moment: "A man has to stand by his comrades."

Janazik nodded, very slowly. "Give me your sword," he said.

"Eh?" Anse looked at him. The blue eyes were unseeing, blind with pain, but he handed over the red weapon. Janazik slipped his own glaive into the human's fingers.

Then he laid a hand on Anse's shoulder and smiled at him, and then looked away.

We Khazaki don't know love. There is comradeship, deeper than any Earthling knows. When it happens between male and female, they are mates. When it is between male and male, they are bloodbrothers. And a man must stand by his comrades.

Ellen came in, pulling her way along the walls by the handholds, and Anse looked at her without saying a word, just looking.

"What happened?" she said. "What is the—*Oh!*"

Carse's body floated in midair, turning over and over in air currents like a drowned man in the sea.

"Carse—Carse—"

Ellen pushed from the wall, over to the dead man. She looked at his still face, and stroked his blood-matted hair, and smiled through a mist of tears.

"You were always good to me, Carse," she whispered. "You were . . : goodnight, brother. Goodnight."

Then turning to Anse and Janazik, with something cold and terrible in her voice: "Who killed him?"

Anse looked at her, dumbly.

"I did," said Janazik.

He held forth the dripping sword. "He stowed away—was going to take over the ship. Alonzo threw him off balance by turning the rockets back on. He killed Alonzo. Then I killed him. He needed it. He was a traitor and a murderer, Ellen."

"He was my brother," she whispered. And suddenly she was sobbing in Anse's arms, great racking sobs that seemed to tear her slender body apart.

But she'd get over it.

Anse looked at Janazik over her shoulder, and while he ruffled her shining hair his eyes locked with the Khazaki's. *This is the end. Once we land, we can never see each other, not ever again. And we were comrades in the old days . . .*

Farewell, my brother.

When the Star Ship landed outside Krakenau's surrendered citadel, it was still raining a little. Janazik looked out at the wet gray world and shivered. Then, wordlessly, he stepped from the airlock and walked slowly down the hill toward the sea. He did not look back, and Anse did not look after him.

So despite centuries of carefully applied sociodynamics, history stubbornly continued to move more by accident than design. Khazak was scarcely a unique case. The experiences of other long-lost colonies repeatedly illustrate this principle.

Surely among the most dramatic—and dangerous—accident that can befall star-farers is exposure to a trepidation vortex. Indeed, it was this space-warping mishap that overtook the original Traveler on her maiden voyage and hurled her into uncharted regions.

What a vortex can do to the continuum, isolation can do to a society.

VIRGIN PLANET

Corporal Maiden Barbara Whitley of Freetoon, hereditary huntress, wing leader of the crossbow cavalry, and novice in the Mysteries, halted her orsper and peered through a screen of brush. Breath sucked sharply between her teeth.

From this edge of the forest, the Ridge mountains rolled away in a green blaze of grass to the wide floor of the Holy River valley. Tall white clouds walked in a windy sky. With midsummer approaching, both suns were visible. Ay was a spark so bright it hurt the eyes, following the great golden fireball of Bee down toward the western horizon. Minos was waxing, huge and banded, in its eternal station a little south of the zenith. The moon Ariadne was a pale half-disc. The other moons had not yet risen, or were drowned by daylight, but the six hours of night to come would be bright.

It was on the thing in the valley, five kilometers away, that Barbara focused her eyes.

It stood upright, like a lean finless war-dart, and

she estimated its height as 40 meters. That was
much smaller than the Ship of Father. But it was
nearly the same shape, if the hints dropped by initiates were truthful . . . and it had been *seen* this
morning, descending from the sky.

A chill went along her nerves. She was not especially pious; none of the Whitleys were. But this
was Mystery. They had always said it, they sang it
in the rituals and they told it to children on rainy
nights when the fires leaped high on the barracks
hearths—

Some day the Men will come to claim us.

If this was the Men.

Barbara's hand strayed to the horn slung at her
waist. She could call the others. Claudia, the Old
Udall, had sent out the whole army to look for the
shining thing, and there must be others within ear-
shot.

The stillness of that big metal beast was un-
nerving. It could well be a vessel of the Monsters.
The Monsters were half folk-tale, it was said they
lived on the stars like the Men and had dealings
with the Men, sometimes friendly and sometimes
otherwise.

A stray lock of rusty-red hair blew from under
Barbara's morion and tickled her nose. She
sneezed. It seemed to crystallize decision.

Surely there were Monsters in that thing! The
Men would arrive much more portentously, landing first at the Ship of Father and then at the various towns. And there would be haloes and other
prodigies about them, and creatures of shining
steel in attendance.

Barbara was rather frightened at the idea of
Monsters—she felt her heart thump beneath the
iron breastshields—but they were less awesome
than Men. If she merely went back to town and re-

ported, she knew exactly how Claudia Udall would take charge—the army would move according to tactics which were, well, simply *rotten*, like the time when it had been led directly into a greendale ambush. And a mere corporal would be just nobody.

She checked her equipment with rapid, professional care: iron helmet, reinforced leather cuirass and kilt, boots, ax, knife, lasso. She cocked her spring-wound repeating crossbow and tucked it in the crook of her left arm. Her right hand picked up the reins, and she clucked to the orsper.

It trotted downhill at the swift rocking pace of its breed, the feathered head, beaked and crested, erect. The wind blew in her face, murmuring of the sea and the Ship whence it came. The object grew nearer—still not a sound from it, not a stirring. Barbara grew quite convinced that there were Monsters aboard. Men would have been out long ago. It was a less terrifying prospect. Monsters had unknown powers, but they were still mortal, limited creatures, but Men. . . .

Barbara had never thought a great deal about the Men. Now the songs and rituals came back to her. "The Men are the males of the human race. We were coming to join them, but the Ship went astray because of our sins. The Men are taller and stronger than we, infinitely wiser and more virtuous, and they have hair on their chins and no breasts . . ."

She came up into the long shadow of the—boat? "Hoy, there!" she cried. No answer. A flock of gray rangers went overhead, calling to each other, incredibly unconcerned.

Barbara rode several times around the thing. There was a circular door in the hull, out of her reach and smoothly closed, and there were blank

ports. Not a face in any of them. Really, it was
getting ridiculous! Fear vanished in a gust of
temper.

The startled screech of the orsper jerked her
back to reality. There was someone running from
the west.

She spurred her mount forward. The person was
approaching the boat . . . must have been looking
around when she arrived. . . . Person? No!

It was strangely dressed in some kind of tunic,
the legs sheathed in cloth, a small packsack on
the shoulders. But the form of it was grotesque,
inhuman. Broad shoulders—not unpleasing, that,
but the hips were of an ugly narrowness. There
was yellow hair cropped short, and a lean face
with too much nose and chin, altogether too much
bone and too little flesh.

Barbara knew what all the 500 families looked
like, and this wasn't any of them. She remembered
from the old stories that Monsters had many
shapes, but some of them looked like deformed
humans.

"Hoy-aaa!" she yelled. "What are you doing
here?"

The Monster drew a small tube from a holster
and pointed it at her. Dashing close, Barbara saw
that its crimson tunic was open at the neck, the
chest was flat and hairy and there was thick hair
on the arms—

Then she hardly had time to think. The Monster
might or might not be peaceful, and she couldn't
just shoot it down. But she knew better than to
take unnecessary risks.

Her knees guided the leaping bird and her hands
whirled up the lariat.

The Monster stood there gaping.

She heard words in a distorted, alien accent:

"Holy Cosmos, what's going on here?" No human had so deep a voice!

Then the lasso snaked out, fell, and drew taut.

Corporal Maiden Barbara Whitley galloped in triumph toward Freetoon, dragging the Monster behind her.

DEFINITIONS AND REFERENCES

"Delta Capitis Lupi: Double. (Coordinates given, indicating its distance from Nerthus as about 200 light-years; Nerthus is a Service base planet, ca. 300 parsecs from Sol.) Primary of type AO, mass 4 Sol, luminosity 81 Sol. Companion Sol-type, average distance from primary 98 Astronomical Units. Unexplored due to trepidation vortex in neighborhood . . ."

—Pilot's Manual, Argus 293 Region (with much expansion of abbreviations)

"Trepidation Vortex: Traveling region of warped space, primary effect being that of violently shifting gravitational fields. Responsible for some planetary perturbations. Spaceships on hyperdrive encountering a vortex are thrown far off course and usually destroyed . . ."

—General Encyclopedic Dictionary

". . . Davis Bertram. Born in Sigma Hominis Volantis system, where father had grown wealthy. (Odd how anachronisms like private ostentation redevelop on the frontier, isn't it?) Basic schooling on Earth; astronautical training on Thunderhouse (the most notoriously slack academy in the known Galaxy—must assemble data and file a complaint when I get the time). Having bought his own robotic cruiser, he came to Nerthus to start a career in stellagraphic survey by going to Delta Wolf's Head—alone! As far as I could gather, his preparations here consisted mostly of bottle hoisting, skirt chasing, and a little amateur landscape painting.

"I could not legally refuse him clearance, since he had the training and a sufficient goodwill quotient to protect any natives he might encounter. I checked the physiological data, hoping for an excuse, but somatically he is first-rate; I presume he makes himself excercise regularly to attract women, but the law does not make this any of my business. He is, in fact (or was), quite a large, good-looking young man of the vanishing Nordic type; his brain is excellent, if he only cared to use it; how can I extrapolate disaster on the basis of mere cocksureness and flippancy?

"I warned him of the vortex, and that the Service did not plan to visit Delta until it was safely gone from the region, in about 30 years. He replied that it was probably safe as of now. I told him that if he did not come back, we could not hazard lives in a rescue party. He could not conceive that he might not return. What he wanted, of course, was the glory. If Delta turns out to have intelligent autochthones or be an uninhabited, colonizable planet, he will go down in history with Carsten.

"In the end, then, he left, and his *At Venture* is now somewhere near the vortex. If he avoids that, and avoids hostile natives, wild beasts, poison, disease—the million traps a new planet lays for us—he will come back and have all the adoring females he can use. So much for Man's Starward Yearning. or am I merely envious in this winter of my own lifetime?"

> —*Diary of Yamagata Tetsuo, Chief of Coordination Service, Argus 293 Region, Stellamont, Nerthus*

Minos was full, drenching Freetoon with cold amber light, and the air had grown chilly. Barbara Whitley walked through silent streets, between darkened buildings, to she cavalry barracks. It formed one side of a square around a courtyard, the stables and arsenal completing the ring. Her boots thudded on the cobbles as she led her orsper to its stall.

A stone lamp on a shelf showed the snoring grooms—all Nicholsons, a stupid family used only for menial work—stirring uneasily on the straw as she tramped in. She nudged one of the stocky, tangle-haired women awake with her toe. "Food," she demanded. "And beer. And take care of the bird."

Afterward, she undressed and washed herself in the courtyard trough. She regarded her face complacently in the water. The Minoslight distorted colors, ruddy hair and long green eyes became something else, but the freckled snub nose and the wide mouth and the small square chin were more pleasing than . . . oh, than that Dyckman build.

Dyckmans were just *sloppy*.

The dying hearthfire within the barrack showed long-limbed forms sprawled on straw ticks. She stowed her weapons and armor, trying to be quiet. But Whitleys were light sleepers, and her cousin Valeria woke up.

"Oh, it's you. Two left feet as always," snarled Valeria, "and each one bigger than the other. Where did you park your fat rump all day?"

Barbara looked at the face which mirrored her own. They were the only Whitleys in Freetoon, their mothers and four aunts having perished in the Greendale ambush 15 years ago, and they should have been as close as relatives normally were. But it was a trigger-tempered breed, and when a new wing leader corporal was required, the sacred dice had chosen Barbara. Valeria could not forgive that.

"I took my two left feet and my fat rump—if you must describe yourself that way—into the valley and captured a Monster in a star ship," said Barbara sweetly. "Goodnight." She lay down on her pallet and closed her eyes, leaving her twin to speculate . . .

Bee had not even risen when there was a clank of metal in the doorway and Ginny Latvala shouted: "Up, Corporal Maiden Barbara Whitley! You're wanted at the Big House."

"Do you have to wake everyone else on that account?" snapped Valeria, but not very loud. The entire company had been roused, and Captain Kim was a martinet, like all Trevors.

Barbara got to her feet, feeling her heart knock. Yesterday seemed unreal, like a wild dream. Ginny leaned on her spear, waiting. "The Old Udall is pretty mad at you, dear," she confided. "We may have all sorts of trouble coming because you roped that Monster." The Latvalas were slim blonde girls, handy with a javelin and so made hereditary bodyguards in most towns.

"I was never ordered not to lasso a Monster," said Barbara huffily.

She let the barracks buzz around her while she dressed for the occasion: a short white skirt, an embroidered green cloak, sandals, and dagger. The air was still cold and the fields below the town white with mist when she came out. A pale rosy light lifted above the eastern Ridge, and Minos was waning. The moon Theseus was red sickle caught in the sunrise.

There were not many people up. A patrol tramped past, all of them husky Macklins, and the farmhands yawned out of their barracks on the way to a day's hoeing. The street climbed steeply upward from the cavalry house, and Barbara took it with a mountaineer's long slow stride. They went by the weavery, she glimpsed looms and spinning wheels within the door, but it didn't register on her mind—low-caste work. The smithy, a most respected shop, lay beyond, also empty; the Holloways still slept in their adjoining home.

Passing a window of the maternity hospital, Barbara heard a small wail. Must be Sarah Cohen's kid, born a few days ago. The sound broke through her worry with an odd little tug at her soul. In another year or so, she would be an initiate, and make the journey to the Ship. And when she came back, no longer called Maiden, there would be another redhaired Whitley beneath her heart. Babies were a nuisance, she'd have to stay within the town till hers was weaned and—and—it was hard to wait.

The stockade bulked above her, great sharp stakes lashed together and six Latvalas on guard at the gate. Inside, there was a broad cobbled yard with several buildings: barracks, stables, sheds, the Father chapel. All were in the normal Freetoon style, long log houses with peaked sod roofs. The hall, in the middle, was much the same, but immensely bigger, its beam-ends carved into birds of prey.

Henrietta Udall stood at its door. She was the oldest of Claudia's three daughters: big and blocky, with sagging breasts and harsh black hair, small pale eyes under tufted brows, a lump for a nose and a gash for a mouth. The finery of embroidered skirt and feather cloak was wasted on her, Barbara thought. None of the Udalls could ever be handsome. But they could lead!

"Halt! Your hair is a mess," said Henrietta. "Do those braids over."

Barbara bit her lip and began uncoiling the bronze mane. It was hacked off just below her shoulders. *Spiteful blowhard,* she thought. *I'm barren if I do and barren if I don't. Come the day, dear Henrietta, you won't find me on your side.*

The death of an Udall was always the signal for turmoil. Theoretically, the power went to her oldest daughter. In practice, the sisters were likely to fight it out between themselves; a defeated survivor fled into the wilderness with her followers and tried to start a new settlement. Day-dreams of heading into unknown country for a fresh start drove the sulkiness from Barbara. If, say, she rose high in the favor of Gertrude or Anne . . .

"All right," said Henrietta as Bee rose. She led the way inside.

The main room of the Big House was long and gloomy. Sconced torches guttered above the Old Udall's seat. Servants scurried around, serving breakfast to her and to the middle-aged high-caste women on the bench below the throne.

"Well!" said Claudia. "It took you long enough."

Barbara had learned the hard way never to blame an Udall for anything. "I'm sorry, ma'm," she muttered, saluting.

The Old Udall leaned back and let her chambermaid comb the stiff gray hair. Elinor Dyckman had gotten that job; an Udall usually took a Dyckman for a lover.

Elinor was in her middle twenties; her baby was dead and she hadn't asked for another. Dyckmans had scant mother instinct. She was medium tall, with a soft curving body and soft bluish-black hair. Her small heart-shaped face smiled sweetly on the chief, and she combed with long slow strokes.

"You'll have to be punished for that," said Claudia. "Suggestions, Elinor, dear?" She laughed.

Elinor blinked incredible lashes over melting dark eyes and said: "Not too severe, ma'm. I'm sure Babs means well. A little KP—"

Barbara's hand fell to her dagger. "I'm in the army, you milk-livered trull!" she exploded. "*Dishwashing*, by Father—!"

"Watch your language," said counsellor Marian Burke.

Elinor smiled and went on combing. "It was only a joke, ma'm," she murmured. "Hadn't we better get down to business?"

The Old Udall gazed at Barbara. *Trying to stare me down, are you?* thought the girl savagely. She would not look away.

"Enough," said Claudia at length. "Yes, Elinor, you're right as usual, we can't stop to quarrel now."

She leaned ponderously forward. "I've heard reports from the scouts who met you," she went on.

Barbara remained silent, not trusting her tongue. Captain Janet Lundgard had emerged from the woods with some troopers and taken charge: set a guard on the ship, slung the unconscious Monster on a spare orsper, and ridden to town with the rest of them for escort. She had reported directly to the Big House—but what had she told? The Lundgards were not as predictable as most families; that was one reason they were hereditary army officers.

"Apparently you attacked the Monster unprovoked," said Claudia coldly. "Father knows what revenge it may take."

"It had drawn a weapon on me, ma'm," answered Barbara. "If I hadn't lassoed it, maybe it would have destroyed all Freetoon. As it is, we have the thing a prisoner now, don't we?"

"It may have friends," whispered Elinor, her eyes very large. A shiver went through the hall.

"Then we have a hostage," snapped Barbara.

The Old Udall nodded. "Yes . . . there is that. I've had relays of guards sent to its ship. None of them report any sign of life. It, the Monster, must have been alone."

"How many other ships have landed, all over Atlantis?" wondered Henrietta.

"That's what we have to find out," said Claudia. "I'm sending a party to the Ship of Father to ask the Doctors about this. We'll also have to send scouts to the nearest other towns, find out if they've been visited too."

Both missions would be dangerous enough. Barbara thought with a tingling what her punishment would be. As a non-initiate, she couldn't go to the Ship, but she would be sent toward Greendale, Highbridge, or Blockhouse, to spy. *But that's terrific! When do we start?*

The Udall smiled grimly. "And meanwhile, for weeks perhaps, we'll have the Monster to deal with . . . and our own people. The whole town must already be getting into a panic.

"We have to learn the truth about the Monster—yes, and all the people had better know the facts. We'll do it this way. The carpenters will set up a cage for the Monster, right in the plaza, and while everybody not on duty watches, someone will go into that cage and we'll see what happens."

"Who's going to volunteer for *that* job?" grumbled Marian Burke.

Elinor smiled gently. "Why, who but our brave Corporal Whitley?" she answered.

Davis Bertram woke when the door was opened and lay there for a minute, trying to remember why his flesh ached in a hundred places. Then he got his eyes unglued.

There was a boot in front of his nose. He rolled over, cautiously, and sent a bleared gaze upward. Above the boot was a shapely knee, and above that a leather-strip kilt reinforced with iron bands; then a belt supporting a knife and pouch, a cuirass of laminated leather with an iron bust bucket, a slim neck, a lot of yellow hair braided under a helmet, and a rather attractive suntanned face.

Cosmos! That girl on the nightmare bird, the lariat and—

"What's going on?" croaked Davis. "Who are you?"

"Father!" stammered one of the girls. "It talks!"

She spoke Basic—a slurred archaic form, but it

was the Basic of all human-settled planets. She must be human, thought Davis groggily; no alien was that anthropoid.

A handsome wench, too, though a bit muscular for his taste. He began to smile through bruised lips at all ten of them.

"Gak!" he said.

The ten were identical.

Well, not quite . . . some leaned on spears and some bore light, wicked-looking axes, and some had a beltful of needle-nosed darts.

He shuddered and grew aware that he had been stripped mother naked. Between the cuts and abrasions, he started to blush, more or less all over. He scrambled to his feet. A jerk at the wrists told him his hands were tied behind his back. He sat down again, lifting his knees and glaring across them.

"I imagine Monsters would have learned the Men language, Ginny," said one of his visitors. On closer observation, Davis saw that she was older and had a scar on one cheek. Some kind of insigne was painted on her breastplate . . . sunblaze, it was the six-pointed star of an astrogator's mate!

"It *looks* fairly harmless," said one of the others doubtfully.

"You, Monster!" The officer raised her battle ax. "Up!" She was tense as a drawn wire. Davis rose.

They marched him out of the shed. He saw a courtyard, rudely paved with stones, a number of primitive wooden buildings, and a high palisade around all. There was a catwalk beneath the stakes, and warriors posted on it with some kind of crossbow.

Beyond the gate, Davis saw quite a small army, alert for whatever he might try to pull. Some were on foot, some mounted on birds like the one he'd seen before: larger and stouter than ostriches, with feathers of blue-tipped white and cruel hawk heads. He decided not to pull anything.

A rutted unpaved street snaked downhill between big, clumsy houses. Outside town it became a road of sorts, wandering through cultivated grainfields. They covered a sloping plateau, which dipped off into forest toward the river valley. Behind the castle, the mountains rose steep and wooded.

Ignoring botanical details, this might almost have been Earth of some elder age. But not when you looked at the sky. It was blue and clear, yes, with towering white clouds in the west; overhead, though, were two crescents, dim by daylight: one almost twice the apparent size of Luna seen from Earth, the other half again as big. And there was the emperor planet, the world of which *this* was only another satellite. When full, it would sprawl across 14 times as much sky as Luna. Now it was a narrow sickle, pale amber. The morning sun was approaching it. That is, the smaller, Sol-type sun, Delta Capitis Lupi B, about which the giant planet moved. The primary sun, bluish-white A, had not yet risen; it would never seem more than the brightest of the stars.

Davis shook an aching head and wrenched his attention back to the ground. Be sundered if this was like Earth, after all, even with the women and children clustered around. Not just their dress—the civilians wore a short skirt, the kids nothing. Their *likeness*. Women and children—all female, the children—seemed to be cast from a few hundred molds. Take two from the same mold, like those gawping dairy-maid types over there, and the only difference was age and scars.

Cosmos, but he was thirsty!

At the farther end of a broad open space were some thousands of civilians, jammed together, craning their necks, held back by a line of guards. Their high-pitched, excited voices sawed on his nerves. In the middle of the square was a large wooden cage.

"In there," said the blonde captain. She drew her knife and cut his bonds.

Davis shuffled through the cage door. "Is this a zoo?" he asked. "Where are all the men, anyway?"

"Don't *you* know?" the captain asked acidly.

"Very well, Babs, let's see how you get out of this one!"

It was a new voice, pleasantly husky in spite of its jeering note. Davis looked through the bars and saw a redhaired girl among the cavalry. Holy Valdaoth, the same one who'd roped him yesterday!

Or was she? Her twin, also in armor, came walking slowly forth across the square. Davis stepped warily back as the newcomer entered. The blonde officer latched the door behind them.

The girl touched her dagger. He could have gone for her in better circumstances. Her greenish eyes widened, and she breathed hard. It would have been an interesting sight if it hadn't been for that iron bra.

"I'll fight if I must," she whispered.

Four women approached the cage, all of the same unprepossessing genotype. The oldest wore a headdress of plumes. "Well, Corporal," she snapped, "question it."

"Y-yes, ma'm," said the girl in a small voice. "I . . . I am Corporal Maiden Barbara Whitley, Monster."

"The same who captured you," said one of the bags.

"Be quiet, Henrietta," said the oldest witch.

With a certain fearless pride: "I am Claudia, the Udall of Freetoon."

"Honored, Citizen," said the man. "My name is Davis Bertram."

"Why . . . that could almost be a human name," said Barbara shyly.

"What else should it be?" asked Davis.

"Oh . . . oh, yes, the stories do say you Monsters learned the arts from the Men." She smiled, the least little bit.

"But I—Who said I was a monster?" He was not, Davis told himself, vain; but more than one woman had informed him she liked his face.

"You are! *Look* at you!"

"Blast it, I'm as human as you are!"

"With all that hair?" rapped Henrietta Udall.

Davis gave her an unfriendly glance.

"Look here," said Barbara reasonably, "we're not blind. I admit you have two legs and five fingers and no feathers. But you're bigger than any of us, and haven't got any more breasts than a ten-year-old."

"I should hope not!" said Davis.

"In fact—" Barbara scratched her neck, puzzledly, and pointed. "Just what *is* that? Do you fight with it?"

"It doesn't look prehensile," said the blonde captain.

Davis told himself wildly that he had not gone insane, that he really was here on the Earth-sized third satellite of Delta Capitis Lupi B I. But somehow it seemed to slip through his fingers.

He put his face in his palms and shuddered.

"Poor Monster." Barbara trod impulsively forward.

He looked up. She paled a little with fright, under the smooth brown skin, and made half a step back. Then her lips—unfairly attractive lips —stiffened, and she stayed where she was.

"We had no way of knowing," she said. "Some Monsters are friendly with the Men and some aren't. We couldn't take chances."

"But I am a man!" shouted Davis.

A groan went through the crowd. Somebody screamed.

Barbara clenched her fists. "Why did you say that?" she asked in a wobbly voice.

"Can't you *see*, girl?'

"But the Men . . . the Men are powerful, and beautiful, and—"

"Oh, Evil!" Davis took her fingers and laid them against his cheek. "Feel that? I haven't got much yet in the way of whiskers, but—"

Barbara turned faintly toward the Udall. "It's true, ma'm," she whispered. "There's hair starting to grow out of his face."

"But you *captured* him!" protested the blonde captain.

Davis took hold of his sanity with both hands. "Look, kenno," he began between clenched teeth. "Let's be reasonable about this. Just what the jumping blue blazes do you think a man is?"

"A Man is . . . is . . . a human male." He could barely hear the Barbara girl's reply.

"All right. Now, have you ever seen a human male before?"

"Certainly not." Her courage was returning. "You must indeed be from far away, Monster, There are no Men on all Atlantis."

"Oh . . . is that what you've called this world? But how do you manage—how long since—"

"Humans came here some 300 years ago. That is, by a year I mean the time Minos needs to go once around the sun Bee."

Minos . . . the big planet, of course. Davis had measured from space that it was about one Astronomical Unit from B, which had nearly the same mass as Sol. So one Minos year was approximately one Earth year. Three centuries—why, they were barely starting to colonize then! The hyperdrive was newly invented and—

"But you have children," he said feebly.

"Oh, yes. By the grace of Father, the Doctors at His Ship can—I don't know any more. I've never been there."

Davis took a while to swallow that one.

Something came back to him. In the few hours he'd been on Atlantis, before this Barbara wench caught him, he had seen plenty of animal life: reptiles, fish, insects, flying and flightless birds. Some of the earthbound avians had been the size of buffalo.

But no mammals. In all those flocks and herds, not a mammal.

Excitement gripped him. "Wait a minute!" he cried. "Are there any . . . I mean, well, does Atlantis harbor any warm-blooded animals with hair that give live birth and suckle their young?"

"Why, no," said Barbara. "Except us humans, of course."

"Ahhh-*ha*. Mammals never evolved here, then. And they're the only terrestroid form where the males are . . . hm—" Davis blushed. "Obviously male. No wonder you didn't recognize—I mean, uh—"

"What do you mean?" asked Barbara innocently.

"This is ridiculous," barked the Old Udall. "It's well understood that the Men will come in all their power and glory. This wretch is a Monster, and the only question is what to do about it."

Another girl trod forth. Even now, Davis felt his eyes bug out. She was dark, throaty-voiced, with gold bangles on slender arms and red flowers in her long hair, high in the prow and walking like a sine wave. "Please ma'm," she said. "I have an idea."

Claudia smiled at her. "Yes, Elinor?"

"It says it is a Man." Elinor waggled her eyelashes at Davis. "Let it prove it."

"How?" demanded Davis.

"By fertilizing the corporal," said Elinor with scientific detachment.

"*What?*"

Barbara stepped back, white-faced. "No!" she gasped.

"Corporal Whitley," said Claudia earnestly, "we've had our little differences, but now the future of Freetoon may depend on you. You won't fail your duty."

"Unless you're afraid, darling," murmured Elinor.

Davis saw Barbara flush red. She knotted her fists. After a very long minute, she looked squarely at him with an air of having but one life to give for her country.

"Yes," she said defiantly. "You may fertilize me, Davis—if you can!"

He looked at several thousand interested faces.

How did you explain the effect of social conditioning to a tribe which had never heard of such matters?

"Not now," he begged hoarsely. "Give me time . . . privacy, for Cosmos' sake . . . can't do anything *here*—"

The Old Udall lifted a skeptical brow.

"Oh, never mind," said Davis. "Have it your way. I'm a monster."

Barbara was not happy.

That sorry business in the plaza had won her a good deal of respect, but she didn't enjoy baiting captives, even Monsters. In the four days since, a growing moodiness had driven her to get permission to go out alone after game. It was not quite safe, but she felt somehow that a companion would be more of a hazard.

We Whitleys are a crotchety lot, she admitted. For once the reflection was less arrogant than gloomy. She had not, before, felt it a loss to have no sweetheart, not even a close friend, and to be forever at odds with her only kinswoman in Freetoon. But suddenly she wanted her mother back . . . Or someone. She couldn't understand the pull she felt, as if her thirteen-year-old self were reaching across seven years of time to invade a body gone all soft and unsure. Ever since those moments in the Monster's cage . . . *Damn* the Monster! Had the thing psyched her?

She headed northward into the woods and steeps of the Ridge, spoored a stamper herd on the second day and caught up to it on the third and shot one of the great grazing birds. She didn't have it cut up before dark, and wasn't sleepy even then.

And she saw that the night was cool, a bright mystery where dewed leaves sparkled gold beneath Minos, a scent of young blossoms, the High

Gaunt rearing its stern stone peak among the stars. An irrational happiness lifted in her, she gathered armfuls of sweetbird and fernish, crooned, threw her arms about a slim white tree and rubbed a hot cheek against it and was near crying when a night-triller began to sing. There was a tingle all through her.

And this was not to be understood either. All at once she wanted very much the harsh sweaty comfort of the barracks. The trail had arced, she could be in Freetoon tonight if she rode hard.

Sleep was no problem. Normally you slept about four hours out of the twelve between a sunset and a sunset, but huntresses could go for days on birdnaps. Barbara loaded her pack orsper, mounted the other, and started at Bee-rise. She ate in the saddle, not stopping even for the holy time of eclipse, when Bee went behind Minos and the stars came out. Ay and Ariadne gave light enough for those ten-plus minutes, and a muttered prayer to Father met minimum requirements.

Shortly afterward she struck the Ironhill road. It was wider than most—all towns, however hostile, met at the mining settlement to trade. Jogging along in her own apprehension, she forgot all care. She rounded a bend and could have been shot by the Greendalers before realizing they were there.

A dozen of them, in full armor, riding toward Freetoon . . . Barbara reined in, gasping, and stared at the crossbows as they swiveled around.

The Greendale leader, a middle-aged Macklin with a broken nose, laughed. "We won't harm you today, darling, if you behave yourself," she said. "Freetooner, aren't you? We're on embassy."

Barbara nodded distantly and joined them. She felt no hatred, but war was as normal a part of life as the harvest festival. She had been in several raids and skirmishes since gaining her growth, and her kin were dead at Greendale hands.

There was a Whitley sergeant among them, about fifty years old. "I'm Gail," she introduced herself.

"What's your mission?" asked Barbara, rather snappishly.

"What do you think?" answered Gail. "You people ought to know better than to send spies our way when I'm on patrol duty."

"Oh . . . you bushwhacked them, then." Barbara felt a chill.

"Every one. Caught three of them alive. One, Avis Damon, got pretty much cut up in the fracas, and rather than bleed to death she told us what she knew."

It was bad news, very bad, but Barbara's first reaction was scorn. "I always claimed those Damons aren't fit for combat." Then, slowly: "So what do you think you learned?"

"A star ship landed in your country." Gail said it with care. "There was a Man aboard."

"A Monster," corrected Barbara. "We made it admit that."

"Mmm . . . yes . . . I thought so myself. You couldn't have captured a Man against his will."

A thin, dark-haired Burke interrupted softly: "Are you sure it was against his will? Maybe as a test of faith, he—"

That was trouble with the Burkes. They thought too much. Barbara's hands felt clammy. "We've sent to the Doctors, of course, to ask what we ought to do," she said defensively.

"And meanwhile you have the Monster and its ship." Anger writhed across the Macklin's leathery face. "Do you think we're going to stand by and let you make an ally of the Monster?"

"What do you want?" replied Barbara.

"We're bringing an ultimatum," said Gail Whitley. "Your Udall has damned well got to turn the Monster over to a joint guard till we get word from the Doctors. If you don't—war."

Barbara thought about if for a while. She ought to make a break for it, try to reach Freetoon ahead of this gang . . . no, that would earn her nothing more than a bolt in the back. There was plaguey well going to be a war, no Udall would cough up a prize like the Monster. *Well, who says we can't defend our own fields? Hell and thunder, we'll toss them out on their fat cans and chase them all the way home.*

The battle would probably start tomorrow. It was about thirty hours' ride to Greendale, but the enemy soldiers must already have left and be bivouacked somewhere in the Ridge.

So be it! Barbara felt a welcome tension, almost an eagerness. It was a pleasant change from her eldritch moods of the past days. She chatted amiably with the others for the rest of the trip.

Bee and Ay were under the horizon when they clattered by the patrols up to Freetoon, but Minos, Ariadne, Theseus, and tiny Aegeus gave plenty of light. The embassy had dismounted in the courtyard and stamped into the Big House when Barbara realized her usefulness was over. She turned her kill over to the servants and put the two orspers in the castle barn. Poor birds, they were so tired. Then she ought to go tell her barracks mates, but—

"Where's the Monster being kept?" she asked, before thinking.

"In the shed under the north wall, ma'm," said the Nicholson groom. "Didn't dare have him anywhere else, they didn't, though he ain't done no harm yet but you can't never tell."

"*He!*" said Barbara with a flash of anger. "Why call it 'he?'"

"Well, he says he's a male, ma'm, and, uh, well, he says—"

Barbara walked off. No reason why the Monster shouldn't be male. They were Man and woman, the wise happy people of the stars, and doubtless Monsters too—But why should the thought of this Davis creature's maleness be so odd, half frightening and therefore resented?

She grew suddenly aware that she had rounded the Big House and was in its mutiple shadow looking toward the Monster's prison.

A door of wooden bars had been erected for the shed. It . . . he . . . Davis stood against the bars, flooded with cool Minoslight and moonlight. He showed sharp and clear in the radiance, and somehow the hollow cheeks and flat hairy breast and bulging muscles were no longer ugly. They had given him clothes, kilt, cloak, and sandals, his hair was combed and a yellow beard was growing out on his face.

He was holding hands between the bars with a girl in a long feather cloak. Their faces drifted to Barbara—Elinor Dyckman, of all foul pests!

"Oh, I really must be going, Bertie. Those awful Greendalers . . . didn't you see them come in? Claudia will be just *furious.*"

"Stick around, beautiful." The Monster's low chuckle was paralyzing, Barbara could not have moved after hearing it. "It's worth all my woes, just to get you here alone at last."

"Really . . . Bertie, let go, you scare me." Elinor tittered.

"Aw, now, macushla. I'm not going to eat you. Let me only feast on your silken hair, your starry eyes, your—" Etc., etc.

"You say *such* things." Elinor leaned closer against the bars. "Nobody says such things here."

"Ah, nobody is able to appreciate you, my little one. To think I crossed the stars and found you. Come here . . . lend me that adorable mouth—"

"Bert! I . . . I . . . mmmmm—"

The night blurred before Barbara. She wondered why, gulped, realized it was tears, and cursed herself.

"I *mustn't*, Bertie, dear! Why you're a—"

"A man. And you're a woman."

"But you said—"

"I had no choice then." Davis leered. "But come in here and I'll prove it to you this time."

"Oh, I can't, Bertie, I just can't! You're locked in and—"

"You can swipe the key, can't you? Here, give me another kiss."

It was too much. And a Whitley was no sneaking spy like a, a, a Dyckman. Barbara strode across the yard, jingling her spurs as noisily as possible. "What's going on here?" she yelled.

"Oh!" Elinor squealed. "Oh . . . Babs, is it? Babs, dear, I was only—"

"I know what you were only. Get out before I knock your teeth down your throat!"

Elinor wailed and fled.

Barbara turned furiously on Davis. "What were you plotting?" she snarled.

The Monster sighed, shrugged, and gave her a rueful grin. "Nothing very evil," he said. "You again, eh?"

Heat and cold chased each other across Barbara's face.

"You know," went on Davis, "this is the kind of thing I used to daydream about in my teens. A brand new world, like Earth but more beautiful, and I the only man among a million women. And holy Cosmos, I've found it, and I want out!"

Barbara raised a fist. "Yes, so you can go home and call your friends to come raiding."

"Look," said Davis earnestly, "we want to help you—blast it all, we're not your kind of blood-thirsty pirate. And I *am* a man, as human as you. If you'd not come along, Elinor Dyckman would have found that out . . . nine months afterward, at most!" His smile grew altogether insolent. "Maybe you'd like to give me another chance? Honestly, you're one of the best-looking girls I've seen any-where."

"Hell spit me out if I do!" Barbara turned her back.

"Don't go away," begged Davis. "It's lonesome as space here. All I've done is argue with that barrel-shaped queen of yours."

Barbara couldn't help laughing. The epithet was too good.

"That's better," said Davis. "Shall we be friends?"

"Why do you claim to be a Man?" she countered hastily. "You've already admitted you aren't."

"I had no choice then, blast it! You and . . . the other girl . . . only ones who might give me a chance to convince them. I tell Siz Claudia that I'm a benevolent Monster and if they'll let me at my boat—under guard, if they want—I'll go home and bring the Men. I mean it, too."

"But she doesn't dare," said Barbara slowly.

"Well, not so far. Can't really say I blame her. Say, have you found my blaster?"

"Your what?"

"My weapon. I had it in a hip holster, dropped it when you—No? I suppose it must be lying out in the grass somewhere. You won't find much in my pack. Medical kit, lighter, camera, a few such gadgets. I've offered to demonstrate them, but the old sow won't let me."

"What were you doing when I . . . found you?" asked Barbara. Really, she thought, he wasn't a bad Monster at heart.

"Just looking around. I analyzed basic surface conditions from space, then came down to let my robots check on the biochemistry, bacteriology, and ecology. That looked safe too, so I violated all doctrine and went for a stroll. I was just coming back to the boat when—Oh, Evil, I don't imagine you understand a word." Davis smiled gently. "Poor kid. Poor little Amazon."

"I can take care of myself!" she flared.

"No doubt. But come over here. I won't hurt you."

Barbara went to the door. He held her hands and pressed his face against the bars. What right had that hairy, jut-nosed, thin-lipped face to look beautiful? Her temples hammered.

"I want to show you something," he said in a grave tone. "Maybe that way . . . one kiss, Barbara."

She couldn't help it, she felt bonelessly weak and leaned toward him.

The main door of the Big House crashed open. Torchlight spilled on the cobbles, Minos became suddenly wan. The Greendale Macklin strode angrily forth, her women bristling about her.

The voice jerked Barbara to awareness, she sprang from the Monster and grabbed for the crossbar slung at her shoulder.

"This means war!"

Civilians and movable property were brought inside the stockade that night, and armed females streamed forth. But the fighting didn't start till well after sunrise.

Davis could just hear the horns and shouts and clash of metal. There was a good-sized battle on the edge of the forest, he guessed. He looked across a courtyard littered with women, children, and assorted dry goods and wondered what the desolation to do.

Claudia Udall tramped over to his jail, in full armor and toting a battle ax. Elinor Dyckman undulated in her wake, thinly clad and scared. Davis would rather have looked at her but thought it more tactful to meet the queen's eyes.

"Well, Monster, now a war has started on your account," said Claudia grimly.

Davis gave her a weak smile. "It wasn't my idea . . . uh, ma'm. What do they want me for, anyway?"

"The power, of course! Any town which had you and your ship could conquer the rest in days. Now we'll have those Greendale pests chased away by eclipse. Then will you help us?"

Davis hesitated. Union law was unreasonably strict about one's relationship with primitives. You could fight in self-defense, but using atomic guns to help a local aggression meant a stiff sentence.

"Let me aboard my boat—" he began.

"Of course," beamed Claudia. "Under guard."

"Hm, yeh, that's what I was afraid of." Davis had intended only to light out for Nerthus and never come back. Let the Service disentangle this Atlantean mess. He gulped and shook his head. "Sorry, I can't use the boat to fight with. You see, uh, well—"

"Bertie!" Elinor wobbled toward him. Her white indoor face was beaded with sweat. "Bertie, darling, you've got to help us. It's death for me if the Greendalers take this place."

"Hm?"

"Don't you understand? The Greendale Udall already has two Dyckman lovers. They won't want a third . . . they'll see to it . . . *Ber-r-rtie!*"

Davis got the idea. A queen's favorite dropped the word to some unsentimental captain—

"Nonsense, child." Claudia glared jealously. "Monster, right now the Greendalers do hold the area where your ship is. Can they get in?"

Davis laughed nervously. "Axes and crowbars against inert steel? I'd like to see them try!"

Short of atomic tools, there was only one way to open that airlock. He had set it to respond to himself whistling a few bars of a certain ballad. And *The Jolly Tinker* was not a song which any lady ought to know.

"You won't help us?" Claudia narrowed her eyes.

Davis began a long, thoroughly mendacious speech about friends who would avenge any harm done to him. He was just getting to the section on gunboats when Claudia snorted.

"If *we* can't have you, Monster, I might decide not to let anybody have you." She swung on her heel and walked off. Elinor followed, throwing imploring looks across her shoulder.

Davis sat down on the straw and groaned. As if he didn't have troubles enough, that sex machine had to slither around in a thin skirt and few beads . . . just out of reach.

Then he found himself wondering about Barbara Whitley. He hoped very much she wouldn't be hurt.

Eclipse came. It happened daily, at high noon in this longitude, when Atlantis, eternally facing her primary, got Minos between B and herself. An impressive sight: the planet, dimly lit by the remote companion sun, fourteen times as wide as Earth's moon, brimmed with fiery light refracted through the dense atmosphere . . . dusk on the ground and night in the sky. Davis looked hungrily at the stars. Civilized, urbane, *pleasant* stars! . . .

An hour later, the battle had ended and the Freetoon girls came back to the castle. Davis noticed that the warriors were divided into about thirty genotypes. When everyone in a single line of descent was genetically identical, a caste system was a natural development. And, yes, he could see why the Atlanteans had reverted to the old custom of putting surnames last. Family in the normal sense couldn't be very important here. For a moment the image of his father drifted across Davis' memory. He'd been rather a disappointment to the old man; it occurred to him that he had spent most of his life trying to justify himself in his father's eyes. But his chromosomes had never intended him for a solid citizen.

The armored lasses, foot and orsper (horse bird?) troops, clamored for lunch and beer. They had casualties and prisoners with them. There weren't many dead or seriously wounded—couldn't be, with these clumsy weapons powered by female muscles—but some had been killed, by ax, knife, dart, bolt—

"Barbara!" Davis whooped it forth.

The tall redhead looked his way and strolled over through the crowd. Her left hand was wrapped in a wet crimson bandage. "Barbara! Cosmos, I'm glad to see you're all right!"

She gave him an unfriendly grin. "Mistake, Monster. I'm her cousin Valeria."

"Oh. Well, how is she?"

"No damage. She's helping mount guard on your ship."

"Then you did win."

"For now. We beat them back into the woods, but they haven't quit." Valeria gave him a hard green stare. "Now I know you're a Monster. The Men would fight."

"Why can't you tribes compromise?"

"Who ever heard of an Udall compromising?" laughed Valeria.

"Then why do you obey them?"

"Why? Why, they're the . . . the *Udalls!*" Valeria was shocked. "When I took arms, I swore—"

"Why did you swear? My people have learned better than to allow absolute rulers. You've got a whole world here. What is there to fight about?"

"A gutless Monster would say that." Valeria spat and left.

The day dragged. Davis was fed, otherwise ignored. Night came, and he tried to sleep, but the refugees made too much noise.

Toward morning he fell into a doze, huddled under his feather quilts against the upland chill. A racket of trumpets and hurrying feet woke him.

Another battle! He strained against the bars, into darkness. And wasn't it getting closer? The sentries were shooting and—

Elinor screamed her way across the courtyard.

The multiple shadows thrown by Minos and the other moons rippled weirdly before her. "Bertie, you've got to help! They're driving us back!"

He reached out and patted her in a not very brotherly fashion. "There, there." When it made her hysterics worse, he shouted. After a struggle, he got some facts.

The Greendalers had returned with allies. Outnumbered three to one, the Freetooners were being hammered back through their own streets.

Newburgh, Blockhouse, and Highbridge banners flew beyond the walls. It was clear enough to Davis. Having learned about the spaceship, and well aware she couldn't take it alone, the Greendale Udall had sent for help, days ago, probably. And the prize looked great enough to unite even these factions for a while.

"But now Claudia will have to make terms," he blurted.

"It's too late!" sobbed Elinor. She moaned and ran toward the Big House. Only warriors were to be seen, the artisans and helots had retreated into their sheds. Davis told himself to stop shaking.

The fighting didn't halt even for eclipse. At midafternoon the gates opened and Freetoon's army poured into the court.

Step by step, their rearguard followed. Davis saw Barbara at the end of the line. She had a round wooden shield on one arm and swung a light long-shafted ax. A red lock fell from under the battered morion and plastered itself to a small, drawn face.

A burly warrior pushed against her. Barbara caught the descending ax-blow on her shield. Her own weapon chopped for the neck, missed, and bit at the leather cuirass. It didn't go through; low-carbon steel got blunted almighty fast. The other woman grinned and began hailing blows. Barbara sprang back and threw her ax between the enemy's legs. Down went the woman. Barbara's dagger jumped into her hand, she fell on top of the other and made a deft slicing motion.

Davis got to his pot barely in time.

When he came back to the door, there was a lull in the battle. The Freetooners had been pumping bolts and javelins from the catwalk, discouraging the allies long enough for the gates to be closed.

Presently Barbara herself came to him. She was a-shiver with weariness, and the eyes regarding him had dark rims beneath. There was blood splashed on her breastplate and arms.

"How is it for you?" she asked hoarsely.

"I'm all right," said Davis. With more anxiety than a neutral party ought to feel: "Are you hurt?"

"No. But I'm afraid this is the end."

"What . . . what do you think will happen? To you, I mean?"

"I'll get away at the last if I can." Her voice was numb.

Davis told himself sternly that this mess wasn't his fault. He had seen from space that there were small towns and agriculture on this continent, and had landed to bring the gift of Union civilization to all its natives. The last thing he wanted was—

The *first* thing he wanted, he thought in self-abasement, had been the glory of finding a new inhabited planet. And the money prizes, and the lucrative survey commissions, and the adoring women.

"Cosmos curse it," he shouted, "I can't help your stupidity!"

Barbara gave him a blind, dazed look and wandered off.

At B-set the battle resumed. Trumpets howled, and by Minoslight he saw Claudia hurry toward the gate.

Its wood groaned. The ladies from Greendale must be using a battering ram. Fire kindled outside, flame ran up and splashed the sky. Somehow a house had been touched off. The top of the stockade loomed black across the blaze, like a row of teeth, the warriors on the catwalk were silhouetted devils. Davis wondered crazily which of them was Barbara, if Barbara was still alive.

The main gate shuddered and a hinge pulled loose.

Someone galloped toward him on a frantic orsper, leading two others. She jumped from the saddle. "Barbara!" he whispered.

"Valeria again." The girl laughed with scant humor. "Stand aside, I'm going to get you out."

Her ax thudded against the bolt.

"But what—why—"

"We're finished," snapped Valeria. "For now, anyway. For always, unless you can help us. I'm going to get you out, Monster. We'll escape if we can, and see if you can remedy matters."

"But I'm neutral!" gibbered Davis.

Valeria grinned unpleasantly. "I have an ax and a knife, my dear, and nothing to lose. Are you still neutral?"

"No," gulped Davis. "Not if you feel that way about it."

Another orsper ran from the stables, with a rider who led a spare mount. Valeria turned, lifted her ax. "Oh, you."

"Same idea, I see," answered Barbara. *Of course*, thought Davis, *genetic twins normally think alike.* He saw that Barbara strove not to weep. It could be no fun to watch your country conquered.

"Put on your cloak, Monster," ordered Valeria

between blows. "Pull the hood up. They won't bother with three people trying to get away . . . unless they know what you are!"

The bolt gave way. Valeria threw the door open. Davis stumbled out, got a foot in a stirrup and swung himself aboard. Valeria mounted another bird at his side. Barbara took the lead. They jogged toward the broken gate where Claudia and a few guards still smote forlornly at a ring of enemies. The orsper's pace was not so smooth as a horse's, and Davis was painfully reminded that a mounted man does well to wear tight pants. This silly kilt was no help. He stood up in the stirrups, swearing.

Someone ran from the Big House. "Help! Ohhh—" Davis glimpsed Elinor's face, blind with terror. He leaned over, caught her wrist, and whirled her toward a spare orsper.

"Get that pantywaist out of here!" yelled Valeria.

Elinor scrambled up. Barbara freed her ax and broke into a gallop. Willy-nilly, Davis followd.

A band of women stood before them. A bolt hummed maliciously past his ear. Barbara's orsper kicked with a gruesomely clawed foot. Davis' mount stumbled on something. Valeria leaned over and swung at a shadowy form, sparks showered.

Then they were out of the melee, on the street, into the fields and the forest beyond.

Davis woke up after eclipse. For a moment he knew only one pulsing ache, then memory of his all-night ride came back and he gasped.

Barbara, crouched over a little smokeless fire,

preparing a meal from what supplies and equipment had been in the saddlebags, smiled at him. "How are you?" she asked.

"I'm not sure. Oof!" Davis crawled from his bedroll. His legs were so sore from standing as he rode that he didn't think he would ever walk again.

Dousing his head in a nearby spring helped, and he looked around. They had come a goodly ways from Freetoon, into a tall country of ancient woods and steep hillsides. Northward the land climbed higher still, with snow on the peaks. The day was clear and windy, sunlight spilled across green slopes and Minos brooded remotely overhead. Ay was a searing spark to the east, daily overtaking the closer sun.

"Bertie!"

Davis lurched to his feet as Elinor came from the forest, sleeking back her long hair. She fell into his arms and kissed him.

"Bertie, you saved my life, oh, I'm *so* grateful . . . do you know, Bertie, *I* believe you're a Man!"

"You might come slice your Man some bread," said Barbara acidly. "Why did you bring her, Davis? Of all the useless— And good women are dead back in Freetoon!"

Valeria strolled into sight, crossbow on her shoulder and a plump bird in one hand. "Hell," she drawled, "all we need to do is leave the Dyckman beast here. Let her make her own way back."

"I'll die!" screamed Elinor. "There are jacklins in these woods! I'll be killed! You can't—*Bertie!*"

"Keep out of this, Davis," snapped Valeria.

He blew up. "I'll be damned to Evil if I will!" he roard. "I've been pushed around long enough!"

In his present mood, he would have welcomed an excuse to clip that coppertopped hellion on the jaw, but Barbara intervened just as Valeria pulled a knife. "Enough out of all of you," she said. "We have to stick together. Davis, if you insist, we'll let this . . . Elinor come along till we reach some town. Now sit down and eat!"

"Yes, ma'm," said Davis meekly.

The food was strengthening, it seemed to give him back his manhood. Now that he was out ot that filthy jail, he ought to start exercising some choice. He would have given much for a cup of coffee and a cigarette, but neither being available, he opened the council. "What are your plans?" he asked.

"I don't know," said Valeria. Both Whitleys had calmed down as fast as they'd flared up, though Elinor remained tactfully inconspicuous. "Last night I only thought about getting away."

Davis tugged his beard. It itched. "Just what will happen at Freetoon?" he asked. "No massacres, I hope."

"Oh, no," said Barbara. "There've been conquests before. As far as the lower castes are concerned, it's only a change of bosses. And some of the soldiers will take a fresh oath to the new Udall—Damons, Burkes, Hausers—" She snorted the names. "But families like us, who don't switch loyalties so easily, have to be killed. Though I imagine a lot of our sort got away into the woods. Outlaw life—" She shrugged, woefully.

"All right," said Davis. "But what do you want to *do?* Claudia and her daughters are most likely dead now. You haven't got any chief to be loyal to."

The cousins stared at him and each other, as if suddenly bewildered. It was a moment before Valeria said savagely:

"Well, the powers of your ship aren't going to be used for Bess Udall of Greendale! Not after she killed barracks mates of mine."

Davis nodded, thinking his own thoughts. If Bess got her hooks on him, the situation would return to what it had been. He wouldn't lift gravs for her without a spear at his back and strict orders to destroy some town which Union law said he must die rather than bombard. He might well be tortured by way of inducement.

Therefore he must recapture his boat, somehow, despite all the guards the victorious allies would mount over it . . . big joke!

Barbara looked at the northern ranges. "We've scant hope of finding help this side of Smoky Pass," she said. "But nobody's crossed the mountains for, oh, generations. They say there are some strange folk living over there. If they'd help . . . we could promise them the loot from the enemy—"

"Wait a minute!" Davis' brain whirred. He was not forbidden by law to use violence against primitives, if it would save himself or rectify an obviously bad turn of affairs. But he doubted that a Coordinator board would see eye to eye with Barbara on what constituted rectification. "Look, look here," he stammered. "Wasn't there a message already sent to this, uh, holy Ship of yours?"

"To the Doctors? Yes," said Valeria. "They would decide—"

"Ah, ha!" Whoever these mysterious Doctors were, they knew enough science to operate a parthenogenesis machine. He'd have a better chance of convincing them of the truth than anyone else. And they could order his boat returned to him!

"Let's go to the Doctors," he said quickly. "They have the final disposition of the case anyway, and we'd be safe there."

"We can't!" said Valeria, quite aghast. "Barbara and I are only Maidens. And *you*—the Ship is sacred to Father!"

"But I'm a man," argued Davis. "Or a monster, if you insist. The rules don't apply to me." He glanced at Elinor. "You're an initiate, aren't you?" She nodded eagerly. "All right. You can escort me through the taboo area."

It took a good deal of wrangling. Being roared down out of bigger lungs was a salutary new experience for the Whitleys. Eventually they agreed, reserving the right to find allies if the Doctors, who seldom mixed in politics, would not order Freetoon liberated. The meaning of "liberation" in such a context was vague to Davis, but the poor lost kids needed something to hope for.

"We'll have to continue north," said Valeria. "Over Smokey Pass and down through the valleys on the other side to the coast . . . because the Holy River route, all this region, will be full of people hunting you, Davis. Once we reach the coast, we can maybe get passage with the sea-dwellers, back to the Ship at Holy River mouth."

The prospect looked strenuous, thought the man dismally.

At least it was summer. The Atlantean seasons were due only to the eccentricity of Minos' orbit, but he had gathered that hereabouts the variation of weather was considerable. A satellite always facing its primary: permanent tidal bulge, terrific mountains on the inner hemisphere and mostly ocean on the outer . . . oh, well.

He remembered an item. "Do you have a sewing kit?" he asked. "I'll need a, uh—" he blushed —"special garment."

"I'll make it for you," said Barbara helpfully. "Just let me get the measurements."

Davis' ears glowed cadmium red. "No, thanks! You wouldn't understand."

Elinor, who had picked up a little self-confidence, piped: "This trip will take just weeks, won't it? But the Freetoon couriers will have reached the Ship pretty soon. The Doctors will send word back. Why, we may meet one of their legates!"

"That's all right," said Valeria. "Just so we don't fall into Greendale hands." She drew a finger across her throat.

"Must you?" said Elinor faintly.

Davis glanced up at Minos. The big planet 5000 Earth masses, was almost half full, its amber face blurred by a crushingly thick hydrogen atmosphere, cloudy bands of dull green and blue and brown, dark blots which were storms large enough to swallow Terra whole. He shivered. It was a long, lonesome way home; the Service wouldn't visit Delta of its own accord for decades, and he didn't think he could survive that long. Why, missing his antigeriatric treatments would alone cut his life down to a lousy century! *In short, me boy, you've got no choice. You're jolly well on the Whitley team.*

He looked at the cousins and then at Elinor; she smiled back at him. It could be a lot worse, he reflected. One man alone with three beautiful girls—if he couldn't make a good thing out of that, he didn't deserve to . . .

Some days later, Davis Bertram shivered on the heights of the Ridge with Elinor.

It had been a cruel trek, through the forests and then up over the glaciers to this pass. Davis wanted to help with the twins' pot-hunting, at least—he soon mastered the spring-powered repeating crossbow—but Valeria told him coldly that he walked too loud. Maybe that had been the worst of the situation, the feeling of uselessness. He had always before taken the lead while women watched and made admiring noises.

However, as they rested atop Smoky Pass, in a mordant wind and whirl of dry snow, Elinor shared his ragged cloak.

The range dropped even more steeply on its north side than the southern approach. Davis looked across a downward-rolling immensity of green, veined by rivers, here and there the flash of a lake, and wished for his paints.

"I don't see any signs of man . . . uh, woman . . . down there," he said, "but there must be some. Haven't you any idea what the people are like? Seems you'd all meet at the Ship."

"Oh, no," replied Elinor. "You see, Bertie, each town sends its own parties to be fertilized. It's seldom that two groups are at the Ship at the same time, and even if they are, they don't talk to—Oh, I mustn't say more. But it's *thrilling!*" She clasped her hands. "And safe. Nobody would dare attack a party going to or from the Ship. If anyone did, why, the Doctors would refuse to fertilize that whole town forever after."

Which would be one form of excommunication that really worked, though Davis. He gave Elinor a sidelong glance. Her nose was frostbitten and peeling, she had lost weight, but she was still an interesting lesson in solid geometry. And he wanted a lot more information from her, whether it was taboo to non-initiates or not. He was going to enjoy persuading her.

Meanwhile, though, they had to get down where it was warm.

Later he remembered the next two days only as a nightmare of struggle. He could hardly believe it when they reached timberline and the nearly vertical descent began to flatten.

This was a conifer forest, trees not unlike jack pines though the smell was different, sweeter and headier. The ground was thick with brown needles, the orsper footfalls a muted *pad-pad*. They saw only small birds, darting red and gold between bluish-green branches, but there was spoor of big game.

At the end of the day, they reached a king-sized lake. It blinked amiably in the low sunshine, reeds rustled on the banks and fish leaped in the water. "We couldn't find a better campsite," said Barbara.

"Skeeterbugs," said Valeria.

"Not this early in the year."

"Yeh? See here, rockhead, I've seen them when—"

There were no skeeterbugs that night. This did not improve Valeria's temper.

In the morning, both Whitleys went out afoot after game. Davis and Elinor were to watch the camp and try for fish: there were hooks and lines in the saddlebags. It was a cool, sun-drenched day and a flock of birds with particularly good voices were tuning up nearby. Davis' grin spread.

"What are you so happy about?" Elinor looked grumpily up from scouring the utensils.

"At having you all to myself," admitted Davis candidly. He knew her type. "Let's take a stroll."

"Bertie! No!" Elinor pouted. "I'm so tired."

"As you wish." He sauntered off. In a moment she pattered after him. He took her hand, squeezing it rather more than necessary.

"Bertie! Bertie, be careful, you're so *strong*—"

Davis wandered along the lakeshore, eyes alert for a secluded spot. He was in no hurry: all day before him, and he was going to enjoy the fishing too.

"You're a brave little girl, Elinor," he said.

"Coming all this way and—" he paused, took a deep breath, and prepared the Big Lie— "never a complaint from you."

"I could complain," she said bitterly. "Those awful Whitleys. Skin and bones and nasty red hair and tongues like files. They're just jealous."

It might have been profitable to agree, but for some reason Davis couldn't backbite Barbara. "I hope the worst is over," he said. "You ought to tell me what to expect when we reach the Ship."

"I can't, Bertie. I mustn't. Nobody who's been there is allowed to talk about it to anyone who hasn't."

"But I'm a Man," he argued. "You do believe that, don't you?"

"Yes . . . you must be . . . even if your whiskers *tickle*."

Davis stroked his short yellow beard patriarchally. "Well, then," he said, "since the Doctors are only filling in for men . . . I mean . . . Sunblaze!" He backed up and started over. "What are they like, the Doctors?"

"I can't—" Davis stopped for some agreeable physical persuasion. "I mustn't—Mmmmm! Bertie!" After a while: "I really *can't* say. They have this big beautiful town, with the Ship in the very middle. But I never saw a Doctor's face. They're always veiled. Bertie, please! I *mustn't* tell you anything!"

"I can guess. The, uh, fertilizing rite—it involves a machine, doesn't it? A lot of tubes and wires and things?"

"If you know that much," said Elinor, "yes."

Davis nodded absently. The picture was taking shape.

Three hundred years ago, the hyperdrive was new and colonization more art than science. You couldn't trust an apparently Earthlike planet; chances were its biochemistry would be lethal to man. It was rare good luck to find a world like Atlantis. Therefore doctrine enjoined caution. First the planet was thoroughly surveyed. Then an all-male party landed, spent two or three years building, analyzing, testing in detail. Finally the women came.

Somewhere in the Service archives of three centuries back lay a record of a female transport with a female crew; you didn't mix the sexes on such a journey unless you wanted trouble. Judging from names, its complement had been purely North American. The ship was bound for a new colony, but vanished. A trepidation vortex, of course, perhaps the same one he had managed to avoid. That was back before anybody knew of such a thing.

The Ship had not been destroyed. It had been tossed at an unthinkable pseudovelocity across hundreds of light-years. The hyperdrive must have been ruined, since it didn't return home. It must have emerged quite near Delta Capitis Lupi, or it would have drifted endlessly at sublight speed till the women died.

Pure good fortune that Atlantis was habitable. But probably the ship had been wrecked in landing, because it seemed never to have lifted gravs again. And there they were, cut off, no way to call for help and no way to get back.

They had little machinery, no weapons, scant technical knowledge. They did their best—discovered what the edible grains and domesticable fowl were, located mines and established crude smelters, named the planets and moons in classical tradition—but that was all, and their knowledge slipped from them in a few illiterate lifetimes.

But in the first generation there must have been
a biochemist. The thought of aging and dying, one
by one, with nobody to help the last feeble survivors, was unwelcome. Human parthenogenesis
was an ancient technique, though little used. The
biochemist had taken what equipment was in the
ship to make such a machine.

The right chemicals under the right conditions
would cause a single ovum to divide. Once that
process was initiated, it followed the normal
course, and in nine months a child was born, genetically identical with the mother.

"Three hundred years of virgin birth!" mumbled
Davis. "An appalling situation. It will have to be
remedied."

"What are you talking about?" asked Elinor.

"You'll find out," he grinned.

They had come to a little bay, with soft grass
down to the water's edge, rustling shade trees, the
mountains looming titanic above. Flowers blos-
somed fiery underfoot and small waves chuckled
against the shore.

It was, in short, an ideal spot for a seduction.

Davis planted his fishing pole in a forked twig,
laid aside his weapons, sat down, and extended an
invitational arm. Elinor sighed and snuggled up to
him.

"Just think," she whispered. "The first Man in
three hundred years!"

"High time, isn't it?" said Davis thickly.

"Ah . . . your kilt . . . what's the matter?"

"Never mind." Davis gathered her in. Their
necking became furious. He fumbled at her belt
buckle. She closed her eyes, breathing hard. His
other hand slid up her thigh.

Something roared behind him.

Davis leaped a meter in the air from a prone position. Elinor screamed.

The thing looked like a saw-beaked, penguin-feathered seal, but bigger. It had swallowed his hook and was quite indignant. The flippers shot it up on the shore and over the grass at express speed.

Elinor tried to get to her feet. The fluke-like legs batted out. She went rolling and lay still. Davis clawed for his ax. He chopped wildly, saw blood run, but the damned soft iron wouldn't bite on that thick skull.

The seal-bird knocked him down and snapped at his face. Jaws closed on the ax haft and crunched it across. Davis got a hand on the upper and lower mandibles, threw a leg over the long sleek back and heaved. The brute roared and writhed. He felt his strength pour out of him, the teeth were closing on his fingers.

A crossbow bolt hummed and buried itself in the wet flank. Another and another. Barbara ran over the grass, shooting as she went. The monster turned its head and Davis yanked his hands free.

"Get away!" yelled Barbara.

Her bow was empty now. She crouched, drawing her knife, and plunged toward the creature. It reared up. She jammed her left arm under its beak, forced the head back, and slashed.

The seal-bird fell on her. Davis glimpsed a slim leg beneath its belly. He picked up his own bow and fired pointblank, again and again, hardly aware of what he did. Blood gurgled in the monster's voice.

Then it slumped, and the arterial spurting was only a red flow across slippery grass.

"Barbara—" Davis tugged at the weight, feeble

and futile. His own throat rattled.

The leg stirred. Barbara forced her way out from under.

She stood up, gasping, adrip with blood, and stared at him. His knees gave way.

"Are you all right?" she whispered. "Bert, darling, are you all right?"

"Yeh." His palms were lacerated, but it was nothing serious. "You?"

"Oh, th-th-this isn't my blood." She laughed shortly, sank to her knees before him, and burst into tears.

"There, there." He patted the bronze head, clumsy and unsure of himself. "It's all over, Barbara, it's finished now . . . Sunblaze, we've got meat for the pot—"

She shook herself, wiped her eyes, and gave him an angry stare. "You *fool!*" she snuffled. "If I hadn't h-h-happened to be near . . . heard the noise . . . oh, you blind gruntbrain!"

"Guess I've got that coming," said Davis.

Elinor stirred, looked around, and started to cry. Since she wasn't much hurt, she got no attention. "Well!" she muttered.

Barbara swallowed her rage. "I never saw a thing like this before," she admitted. "I suppose you couldn't have known, Bert. You were giving it a hell of a good fight. And it *is* meat."

"Thanks," he said weakly. . . .

When Valeria had blown off enough pressure by a magnificent description of Davis' altogether negligible intelligence, she finished: "We'll start out again tomorrow."

"Oh, yes!" babbled Elinor. "Those *things* in the lake—"

"What about the orspers?" demanded Barbara.

"Ride 'em till they drop, child, and continue on foot," said Valeria. "It'll be quicker."

"Don't call me child!" exploded Barbara. "I'm only three days younger than you, and my brain is twenty years older!"

"Girls, girls," began Davis. Valeria's scarred left hand dropped to her dagger, and he shut up and let the twins argue.

Barbara gave in at last, against her better judgment . . . after all, if they camped longer, Davis and Elinor were sure to— Only why should she care? What was a Monster to her?

She regarded him with concern. He had seemed such a big coward, she reflected; and yet he had fought the lake bird to save Elinor's life . . . Damn Elinor! If Davis had died on her account—Maybe, she thought, his unwillingness to fight was only a different way of thinking. A Man wouldn't think like a woman.

But it was heresy to admit this creature barely two meters tall, who could sweat and bleed and be afraid, was a Man!

And yet, when you got used to him, he was a beautiful creature, beard like spun gold and blue eyes that crinkled when he laughed . . . his hand brushed her knee, accidentally, and for a moment it seemed to burn and she got all weak and the world wobbled. What was wrong with her? She wanted to laugh and cry at the same time. Vague dreams chased through her head, she performed heroic deeds before his eyes, now they were together under a full Minos—

"Damn!" said Barbara.

"What's the matter?" asked Davis.

"Oh, nothing." His gaze made her want to squirm. "Leave me alone, will you?— No, I didn't mean that!"

All the next day, as they rode deeper into the valley, she churned over a new thought. Just suppose Davis *was* really a Man. What then? Yes . . . voice the thought, wait for Father's thunderbolt . . . when none came, Barbara's universe quivered and lost a few bricks.

He was at least a very dear Monster, with his songs and laughter, and he came from the stars. The stars! Man or no, he could bring the Men, and Atlantis would never be the same again.

Even if no Men ever came, she thought with sudden tears, her own Atlantis was dead. Let her return in triumph, driving out the enemy from Freetoon, return to the comradeship of the barracks and the unforgotten forest, Holy River below her like a dawn knife and the remote lance of the High Gaunt wreathed with cloud—for her, after knowing Davis, it would be too narrow and lonesome. She could never really go home.

She wanted to blurt her woe to him. It was not the Whitley way, but there would be a strange comfort, like having her mother back . . . only he would not hold her like her mother—

For lack of anyone else, she confided in Valeria. They were sitting up by the campfire while the others slept.

"It would be better if the Men came," agreed her cousin. "We've never lived as Father meant us to. We've just hung on, hoping, for three hundred years."

Barbara felt a smile tug her mouth. "It would be fun to have a Man-child," she murmured. "A kid like his father—like both of us mixed together—"

Suddenly: "Val! I've been thinking . . . I almost believe Bert *is* a Man!"

"Rotten specimen of one, then," snapped Valeria.

Barbara felt puzzled. Her twin was an obstinate nuisance, yes, but so was she. They had never thought so unlike before now.

On the following day, the descent became so steep that they had to lead the orspers. Toward evening they found themselves on the stony floor of a large canyon. The river flowing through it was broad as a lake, brown and swift, toppling in a kilometer-high waterfall over a cliff behind them. The air was subtropically warm, this was a much lower country than Freetoon's.

"These birds are about finished if they don't get a long rest," ventured Elinor. She sighed. "So am I."

"Maybe we can find someone around here who'll trade us," suggested Davis. "Look, whether you believe I'm a Man or not, I can sure as Evil act the part, overawe them, demand their help."

"It's blasphemy!" said Valeria.

Barbara looked down at her own tanned form, saw no signs of shriveling, and grew skeptical of Father with a speed that astonished her. "Are you afraid to try, Val?" she purred.

"All right, then!" snarled the other Whitley. "If this oaf can act like a Man, all right."

They were up before Bee-rise the next day, trudging downstream along the barren riverbank. The first dawn-glow showed the end of their search.

An island, some ten kilometers across, lifted sheer cliffs from the water to a luxuriance of trees on its crown. There was no access but a suspension bridge from the shore to the heights. Barbara's crossbow clanked into position. "So we've found somebody," she murmured.

"The question," said Valeria, "is who, and what can we talk them out of? Go to it, Davis."

He advanced to the foot of the bridge, cupped hands around his mouth, and bawled: "Hello, up there! We come in peace!" Echoes clamored from the canyon wall. There was a waiting.

Then a slender girl clad in long brown hair and a few flowers stepped from beneath the trees to the bridgehead. She carried an arbalest, but didn't aim it. "Who are you?" she called timidly.

"She's a Craig," muttered Barbara to Davis. "At home they're all poets and weavers. Now why would a Craig be on sentry-go?"

Davis drew himself up. "Know that I am a Man, come from Earth to redeem the old promise," he intoned. Barbara smothered a giggle.

"Oh!" The Craig dropped her bow and broke into a tremble. "A Man—*Ohhhh!*"

"I come as the vanguard of all the Men, that they may return to their loyal women and drive evil from Atlantis," boomed Davis. "Let me cross your bridge that I may, uh, claim your help in my, er, crusade. Yes, that's it, crusade."

The Craig squeaked and fell on her face. Davis led his tatter-demalion party over the bridge. The timing was perfect: Bee just rising in a golden blaze over the great waterfall above them. On the other side of the bridge, there was a downward path. The island was cup-shaped, holding trees in orderly groves, clipped grass, brilliant flowerbeds.

A few more women emerged from the foliage. They were as sleek, sun-tanned, and informally clad as the first one. And their reactions were just as satisfactory, a spectrum from abasement to awed gaping.

"More Craigs, couple of Salmons, a Holloway, an O'Brien," murmured Valeria. "Artist, artisan, entertainer classes at home—where are the warriors?"

A Holloway cleared her throat shyly and blushed. "We never thought there would be such an honor for us," she said. "We thought when the Men came, they'd—I mean—"

Davis puffed himself up. "Do you doubt I am a Man?" he roared.

"Oh, no, ma'm!" The Holloway cringed back from possible thunderbolts. Her voice, like that of all the islanders, had a melodiousness which betokened long training.

"Where's your Udall?" asked Valeria impatiently.

"Udall, ma'm?" The Craig they had first seen looked confused. "No Udalls here. Just us, ma'm."

No Udall! Barbara's mind staggered. But, but it wasn't possible!

"We'll take you to Prezden Yvonne Craig, ma'm," offered the Holloway.

"Do so." Davis beamed. "Incidentally, 'sir' would be more suitable than 'ma'm'. And don't . . . I mean, be not afraid. Rejoice!"

Another puzzling alienness—the islanders needed no more than the Man's consent to start rejoicing! Like children! When they had walked through two kilometers of parkscape, the whole population swarmed out to meet them, laughing, singing, dancing, striking up music for them. Altogether they numbered about a thousand, including children, and all bore plain signs of good, easy living.

Their village was surprisingly large. Barbara decided dazedly that they didn't have barracks at all.

Each of these simple grass huts was for no more than one woman and her children. The concept of privacy was so new it felt like a hammerblow.

She was led to a hut, and goggle-eyed girls brought her eggs, fruits, small sweet cakes, and sang to her while she ate. Only slowly did her mind stumble from the wreckage of its own axioms and wonder what Davis was up to. . . .

As a matter of fact, Davis, the past weeks catching up with him, had gone to sleep. He woke near sunset, donned the embroidered kilt, plumed headdress, and gold ornaments laid out for him, and strolled from the shack to find a banquet in preparation.

Valeria stood waiting for him in the long mellow B-light. She has loosened her red hair and discarded armor for a kilt and lei, but the scarred left hand rested on her dagger. They started together across the green toward a dais draped with feather cloaks, where Barbara stood talking to a Craig who held a carved staff.

"We seem to have found the kind of place we deserve," he said.

Valeria snorted. "Oh, yes, they're friendly enough—but gutless. This island is *too* easy to defend. They fish, raise fowl, have fruits the year round, all the metal they need . . . spend their time on arts, poetry, craft, music—" She ended her list with a vulgarity.

Glancing at delicately sculptured wood, subtly designed decoration, intricate figure dancing, listening to choral music which was genuinely excellent, Davis got fed up with Valeria. Narrowminded witch! Her own rather repulsive virtues, hardihood and fearlessness, would be as redundant here as fangs on a turtle.

"What's the place called?" he asked coldly.

"Lysum. There was a conquered town about a hundred years ago that a lot of its people ran away from. Up the river there's a settlement of nothing but Burkes. These people are all from the same class . . . Oh, here we are. Prezden Yvonne Craig, Davis Bert."

The woman stood up for him. She was in her middle thirties, and given a stronger chin would have been quite pretty—though Barbara, in kilt and lei, was unfair competition. "Be welcome among us, Man." Now that the first shock had worn off, she spoke with confidence. "Atlantis has never known a happier day. Oh, we're so thrilled!"

Davis looked around. "Where's Elinor?"

"Still pounding her ear," clipped Barbara. "Want to wait?"

"Cosmos, no! When do we—I mean, let the banquet begin."

Rank, as the women of Lysum settled themselves on the grass, seemed strictly according to age. It was pleasant to be in a casteless society again. The food was delicious, and there was course after course of it, and the wooden winebowls were kept filled.

Suppressing a burp, Davis leaned toward Yvonne. "I am pleased with what I have seen here," he told her.

"You are *so* sweet . . . er, gracious," she trilled happily.

"But elsewhere there is devilment on the loose. I am only the vanguard of the Men. Before all of them can come, the wrongdoers of Atlantis must be punished."

Yvonne looked alarmed. Valeria, flanking Davis

on the seat with Barbara, leaned over and hissed:
"No help here. I told this featherbelly we'd want
some spears to follow us, and she damn near
fainted."

"Mmmm . . . yes." Davis felt a moment's grim-
ness. He couldn't stay holed up here forever. No
wonder Val was so down on the islanders. Not a
bad girl, Val, in her waspish way. Davis tilted his
winebowl. His free arm stole around Barbara's
waist. She regarded him mistily.

"Strong, this drink," she said. "Not beer. Wha's
it called?"

"A jug of wine, and thou," smiled Davis.

"Bubbles in my head . . ." Barbara leaned
against him.

The Prezden gave him a large-eyed look. Minoslight streamed over sprawling feminine shapes.
"Will you take your pleasure of us all tonight,
sir?" she inquired.

"Yipe!" said Davis.

"Like hell you will!" Barbara sat straight up and
glared at him.

Yvonne looked bewildered. Barbara was quite
tight enough to start an argument, which would
never do. Davis gritted his teeth and said: "No,
thanks. Tonight I must, urp, think on weighty
problems. I would be alone."

Yvonne bent her long-tressed head. "As the Man
wishes. My house is his." Her dignity collapsed in
a titter. "I am his, too, if he changes his mind. Any
of us would be so *thrilled*—" She rose and clapped
her hands. "The Man wishes to be alone tonight,"
she called. "All you girls scat!"

Davis gaped. It was not what he had meant. Too
late now, of course. A god couldn't say, "Hoy,
wait!"

Valeria stood up, put an arm under Barbara's shoulders, and raised her tottery cousin. "I'll see her to bed," she said frostily.

Davis watched them disappear into one of the huts. "Death and destruction!" he said, and poured himself another drink.

He was tipsy, but there was no sleep in him. Presently he wandered off across a dewed sward, under the light-spattered shade of high trees, and stood on the island rim looking across a broken wilderness of stone and water and moonlight.

The fact is, me boy, and we might as well face it with our usual modesty, Barbara is in love with me. Maybe she doesn't quite realize it yet, but I know the symptoms. Well?

Well, so if they could only shake that Valeria hornet and that rather cloying Elinor, they could have a lot of fun. Only somehow Barbara Whitley wasn't a person you could simply have fun with. Davis grew a little scared. Cosmos sunder it, he didn't want to be tied down yet!

So, since he couldn't get away from her, he'd have to remove temptation by curing her of her feelings. In the absence of electronic psych-adjusters, he thought woozily, he could do that by making her mad at him—say, by exercising his Man's prerogatives with, yes, with Yvonne . . . who must be very disappointed in him . . . he grinned and started down toward the village.

As he emerged from a grove into the unreal light, he stopped short. A tall form approached him. "Barbara," he stammered.

She came to him, smiling and shaking the loose red hair down over her back, but her eyes were big, solemn, a little afraid. "Bert," she said. "I have to talk to you." She halted and stood with hands clasped behind her, like a child. Davis swallowed, because she was not at all like a child in other respects.

"Uh . . . sure . . . you got rid of that spitcat cousin of yours, I see," he began feebly.

"She's asleep. I wanted this to be between us two."

"Uh, yes, of course. Can't settle anything with Valeria around. Ask her a civil question and you get a civil war."

"Val . . . oh." Light and shadow flowed across the girl. Suddenly: "What do you have against Valeria?"

"She's just a natural-born shrew, I suppose," he shrugged.

"She means well. It's only that she—never quite knows what to say . . . we are of the same blood, I know her and—"

"Scuttle Valeria!" said Davis impulsively. "Come here, you!"

She crept into his arms, her hands stole around his neck and he kissed her. She responded with an endearing clumsiness.

"I couldn't stand it, Bertie," she gulped. "You and all those other women—what's happened to me?"

"Poor little Babs." He stroked her hair. "Sit down."

They spent a while without words. He was delighted to see how fast she learned. Here in the shadow of the frondtrees, she was only a warm breathing shape close to him.

After a time, she blurted: "Do whatever you want, Bertie."

Davis reached for her—and pulled up cold.

It was one thing to seduce an Elinor or an Yvonne. Barbara was a different case entirely: too whole-hearted, it would hurt her too much when he finally left. And . . . and . . . oh, there were all the practical objections, a long dangerous road ahead and so on. At the same time—no he *could* not rebuff her or humiliate her into storming off.

"Well?" she asked with a hint of testiness.

"Well, this is a serious matter," said Davis frantically. "You should think it over . . . look here . . . but—"

"But nothing!" Small calloused hands closed on his wrists.

Davis talked. And talked. And talked. He wasn't sure what he said, but it included words like sanctity. At the end, sweating, he asked her if she understood at all.

"No," she sighed. "But I imagine you know best."

"I wonder—never mind! Of course I do."

"There'll be other times, darling. Whenever you want to fer—"

"Cut that out!" groaned Davis. "Give me a kiss and go to bed."

She gave him a lengthy one. Then, rising: "There's one thing, dearest. The others in our party—you know it could make trouble—don't let's let on to *anyone*. Don't even talk to me about it unless I say the coast is clear."

"All right. That does make sense. Run along, sweetheart."

"Goodnight, Bertie. I care for you."

"The word," he said, "is 'love.' "

"I love you, then." She laughed, with a little sob, and sped off.

She ran like a deer, Davis thought. Evil, why couldn't she be trained for spatial survey? Married teams were common enough.

The girl stumbled. She spread her hands, regained balance, and continued.

Davis felt the wind go out of him. There had been a scar on her left hand. . . .

Barbara woke up and wished she hadn't. What had she been *drinking?*

She rolled over on her stomach and buried her face in her hands. Foggy recollections came back, yes, Val had helped her to bed and then she passed out . . . Davis making eyes at that Yvonne trollop—Father!

A young O'Brien entered with breakfast, which helped. Barbara tottered out into the open. It was a little past eclipse, and the islanders were going leisurely about their business. Prezden Yvonne ran warbling to greet her, received a bloodshot glare, and backed off. Barbara smoldered her way toward a fruit grove.

Valeria came into sight, wringing out her hair. "O, hello, little one," she grinned. "I recommend a swim. The water's fine."

"What have you got to be so Father-damned happy about?" grouched Barbara.

Valeria did a few steps of the soldier's ax dance. "Beautiful, beautiful day," she caroled. "I love this place!"

"Then it's too bad we're getting the hell out of here."

"Whatever for?"

"What reason is there to stay?" Barbara kicked miserably at the turf. "So Davis can make up to all the women in Lysum? I suppose he's still sleeping it off."

"Well, he did go to bed quite late, poor dear. But he just walked around, thinking." Valeria flushed at Barbara's look. "I couldn't sleep—sat up watching." Quickly, she jumped after a red fruit and crunched it between small white teeth. "Look, Babs, we do need a rest. So do our orspers; there aren't any here."

"Don't you know?" said Barbara. "One of those yuts told me yesterday. This river runs straight to the sea. They have boats here, we'll take one and make the trip twice as fast. The Lysumites get to the Ship that way—buy passage from—"

"Oh, hell, Babs. Life's too good to waste. I say let's stay here a few more days, at least." Valeria wandered off.

Barbara drifted glumly to the bridge. She didn't like the idea. That Yvonne—ugh!

A swim did help. Seated again on the rocky bank, she found her head clear enough to hold the problem. Which was that she wanted Davis for herself.

Just what that would mean, she wasn't sure, but the thought made her hot and cold by turns. She no longer doubted he was a Man, but it wasn't just any Man, it was *him*. Hell fry her if she let anyone else get him!

Then the thing to do was sneak out tonight, find him and— It took more courage than facing a wounded stamper. But to know where she stood and what she meant to do about it was like a fresh cup of that wine drink. She put her kilt back on and returned almost merrily.

Davis was just emerging from his hut. He looked wretched. Barbara's heart turned over with pity, she ran toward him calling his dear name and wondered why he jerked.

"Bert, what's the matter? Don't you feel well?"

"No," said Davis, hollowly.

Valeria joined them, walking in a new undulant fashion. Was everybody falling sick? "Lemme out of here," Davis muttered.

The musical winding of a horn interrupted them.

"Somebody's coming," said Barbara. "Over the bridge."

"It may not mean anything," said Valeria, "but let's get out of the way, just in case. Better collect the Dyckman."

Barbara nodded and ran off. Elinor, stretching herself langorously before a burly Holloway, found herself suddenly prodded up the slope at dagger point. Valeria and Davis joined them in a tanglewood stand on the rim. They stood peering through the leaves at a bustle down in the village, the Lysumites leaping to form ceremonial ranks.

"Father!" breathed Valeria. "It's a legate—messenger from the Doctors!"

The awe of a lifetime rose within Barbara. She had rarely seen a legate; now and then one had come to Freetoon to discuss such matters as the payment of annual tribute.

This was a tall woman. She wore a travel-stained uniform: hooded blue cloak, trousers and boots under a white gown, heavy veil. She was mounted on an orsper and led remounts and a packbird. As she stepped to earth, Yvonne prostrated herself.

Valeria snapped her fingers. "Of course!" she said excitedly. "Messengers from Freetoon to the Ship . . . remember? The Doctors must have sent to every town to inquire—"

"Well," said Davis. "Well, this is terrific! Our troubles are over, girls."

The veiled woman entered a hut. Her baggage was brought in after her, then she was alone. A party of women ran up the slope calling: "Man!

Man, the legate wants to see you!"

Davis smiled importantly and led the way down. He seated himself on the dais, much to the shock of the crowded islanders—nobody sat in a Doctor's presence!—and waited. Stillness lay thick.

When the legate finally emerged, Barbara's knees bumped together.

The woman had changed into ceremonials: green robe, gloved hands holding a metal staff, a plumed mask in the shape of an orsper head covering her own and making it coldly unhuman.

Daivs got up. "Hello, ma'm," he smiled. There was no answer. He faltered. "I am the Man," he stumbled. "You, uh, know about me?"

"Yes," said the legate. She had a low voice and a stiff accent. "The Ship and all Atlantis have awaited the Men for three hundred years. How many of you are there?"

"Just me," said Davis. "I need your help—the Doctors' help. Otherwise," he finshed dramatically, "there won't be any Men coming for a long time yet."

The legate neither moved nor spoke. Davis looked disconcerted, but launched into his story. He warmed up to it as he went along, and clenched his fists to emphasize the main point: the Doctors could order his boat returned to him, and he would fetch the Men. Barbara thought he looked much too smug, but lovable all the same.

At the end, the legate asked cooly: "Have you any weapons?"

"No, I told you. Just this dirk here. But—"

"I understand."

She strode from him, toward the bridge guards who stood holding their bows in what Barbara considered a miserable approximation of dress parade. Her voice rang out:

"This is no Man, it's a Monster. Kill it!"

For a moment nobody stirred.

The legate whirled on Yvonne. "I order you in the name of Father," she cried. "Kill the filthy thing!"

Barbara had no time to think. She jumped, snatched a bow from a half paralyzed guard, and lifted it to her shoulder. "The first one of you to move gets a bolt in the belly," she announced.

Valeria's dagger flared directly before the legate. "And this witch gets a slit throat," she added. Her voice cracked across. "Hold still, you!"

In Freetoon the arbalests would have been snapping already. But these were a timid folk who had not known battle for generations. "Drop your weapons," said Barbara. She swiveled her own from guard to guard. Armament clattered to the grass. A moan went through the densely packed crowd.

Davis shook a benumbed head. "What's the matter?" he croaked. "I am a Man. Give me a chance to prove it!"

"You've already proved yourself a Monster by assaulting the Ship's own envoy," shouted the legate. "Prezden, do your duty!"

Yvonne Craig shuddered her way backward, lifting helpless hands. "You mustn't," she whimpered. "You can't—"

Through a haze of terror, Barbara saw Davis shake himself. He spoke swiftly then: "Unless you want to die, lady, you'd better tell these people to obey us."

Valeria emphasized the request with a dagger flourish. Malevolence answered him: "So be it, then . . . for now! Don't think you'll escape Father."

Davis turned to the Whitleys. He was pale and breathed hard, but the words rattled from him: "We have to get out of here. Keep these people covered. I'll take charge. You, you, you, you—" his finger chose young, horror-smitten girls. "Fetch out all our stuff. And the legate's pack. And food, plenty of it. Elinor, pick up some bows."

"No—no, you Monster," she gasped.

"Suit yourself," he laughed harshly. "Stay here if you want to be torn to pieces as soon as we're gone."

Shaking, she collected an armful of weapons.

When the supplies were ready, Davis led his group up the path, a scared and sullen village trailing them several meters behind and staring into the Whitley bowsights. Once over the bridge, he cut the cable with a few hard ax strokes. The bridge collapsed into the water and broke up.

"How do we get back?" cried a young Holloway.

"You can swim out and let 'em lower ropes for you," said Davis. "Now, take us to those boats I heard somebody mention."

The burdened women trudged along the shaly bank while Yvonne stood on the cliffs and howled loyal curses. On the other side of a bluff, jutting into the river, a score of long slim bark canoes with carved stemposts were drawn up. Davis told his prisoners to load one. "And set the others afire," he added to Barbara.

She nodded mutely and took forth tinder and fire piston from her pouch. Flame licked across the hulls. Her mind felt gluey, she didn't know if she could have moved without him to think for her.

"All right," said Davis when the job was done. "Scram, you females. Boo!" He waved his arms and the youngsters fled screaming.

Barbara took a certain satisfaction in binding the legate's wrists and ankles and tossing her among the bundles. Elinor huddled near the captive, big help she'd be! They shoved the canoe into the river and climbed aboard. Davis demonstrated the use of paddles, set Valeria in the bow and Barbara in the stern, and said he and Elinor could spell them.

Ariadne rose above Ay-set, and Theseus was already up. It would be a bright night. Father! Barbara could have wished for clouds, she felt so exposed under the naked sky. There was a blotch on Minos like a great bloodshot eye glaring down at her.

No, she told herself, Father was a lie . . . at least, the stiff lightning-tossing Father of the Ship did not exist, or if he did then Bert with his long legs and blue eyes and tawny beard was a stronger god. Merely looking at him made her want to cry.

He grinned and wiped sweat off his face. "Holy Valdaoth, I don't want to go through that again!" he said.

Valeria looked over her shoulder. "But we got away," she whispered. "Thanks to you, we got away."

"To me? Thunderation! If you two hadn't— Well, let's take the cash and let the credit go." He regarded the legate thoughtfully. "I wonder what's beneath that helmet," he said.

He lifted the gilt orsper head. Barbara, who had half expected haloes or some such item, was almost disappointed when the ash-blonde hair and coldly regular features of a Trevor appeared.

Elinor covered her eyes and crouched shivering.

"I d-d-didn't want to see, ma'm," she pleaded.

"You've fallen into bad company, child," said the Trevor. Then, to Davis: "Are you satisfied, Monster?"

"No." He ran a hand through unkempt yellow hair and asked plaintively: "What have you got against me? Don't you know I'm a Man? You must have *some* biological knowledge to operate that parthenogenetic wingding."

"You aren't a Man." The Trevor lay back, scowling in the light that spilled from the sky.

After a moment, Davis murmured: "I see. It's a common enough pattern in history. You Doctors have had it soft for a long time. You must always have dreaded the day when the Men would finally arrive and upset your little wagon. When I told you I'm alone and there won't be any others for a long time yet it I don't return—well, your bosses at the Ship must already have told you what to do if that was the case."

"You're a Monster!" said the Trevor. Dogmatic as ever.

"Even if you honestly thought I was, you wouldn't have ordered them to cut me down. Even a Monster could go home and call the true Men. No, no, my friend you're a pretty sophisticated lot at the Ship, and you've just decided to rub out the competition."

"Be still before Father strikes you dead!" she cried.

"Legates sent to every town," went on Davis. "Orders to learn what the facts are—dicker with the Men if there really are a number of them or if they can call for help; otherwise kill them and deny everything."

"I'd like to kill *her*," said Barbara between her teeth.

"Babs, have you any idea who the Doctors are
. . . how many, what families?"

She frowned, trying to remember. A child always picked up scraps of information meant only
for initiates . . . she overheard this, was blabbed
that by a garrulous helot. "There are a few thousand of them, I believe. And they're said to be of
the best families."

"Uh-huh. I thought so. Inferior types couldn't
maintain this system. Even with that tremendous
monopoly of theirs, there'd have been more conflict between Church and State unless— Yeh.
Trevors, Whitleys, Burkes, that sort—the high
castes of Freetoon, with the wits and courage and
personality to override any local chief. Well."

Barbara shoved her paddle through murmurous
moonlit waters. "But what are we going to do?"
she asked in helplessness.

"I think—yes. I really think we can get away
with it." Davis took a long breath. "The word from
Lysum will be far behind us. Now, either of you
two is about the size of this dame. You can pass for
a legate yourself—"

Barbara choked. After a moment, Valeria shook
her head. "No, Bert. It can't be done. Every child in
the soldier families gets that idea as soon as it can
talk: why not pass a Freetoon Whitley off as a
Greendaler? There are countersigns to prevent
just that."

"It isn't what I meant," said Davis. "Look here.
How are the sea people to know you're not a genuine legate, bringing back a genuine Man? Only, on
his behalf, you requisition an escort and a lot of
fast orspers. We ride back to Freetoon, demand my
own boat—oh, yes, our pseudo-legate can also order your town set free. Then we all hop into my
spaceship and ride to Nerthus—and return with a

thousand armed Men!"

Barbara thought dazedly that only he could have forged such a plan.

Eighteen Atlantean days later, the canoe nosed into Shield Skerry harbor.

The enormous, shifting tides raised by the other great moons turned the coasts into salt marshes at ebb, brackish lakes at flow. But the local life had adapted, there were even trees and grass, and a few of the low-caste families lived here, sunken to a naked neolithic stage but available as guides. Valeria, impressive in robe and veil, commandeered their help.

Davis had tried to quiz the legate. Beyond the information that her name was Joyce and he was a Monster destined for hell's hottest griddle, she would tell him nothing.

For Davis, lack of privacy and the weariness of incessant paddling had its good points. It staves off his own problem. The notion that someday he'd face it again—maybe alone in space with two jealous Whitleys, because he couldn't leave them defenseless against the Doctors' revenge—made his nerves curl up and quiver at the ends.

Unless he gave himself to a psychadjuster on Nerthus and had his own hankerings electronically exorcised—which he didn't want to do—he would have to pick one or the other. And now that he knew them both, he couldn't chose!

What have I done to deserve this?

Elinor had been very quiet on the trip. She made herself useful to Joyce, probably too scared of both sides to reach a decision. Davis felt sorry for her, in a patronizing fashion.

And then finally they were out of the marsh.

The chief Nicholson had told him in her barely intelligible argot that there were many many seafolk on many many islands, that Shield Skerry was only a port for the inland trade. Davis looked eagerly ahead. Behind him the swamps were a vaporous gray, low in the sea, a storm of shrieking birds made a white wing-cloud under Minos and the two suns—otherwise there were only the huge foam-flanked waves that marched out of the west. The water was a chill steely bluish-gray, the wind shrill in his ears.

The rock was nearly hidden by the stone walls erected on its back: massive blocks cut square, a primitive lighthouse where oil fires behind glass burned in front of polished copper reflectors, two long jetties enclosing a small harbor. As they entered this, Davis saw that a good-sized ship—by Atlantean standards—was in. A capstan-powered crane was unloading baled cargo. Strong suntanned women bustled about, barefoot, clad in wide trousers and halters, their hair cut off just below the ears. Beyond the dock were warehouses and dwelling units. They were of stone, with shingle roofs, in the same uncompromising angular style as the town wall and the pharos.

The ship was carvel-built, with a high poop and a corroded bronze winged-fish figurehead. Davis guessed it had a deep draught and a centerboard, to maintain freeway in these tricky waters. There was no mast, but a windmill arrangement turned idly amidships. What off Earth—? Otherwise the harbor held only a few boats, swift-looking, more or less yawl-rigged.

"Highest technology I've seen here," he remarked.

"What? Oh, you mean their skills," said Barbara. "Yes, they say the seafolk are the best smiths in the world. It's even said their captains can read writing, like Doctors."

Davis assumed that the pelagic colonies were old, founded perhaps before the final breakdown of castaway civilization. The sea held abundant food if you knew how to get it. "What kind of people are they?" he asked.

"We don't know much about them in the uplands," said Barbara.

"Well," said Davis, "we'll find out pretty quick." His stomach was a cold knot within him.

Work at the dock was grinding to a halt. Women swarmed from the buildings and hurried down tortuous cobbled streets. *"A legate, another legate, and who's that with her?"*

Valeria did not thank their guides, it wouldn't have been in character. She stepped haughtily onto the quay. Davis followed. Barbara nudged the wrist-bound Trevor with a knife and urged her after. Elinor slunk behind.

There was a crowd now, pushing and shoving. A few must be police or guards—they wore conical, visored helmets and scaly corselets above their pants. Davis noticed flamboyant tattoos, earrings, thick gold bracelets . . . and on all classes. A Nicholson stood arm in arm with a Latvala, a Craig pushed between a Whitley and a Burke, a Holloway carrying a blacksmith's hammer gave amiable backchat to a Trevor with spear and armor.

Valeria raised her staff. "Quiet!" she shouted.

The babble died away, bit by bit. A gray-haired

woman, stocky and ugly, added a roar: "Shut up, you scupperheads!" She was an Udall, Davis recognized uneasily. She turned to Valeria and gave a crude salute.

"Are you in charge?" asked the girl.

"Reckon I am, ma'm, being the skipper of this tub . . . *Fishbird* out o' Farewell Island, she is. Nelly Udall, ma'm, at your service."

Joyce Trevor opened her mouth. She was white with anger. Barbara nudged her and she closed it again.

Valeria stood solemnly for a moment. It grew quiet enough to hear the waves bursting on the breakwater. Then she lifted her veiled face and cried: "Rejoice! I have brought a Man!"

It had the desired effect, though a somewhat explosive one. Davis was afraid his admirers would trample him to death. Nelly Udall cuffed back the most enthusiastic and bellowed at them. "Stand aside! Belay there! Show some respect, you—" What followed brought a maidenly blush to Barbara herself, and she was a cavalry girl.

When the racket had quieted somewhat, Davis decided to take charge. "I am a Man," he said in his deepest voice. "The legate found me in the hills and brought me here. She knows you are a pious people."

"Bless you, dearie," said the Udall through sudden tears. "Sure, we're pious as hell. Any Father-damned thing you want, ma'm, just say so."

"But there is evil afoot," boomed Davis. "Before all the Men can come, you must aid me to destroy the evil in Atlantis."

A certain awe began to penetrate those hard skulls. The show was rolling. Davis turned to Nelly Udall. "I would speak with you and your counselors in private," he said.

She looked confused. "Sure . . . sure, ma'm. Yes, your manship. You mean my first mate?"

"Oh . . . no authority here, is there? Well where does the Udall of the seas dwellers live?"

"What Udall? I'm just me."

"Who is your queen, chief, president—who makes the decisions?"

"Why, why, Laura Macklin is the preemer, ma'm," stuttered Nelly. "She's at New Terra, that's the capital. Did you want everybody to come there and vote, ma'm?"

A republic was about the last thing Davis had expected to find. But it was plausible, now that he thought about it. Even under Atlantean conditions, it would be hard to establish despotism among a race of sailors. The cheapest catboat with a few disgruntled slaves aboard could sail as fast as the biggest warship.

"Never mind," he said majestically. "I'm afraid you misunderstood me, Captain Udall. Take us to a place where we can talk alone with you."

"Yes, *ma'm!*" Nelly's eyes came to light on Joyce Trevor's sullen face. She jerked a horny thumb toward the prisoner. "Enemy of yours, ma'm? I'll chop her up personally."

"That will not be required," said Davis. "Bring her along."

"Awright, awright, clear a way!" roared Nelly. "Stand aside there, you bilge drinkers!" Her fist emphasized the request, but nobody seemed to mind. Tough lot.

Davis led his party after her, through a narrow street to a smoky kennel with an anchor painted on the gable. "We'll use this tavern," said Nelly. "Break open a keg of— *No*, you fishbrains! This is private! Git!" She slammed the door in a hundred faces.

Davis coughed. When his eyes were through watering, he saw a room under sooty rafters, filled with benches and tables. A noble collection of casks lined one wall, otherwise the inn was hung with scrimshaw work and stuffed fish. A whole seal-bird roasted in the fireplace.

Nelly fetched heroic goblets and tapped a brandy cask. "Now then, your maledom, say away." She leaned back and sprawled columnar legs across the floor. "Death and corruption! A Man, after all these years."

Formality was wasted on her, Davis decided. He told her the same censored tale he had given Lysum.

"Heard of those wenches." Nelly snorted. "Well, ma'm . . . sorry, you said it was 'sir,' didn't you? What happened next?"

"This Trevor showed up," said Davis. "She was one of the agents of evil, the same who had whipped Greendale and the other towns into attacking Freetoon. She stirred up Lysum against me. I made her captive and we went down the river till we came here."

"Why didn't you see her gizzard, sir?"

"The Men are merciful," said Davis with a slight shudder. "Do you have a place where she can be held incommunicado?"

"A what? We've got a brig."

"That'll do." Davis continued with his demands: passage to the Holy River mouth and an escort to Freetoon, where the lady legate would give the orders of the Ship.

Nelly nodded. "Can do, sir. There are twenty good crewgirls on the *Fishbird,* and a causeway from the Ship over the swamps—"

"We needn't stop at the Ship," said Valeria quickly. "In fact, I'm commanded not to come near

it till the rest of the Men arrive. And you understand, this has to be kept secret or we may have
more trouble with the, uh, agents of hell."

"Awright, ma'm. We'll just leave the *Fishbird* at
Bow Island and get orspers and ride straight to
Freetoon. There's a ridge we can follow through
the marshes."

Davis frowned. Whatever legate had gone to
Freetoon might have planted a story that he really
was a Monster, to be killed on sight. Or no, probably not . . . *that* legate had no way of knowing he
was the only male human on Atlantis; she'd have to
ride back for orders. . . .

"The faster the better," he said.

"We'll warp out at Bee-rise tomorrow, ma'm,"
said Nelly Udall. She shook her head and stared
into her goblet. "A Man! A real live Man! Father
damn it, I'm too old . . . but I've seen you, sir.
That's enough for me, I reckon."

After Joyce Trevor had been safely locked in the
town jail, with the guard ordered not to speak to
her or let anyone else do so, Nelly led Davis' party
down to the dock, where he made a short but telling speech to the assembled women. The inquiries
of the preceding legate as to whether a Man had
been seen had paved the way for his arrival; no one
disbelieved him.

Cloud masses piled blackly out of the west, wind
skirled, and scud stung his face. He felt the weariness of being hunted. "I would retire," he said.

"Yes, sir, this way, sir," said Nelly. She gave him
a wistful look. "Sure you won't come down to the
Anchor with us and fer—"

"Quite sure!" said Barbara and Valeria
together.

The crowd trailed them to a long house reserved

for ships' captains. Beyond a common room, there
was a hall lined by small bedchambers. Elinor
slipped into the first, then Valeria, then Davis,
then Barbara . . . he closed the shutters against
the gale, turned off the guttering oil lantern, and
crept through a sudden heavy darkness into bed.
Ahhh!

But it wasn't easy to sleep. Too much to think
about . . . it would be good to be among men again
. . . what to do about the Whitleys?—oh, blast, face
that problem later . . . he'd be coming back to Atlantis, surely, to help these forlorn female devils
through the difficult period of readjustment . . .
*Hello, Dad! I seem to've been pounded into a sober
well-integrated citizen after all* . . . But nobody
mated to a Whitley would ever get *too* sober—

Drowsiness spilled from him when the door
opened. He sat up. "Who's that?" Bare feet groped
across the floor. His scalp prickled.

"Shhh!" The husky voice was almost in his ear.
He reached and felt a warm roundedness. "Bertie,
I just had to come to you—"

Davis made weak fending motions. The girl
laughed shyly and slid under his blankets. Two
strong arms closed about him.

His morality stood up in indignation, slipped,
and tobogganed whopping down his spinal col-
umn. "C'mere!" he said hoarsely.

Her lips closed against his, still inexpert, her
hands shuddered their way along his back. Well,
he thought with an intoxicating sense of release, if
Valeria chose to enter his bed, why, Val was a wonderful girl and he'd make a more or less honest
woman of her when he got the chance.

"Bert . . . Bert, darling, I don't know what . . .
what this is, to be with a Man . . . but I care for you
so much—"

"I told you the word was 'love,' " he chuckled.

"Did you? When was that?"

"You remember, Val, sweetheart . . . you didn't fool me—"

"*Val!*" She sat bolt upright and screeched the name. "*Val?* What's been going on here?"

"Oh, no!" groaned Davis. "Barbara, listen, I can explain—"

"I'll explain you!" she yelled.

Davis scrambled to get free. The blankets trapped him. Barbara got her hands on his throat.

The door opened. The tall red-haired girl carried an ax in her right hand; the left, holding a lantern, was scarred.

"What's happening?" barked Valeria.

To the untrained eye, a wrestling match is superficially not unlike certain other sports. Valeria cursed, set down the lantern, and strode forward with lifted ax. Barbara sprang out of bed, snatched up Davis's knife, and confronted her tiwn.

"So you've been mucking around!" she shouted.

"I wouldn't talk," answered Valeria from clenched jaws. "The minute my back is turned, you come oozing in and—and—"

"Now, girls," stammered Davis. "Ladies, ladies, please!"

They whirled on him. Something intimated to him that this was not just the correct approach. He got out of bed one jump ahead of the ax and backed into a corner. "It's all a mistake!"

"The mistake was ever bringing you along," snarled Valeria.

The wind hooted and banged the shutters. Above it, suddenly, he heard a roar. It swept closer, boots racketing on cobblestones, clattering iron, a mob howl.

The Whitleys reacted fast. Valeria whirred her

ax, Barbara darted back to her room for a bow. The vague light threw their shadows monstrous across the walls.

Feet pounded down the hall. Nelly Udall burst into the chamber. There were gashes on her squat body, and the ax in her hand dripped blood. "Hell and sulfur!" she bawled. "Grab your weapons! They're coming to kill you!"

A Macklin and a youthful Lundgard followed her. They were also wounded, hastily armed, and they were crying.

"What happened?" rattled Davis.

"I bolted the outer door," panted Nelly. "They'll break it down in a minute." A groan of abused wood came from behind her. "I believe you're a Man, dearie . . . that's how I got these cuts . . . but the Trevor— Why didn't you kill that snark when you had the chance?"

"*Trevor!*" Davis grabbed the Udall's shoulders. "Is she loose?"

"Yeh," said Nelly in a flat voice. "We was all down at the Anchor, drinking your health, and this Trevor walks in with that Dyckman of yours, says she's the legate and you're a Monster. Proves herself by running through the rites every mother knows are said at the Ship—challenges your Whitley to do the same—" Nelly shook her head. "It was quite a fight. We three here beat our way out o' the tavern and got here ahead of 'em."

"Elinor!" Barbara's voice seethed.

"She must have sneaked out," said Davis wanly. "Gone to the brig, told the guard she had new orders from me, set Joyce free. . . . Oh, almighty Cosmos, what're we going to do now?"

"Fight," answered Nelly. She planted herself in the doorway.

There was a final crash, and the mob came down

the hall. A Salmon leaped yelling, with drawn knife. Nelly's ax thundered down, the body rolled at her feet. A Hauser jabbed at her with a spear. Barbara shot the Hauser through the breast.

It dampened them. The women milled sullenly in the narrow corridor, the noise quieted to a tigerish grumble.

Davis stepped forward, trying not to shake. A scarred elderly Damon faced him boldly. "Will you call a truce?" she asked.

"Yes," said Davis. "Hold your fire, Barbara. Maybe we can—"

Joyce Trevor pushed her way through the crowd and regarded him over Nelly's shoulder. Ragged skirt and matted hair took away none of her frozen dignity. "I say you are a Monster," she declared.

"Elinor," said Davis, very quietly, still not believing it. "Elinor, why did you do this?"

He glimpsed her in the mob, thin, shaking, and enormous-eyed. Her lips were pale and stiff. "You are," she whispered. "You attacked a legate. The legate says you're a Monster."

Davis smiled wryly. "I was alone, and there were a lot of Doctors," he murmured. "That's why, isn't it?"

"Shut up, you Monster!" screamed Elinor. "You and those Whitleys kicked me around once too often!"

"This is a waste of time," snapped Joyce. "If that Whitley is a true legate, let her prove it by reciting the rites."

"Never mind," sighed Davis. "She isn't. But I am a Man. I can bring all the Men here. The legate lies about me because the Doctors don't want them. It would mean the end of Doctor power."

"I sort of thought that," muttered the Lundgard beside him.

"Let me go to my spaceship," said Davis. "That's all I ask."

Joyce whirled on the crowd. "Let him summmon the other Monsters?" she yelled. "I lay eternal barrenness on anyone who helps this thing! I order you to kill it, now!"

Nelly hefted her ax, grinning. "Who's next?" she inquired.

Davis heard feet shuffle in the corridor, voices buzz and break, spears drag on the floor. And there was the sound of new arrivals, a few pro-Davis women stamping in and making their own threats. Women have slightly less tendency to act in mobs than men do; the crowd was wavering, uncertain, afraid.

He straightened, licked his lips, and walked forward. "I'm going out," he said. "Make way."

Barbara, Valeria, Nelly and her two companions, followed at his heels. A handful of determined roughnecks shoved through the pack, toward him, to join him. Otherwise no one stirred. Joyce boiled under the menace of Barbara's cocked bow, Elinor hid her eyes. If nothing broke this explosive quiet—

The wind raved in coalsack streets. A lonely score of women tramped in a circle about Davis, toward the dock. He heard the crowd follow, but it was too dark to see them.

Barbara—he felt the hard stock of her arbalest—whispered venomously: "Don't think I'm coming along for your sake, you slimy double-face. I haven't any choice."

When they emerged from canyon-like walls, onto the wharf, enough light to see by trickled down from the pharos. Nelly led the way to her ship.

"I'm staking one hell of a lot on your really being a Man," she said desolately, into the wind. "I don't dare believe anything else."

The Shield Skerry folk swirled on the edge of darkness, still paralyzed. He had to get away before the shooting began. He crossed the gangplank to the deck. Valeria edged close to him and hissed: "Yes, I'll believe you're a Man too . . . and the hell with all Men! I'm only coming because I haven't any choice."

Nelly seemed to draw strength from the planks booming beneath her feet. "All aboard, you scuts! Man the capstan! Look lively now!"

She went aft, up on the poop to a nighted helm. The other women scurried about, doing incomprehensible things with ropes and pulleys. The great windmill jerked, gears whined as they engaged, there was a white threshing at the stern. The *Fishbird* moved slowly out of the harbor.

Morning was gray over an ice-gray sea, where waves snorted from horizon to horizon and the ship wallowed. Davis emerged from one of the little cabins under the poop to find the crew—mostly young women of the more war-like families—chattering happily. Barbara and Valeria sulked on opposite sides of the deck, elaborately ignoring him.

The windmill, facing into the stiff gusts, turned, driving a propeller through a set of gears and shafts. As he waited for breakfast, Davis tried to lose his gloom by admiring the arrangement—it made the ship independent of wind direction. Evil! Who cared?

Nelly Udall waddled into view. "Morning,

dearie," she boomed. "Not seasick, I hope? No? Good—kind of hard to believe in a seasick Man, eh? Haw, haw, haw!" She slapped his back so he staggered. Then, seriously: "Come into my cabin. We got to talk."

They sat on her bunk. She took out a pipe and stuffed it with greenish flakes from a jar. "We can't go on to Holy River now, that's for sure, chick. That Father-damned legate's been preaching hellfire to 'em back at Shield. The boats must already be headed for the Ship to bring the glad tidings. With a wind like this, a yawl can sail rings around us. Time we get to Bow Island, even, all the country will be up in arms."

"Glutch!" strangled Davis.

Nelly kindled her pipe with a fire piston and blew nauseous clouds. "Sure you aren't seasick, duck? All of a sudden you don't look so good."

"We've got to raise help," mumbled Davis. "Somewhere, somehow."

Nelly nodded. "Figgered as much. I'm bound for Farewell, my home port. Got plenty of friends there, and nobody to conterdick whatever you say.'

"But when they hear the Ship's against us—"

"I know a lot who'll still stick by us, dearie. Girls like our present crew. We've gotten almighty sick of the Doctors. We see more of 'em than the uplanders do, the—" Nelly went into a rich catalogue of the greed, arrogance, and general snottiness of the Doctors. Davis guessed that a mercantile culture like this would naturally resent paying tribute . . . and then, generations of sexual frustration had to be vented somehow.

The Doctors could not all be villains. Doubtless many were quite sincere. But Davis knew enough Union law to be sure that anything he did to them would be all right with the Coordination Service. It was they who stood between Atlantis and civilization—more important, a normal family life.

The idea grew slowly within him as the Udall rumbled on:

"I reckon we can raise quite a few shiploads, then go far up the coast and strike inland toward your boat."

"No!" said Davis. Words poured from him. "Too risky. It'll be guarded too heavily; and they may have tools enough left in the Ship to demolish it. We've got to act fast. If you think your friends are willing to hazard their lives to be free—"

Nelly smiled. "Chick, with that beard and that voice you can talk 'em into storming hell gate."

"It won't be quite that bad," said Davis. "I hope. What we're going to do is storm the Ship."

The rebel fleet lay to at Ship city at high tide, just after B-rise.

Davis stood on the *Fishbird's* deck and watched his forces move in. There were about forty vessels, their windmills and sails like gull wings across waters muddy-blue, rippled and streaked by an early breeze. At their sterns flew the new flag he had designed. His girls were quite taken with the Jolly Roger.

The rebels numbered some 2,000 women from the Farewell archipelago. There were more than that to guard the Ship, but less tough, less experienced in fighting—the seafolk were not above occasional piracy. The odds didn't look too bad.

Valeria stamped her feet so the deck thudded. "I'm going ashore," she said mutinously.

"No, you don't, chicakabiddy." Nelly Udall twirled a belaying pin. "Got to keep some guard over the Man. What's the bloody-be-damned use of it all if he gets himself skewered?"

Barbara nodded coldly. "She's right, as anyone but you could see," she added. "Not that I wouldn't rather guard a muck-bird!"

Davis sighed. In the three Atlantean weeks since they left Shield Skerry, neither of the cousins had spoken to him, or to each other without a curse. After the hundreth rebuff, he had given up. Evil take all women anyway! He just wanted to to go home, go back and get roaring drunk and have the psych machine numb the pain which went with red hair and green eyes.

He twisted his mind elsewhere. The Ship must have been badly crippled, to land here; probably it had come down where it could, on the last gasp of broken engines. The walls which now enclosed it had been built on a hill that just barely stuck out over high tide. Eastward lay the marches, a dreary gray land where a stone causeway slashed through to the distance-blued peaks of the Ridge.

There must have been heavy construction equipment in the Ship's cargo. A few thousand women could not have raised this place by hand. The machines were long ago worn out, but their work remained.

The city was ringed by white concrete walls five meters high, with a square watchtower at each corner. The walls fell to the water of high tide or the mud of ebb: inaccessible save by the causeway entering the eastern gate or the wide quay built out from the west side. Against this dock the rebel boats were lying to. Gangplanks shot forth and armored women stormed onto the wharf.

Davis let his eyes wander back to the city. he could see the tops of buildings above the walls, the dome-roofed architecture of three centuries ago. And he could see the great whaleback of the Ship itself, 300 meters long from north wall to south wall, metal still bright but a buckled spot at the waist to show how hard it had landed.

Barbara looked wistfully at the yelling seafolk. She was clad like them: visored helmet on her ruddy hair, tunic of steely-scaled orcfish hide, trousers, spike-toed boots. The accessories included lasso, knife, ax, crossbow and quiver, she had become a walking meat grinder.

Davis, likewise armored, felt the same sense of uselessness. Not that he wanted to face edged metal, the thought dried out his mouth. But when women were ready to die for *his* sake—

Bee struck long rays into his eyes. Ay was so close as to be hidden by the glare of the nearer sun. Minos brooded overhead in the gigantic last quarter. There was a storm on the king planet—he could see how the bands and blotches writhed.

Horns blew on the walls, under the Red Cross flag. Women, lithe tough legates and acolytes, were appearing in cuirass, greaves, and masking helmet, all of burnished metal. Crossbows began to shoot.

There was no attempt to batter down the iron door at the end of the quay. A howling mass of sailors raised ladders and swarmed skyward.

"Cosmos!" choked Davis.

A Doctor shoved at one of the ladders, but there was a grapnel on its end. Davis saw her unlimber a long rapier. The first rebel up got it through the throat and tumbled, knocking off the woman below her, they fell hideously to the ground.

"Let me go!" yelled Valeria.

"Hold still," rapped Nelly. Her worried eyes went to Davis. "I didn't think they'd have so good a defense, chick. We'd better get them licked fast."

He nodded. They had only a couple of hours before the tide dropped so far that any ship which remained would be stranded, in mud or the harbor locks, till the next high.

"So we stay," growled Barbara. "Isn't that the idea?"

"Yeh," said Davis. He drew hard on a borrowed pipe. "Only the Doctors must have called in a lot of upland warriors, to patrol between here and Freetoon. Now they'll send for their help. If things go badly, I'd like a way to retreat."

"You would," she agreed, and turned her back on him.

Axes, spears, swords clashed up on the wall, bolts and darts gleamed in the cool early light. The Doctor fighters were rapidly being outnumbered. One of them, in a red cloak of leadership, winded a horn. Her women fought their way toward her.

Davis gulped. It couldn't be that simple! Yes, by all creation, the Doctor forces were streaming down a stairway into their town. A slim young Burke cried triumph, he could hear the hawk-shriek above all the racket and see how her dark hair flew in the wind as she planted the Jolly Roger on the city wall.

Now down the stairs! There was a red flash of axes. The last legate backed out of view, thrusting and slicing at sailor shields.

Nelly grabbed Davis and whirled him in a wild stomp around the dock. "We got 'em, we got 'em, we got 'em!" she caroled. Planks shuddered beneath her.

The man felt sick. His whole culture was conditioned against war, it remembered its past too well. If he could have been in the action, himself, taking his own chances, it wouldn't have been so gruesome. But he was the only one on Atlantis who

could bring the Men. He had to hold himself
back—

"Scared?" jeered Valeria. "If it looks like you
might get hurt after all, we'll take you away where
it's safe."

"I'm not going to retreat!" he said in a raw voice.

"Yes, you will, duck, if we got to," said Nelly. "If
you get killed, what's for us?" Her seamed face
turned grimly inland. "We've got to win . . . no
choice . . . if the Doctors win, there'll never be another baby on the islands."

That was what drove them, thought Davis. Below all the old grudges and the glamor of his cause,
there was the primeval mother urge. The seafolk
had not told it to themselves in so many words, but
their instincts knew: a machine was too unsafe a
way of bringing life into the world.

The iron harbor doors were flung open. So the
west end of town was firmly held by his side. The
noise of battle was receding, the Doctors being
driven back . . . So what? A victory where you
yourself did nothing was no victory for a man.

Damn! His pipe had gone out.

"I think we'll have the mucking place before
ebb," said Nelly. "But then what do we do?"

"We'll have the parthenogenetic apparatus,"
Davis reminded her. "Not to mention the prestige
of victory. We'll own the planet."

"Oh . . . yeh. Keep forgetting. I'm growing old,
dearie—huh?"

There was a shriek through the gateway.

Sailors poured out of it, falling over each other,
hurling their weapons from them in blind panic. A
couple of hundred women made for the ships.

"What's happened?" bawled Nelly. "Avast, you
hootinanies! Stop that!" She went into a weeping
tirade of profanity.

Barbara snatched her megaphone from the captain. "Pull in!" she cried. "We're going ashore now!"

The helmswoman looked ill, but yanked a signal cord. The ship moved across a narrow stretch of open water and bumped against one of the docked schooners.

"Let's go," snapped Valeria. She leaped onto the schooner deck.

Barbara saw Davis follow. "No!" she yelled.

"Yes," he answered harshly. "I've stood enough." Blind with fury, he dashed to the wharf.

The mob was still coming out of the door and over the quay to mill on the ships. Davis grabbed a Craig and whirled her around.

"What's the matter?" he shouted. She gave him an unseeing look. He slapped her. "What happened in there?"

"We . . . street fighting . . . Doctor troop . . . flame, white flame and it *burned* our forward line—" The Craig collapsed.

"It's Father himself!" gasped a Macklin.

"Shut up!" rapped Davis. He felt sick. "I know what it is. They must have found my blaster up by Freetoon, and the legate took it back here. Maybe records in the Ship describe blasters." He shook his head numbly. "Chilluns, this is not a good thing."

"What are we going to do?" breathed Barbara.

Davis thought, in a remote part of his mind, that later on he would break out in the cold shakes. If he lived! But for now he had to keep calm—

"We're going to get that blaster," he said. "There's nothing supernatural about an ion stream. And there's only one of them."

"You'll be killed," said Valeria. "Wait here, Bert—"

"Follow me," he said. "If you dare!"

They trotted after him, a dozen from the *Fishbird* and as many more from the retreat whose morale had picked up. He went through the doorway and saw an ordered gridiron of paved streets between tall concrete houses. The Ship rose huge at the end of all avenues. From two other streets came the noise of fighting. The battle had spread out, and few had yet seen the gun fire. They would, though, if he didn't hurry, and that would be the end of the rebellion.

"We went down this way," pointed a Latvala.

Davis jogged between closed doors and broad glass windows. Looking in, he saw that the inhabitants did themselves well, no doubt luxury existed elsewhere on Atlantis. He could understand their reluctance to abandon such a way of life for the untried mythic civilization of Men.

He skidded to a halt. The Doctors were rounding the corner ahead.

There were about twenty. A line of legates, their helmets facelessly blank, spread from wall to wall with interlocked shields. Behind them lifted swords and halberds.

"Get them!" shouted Nelly.

Three girls sprang ahead of Davis. One of them was a Whitley, he thought for a moment she was one of *his* Whitleys and then saw Barbara and Valeria still flanking him.

Over the shield tops lifted a Burke face. It was an old face, toothless and wrinkled below a tall bejeweled crown, and the body was stooped in white robes. But his blaster gleamed in a skinny hand.

Davis flung out his arms and dove to the ground, carrying Barbara and Valeria with him. Blue-white fire sizzled overhead.

The three young girls fell, blasted through. It

could have been Val or Barbara lying there dead and mutilated on the the pavement, thought Davis wildly. He remembered how he loved them.

He rolled over, into a doorway. His gang were already stampeded. Nelly stood firm in the street, Barbara and Valeria were beside him. Nelly threw her ax, it glanced off a shield, the legate stumbled against the old Doctor. Her next shot missed, and Nelly pumped thick legs across the street.

She hit the door with one massive shoulder. It went down in splinters. Davis sprang into a sybarite's parlor.

Two legates appeared in the doorframe. Barbara's crossbow snapped twice. Valeria and Nelly led the way through another door.

Davis followed and saw a stair. "Uncoil me your lasso, Babs," he said. "I have an idea." They pounded up after him.

A bedroom overlooked the street. Davis shoved up the window. The blaster party was just underneath. Barbara nodded, leaned out—her lariat closed around the chief Doctor.

"Help!" screamed the Burke. "I've been roped!"

Davis sprang into the street. He landed on an armored legate and both went down with a rattle and a gong. She didn't move. Davis jumped up and sent a left hook to the nearest jaw. Valeria's rope snaked from the window, fastened to something. She came sliding down it with her ax busy. Valeria and Nelly followed.

The old Burke snarled. She fought free and reached for the blaster. "Oh, no, you don't!" Davis put his foot on it. A rapier struck his scaly coat and bent upward, raking his cheek. He kicked, and the woman reeled off to trip somebody else.

Nelly had picked up an ax. "Whoopee!" she bawled, and started chopping. Barbara and

Valeria stood back to back, their weapons a blur in front of them. Davis was still too inhibited to use whetted steel on women, but every blow his fist dealt shocked loose some of his guiltiness.

The fight was over in a few minutes. Male size and female skill had outweighed numbers. Davis stooped for this blaster. "Let's go," he panted.

They went down the street. There was a narrow passage between the Ship and the wall. On the other side lay a broad open square, lined with impressive temples. . . . No more sound of fighting. Odd!

A sailor troop emerged from behind one of the columned sanctuaries. "It's the Man!" squealed somebody. they ran toward him and drew up, flushed. The leader gave a sketchy salute.

"I think we just about have the town, sir," she puffed. "I was patrolling on the east end. Didn't see anyone."

"Good!" Davis shuddered his relief. He could *not* have used a blaster on women, the memory of the dead Whitley girl was burned too deeply in him.

"Get our people together here," he said. "Post guards. Round up all the Doctors left, herd 'em into one of these chapels . . . and don't use them for target practice! Set up a sickbay for the wounded, and that means enemy wounded too. Nelly, you take charge, I want a look around."

He walked through empty avenues. Behind him he could hear cheers and trumpets, the tramp of feet and triumphal clang of arms, but he was in no mood for it.

Minos was a thin sliver, with Bee sliding close. Nearly eclipse time . . . had all this only taken three hours?

The Whitleys trailed him. He heard: "I take a lot back, Val. You fought pretty good."

"Hell, Babs, you're no slouch yourself. After all, darling, you are identical with me."

The street opened on a narrow space running the length of the east wall. There was a doorway in the center, with wrought-iron gates. Davis looked through the bars to the causeway and the marshes. Mud gleamed on the ridge which the road followed, birds screamed down after stranded fish. The tide was ebbing, the ships already trapped . . . but what the Evil, they had won, hadn't they?

Hold on there!

The highway bent around a clump of saltwater trees three kilometers from the city. Davis saw what approached from the other side and grabbed the bars with both hands.

"An army!" he croaked.

Rank after rank poured into view, with war-cries and haughty banners; now he saw leather corselets, iron morions, boots and spurs and streaming cloaks. They were the hill people and they were riding to the relief of the Doctors.

"A couple of thousand, at least," muttered Barbara. "The legates must have gone after them as soon as we attacked. They've been waiting around to kill you, my dearest—" She whirled on him, her visored face pressed against his side. "And it's too late to retreat, we're boxed in!"

"Not too late to fight!" shouted Valeria. Sea women on the walls lifted horns to lips and wailed an alarm.

Davis looked at the gate. It was locked, but it

could be broken apart. His hand went to the blaster. Before Cosmos, that would stop them. No!

The rebel army pelted into the open space. Right and left, arbalestiers swarmed up the staircases to the walls. *Hasn't there been enough killing?* thought Davis.

Behind him, Nelly Udall scurried along the ranks, pushing them into a semblance of order. Davis regarded them. Tired faces, hurt faces, lips that tried to be firm and failed; they would fight bravely, but they hadn't a chance against fresh troops.

Up on the parapets, crossbows began to snap. Orspers reared, squawked, went off the road into the mud and flapped atrophied wings. The charge came to a clanging halt, broke up, fought its way back along the road . . . it stopped. Leaders trotted between panicked riders, haranguing them.

Hill women dismounted. Their axes bit at a roadside tree. It wouldn't take them long to make a battering ram. They would slog forward under fire, they would be slaughtered and others take their place, and the gate would come down.

"When they're in range," leered Nelly to Davis, "burn 'em!"

Bee slipped behind Minos. The planet became a circle of blackness ringed with red flame. Of all the moons, only firefly Aegeus was visible. Stars glittered coldly forth. A wind sighed across the draining marshes, dusk lay heavy on the world.

Davis fired into the air. Livid lightning burned across heaven, a small thunder cracked in its wake. Screams came from the shadow army on the road, he fired again and waited for them to flee.

"Hold fast! Stay where you are, Father damn you!" The voices drifted hoarse through the gloom. "If we let the Monster keep the Ship, you'll die with never another child in your arms!"

Davis shook his head. He might have known it.

Someone clattered up the road. Four short trumpet blasts sent the sea birds mewing into the sudden night. "Truce call," muttered Valeria. "Let her come talk. I don't *want* to see them fried alive."

The mounted woman approached. She was an Udall. Barbara squinted through the murk at the painted insignia. "Bess of Greendale!" she hissed. "Kill her!"

Davis could only think that the Doctors' desperation had been measured by their sending clear up to Greendale for help. The swamp and the upper valley must be alive with armies intent on keeping him from his boat.

"No," he said. "It's a parley, remember?"

The Udall rode scornfully up under the walls. "Is the Monster here?" she asked.

"The Man is here," said Barbara.

Davis stepped into view, peering through iron bars and thick twilight. "What do you want?" he asked.

"Your head, and the Ship back before you ruin the life machine."

"I can kill your whole army," said Davis. "Watch!" He blasted at the road before him. Stone bubbled and ran molten.

Bess Udall fought her plunging orsper to a halt. "Do you think that matters?" she panted. "We're fighting for every unborn kid on Atlantis. Without the machine we might as well die."

"But I'm not going to harm the damned machine!"

"So *you* say. You've struck down the Doctors. I wouldn't trust you dead without a stake through your heart."

"Oh, hell," snarled Valeria. "Why bother? Let

'em attack and find out you mean business.''

Davis stared at the blaster. "No," he said. "There are decent limits.''

He shook himself and looked out at the vague form of the woman. "I'll make terms," he said.

"What?" yelled Barbara and Valeria together.

"Shut up. Bess, here's my offer. You can enter the town. The sea people will go back to their ships and sail away at next high tide. In return, they'll have access to the life machine just as before.''

"And you?" grated the Udall. "We won't stop fighting till you're dead.''

"I'll come out," said Davis. "Agreed?''

"*No!*" Barbara leaped at him. He swung his arm and knocked her to the ground.

"Stand back!" His voice rattled. "I'm still a man.''

Bess Udall stared at him through the darkness. "Agreed," she said. "I swear to your terms by Father.''

The rebels shuffled forward, shadow mass in a shadow world. "Don't move," said Davis. "It isn't worth it . . . my life . . . Evil! The men will be here in another generation anyway.''

His blaster boomed, eating through the lock on the gate. He pushed it open, the hot iron burned his hands, and trod through. With a convulsive gesture, he tossed the blaster into a mudpool.

"All right," he said. "Let's go.''

Bess edged her orsper close to him.

"Move!" she barked. A few women surged from the gateway. She brandished her spear. "Stand back, or the Monster gets this right now!''

Minos was a ring of hellfire in the sky.

"*Wait!*"

It was a Whitley voice. Davis turned. He felt only an infinite weariness, let them kill him and be done with it.

He couldn't see whether it was Barbara or Valeria who spoke: "Hold on there! It's us who make the terms."

"Yes?" growled the rider. Her spear poised over Davis.

"We have the life machine. Turn him back to us or we'll smash it and kill every Doctor in town before you can stop us!" They faced the crowd defiantly.

A sighing went through the rebels. Nelly cursed them into stillness. "That's right, dearie," she cried. "What the blazes is a bloody machine worth when we could have the Men?"

The Whitley walked closer, cat-gaited. "These are our terms," she said flatly. "Lay down your arms. We won't hurt you. By Father, I never knew what it means to be a Man till now! You can keep the town and the machine—yes, the Doctors—if you want. Just let us bring the Man to his ship to bring the Men back for us!"

Bess Udall's spear dropped to the ground.

"You don't know he's a Man," she stammered.

"I sure as hell do, sister. Do you think we'd have stormed the Holy Ship for a Monster?" She waited.

Night and silence lay thick across the land. A salt wind whined around red-stained battlements.

"Almighty Father," choked Bess. "I think you're right."

She whirled her orsper about and dashed down the road to the army.

Davis heard them talking in the orsper host. It seemed to come from very far away. His knees were stiff as he walked slowly back toward the gate.

Several riders hurried after him. They pulled up

and jumped to the ground and laid their weapons at his feet.

"Welcome," said a voice. "Welcome, Man."

The sun swung from behind Minos and day burned across watery wastes and the far eastern mountains.

Davis let them cheer around him.

Barbara knelt at his feet, hugging his knees. Valeria pushed her way close to lay her lips on his. "Bert," she whispered. He tasted tears on her mouth. "Bert, darling."

"Take either of us," sobbed Barbara. "Take us both if you want."

"Well, hooray for the Man!" said Nelly. "Three chee—whoops! Catch him there! I think he's fanted!"

It had been a slow trip up through the valley. They had to stop and be feasted at every town along the way.

Davis Bertram stood in tall grass, under a morning wind, and looked up the beloved length of his spaceship. He whistled, and the airlock opened and the ladder descended for him.

"I'll be back," he said clumsily. "Inside a hundred of your days, the Men will be here."

And what would they say when he walked into Stellamont wearing this garb of kilt, feather cloak, and warbonnet?

The Freetoon army was drawn up in dress parade a few meters off. Sunlight flamed on polished metal and oiled leather, plumes nodded and banners fluttered in the breeze. More of their warriors had survived the invasion than he expected. They came out of the woods to worship him as their deliverer when he ordered the town set free.

Gaping civilians trampled the meadows behind them. Davis wondered how many of their babies he had touched, for good luck. Well, it beat kissing the little apes . . . not that it wouldn't be nice to have a few of his own someday.

Barbara and Valeria stood before him. Under the burnished helmets their faces were drawn tight, waiting for his word.

His cheeks felt hot. He looked away from their steady green eyes and dug at the ground with his sandals.

"You're in charge here," he mumbled. "If you really want to make Freetoon a republic—and it'd be a big help, you folk have a difficult period of adjustment ahead—at least one of you has to stay and see the job is done right. There has to be someone here I can trust."

"I know," said Valeria. Her tone grew wistful. "You'll bring that machine of yours to . . . make her forget you?"

"Not forget," said Davis. "Only to feel differently about it. I'll do better than that, though. I'll bring a hundred young men, and you can take your pick!"

"All right," said Valeria. "I pick you."

"Hoy, there!" said Barbara.

Davis wiped sweat off his brow. What was a chap to do, anyway? He felt trapped.

"It'd be better if you both stayed," he groped. "You'll have a . . . a rough time . . . fitting into civilization—"

"Do you really want that?" asked Barbara coolly.

"No," said Davis. "Good Cosmos, no!"

After all, he was a survey man. He wouldn't be close to civilization for very long at a time, ever. Even a barbarian woman, given spirit and intelligence, could be trained into a spacehand.

And a few gaucheries wouldn't matter. A Whitley in formal dress would be too stunning.

"Well, then," said Valeria. Her knuckles tightened around her spearshaft. "Take your choice."

"I can't," said Davis. "I just can't."

The cousins looked at each other, They nodded. One of them took a pair of dice from her pouch.

"One roll," said Barbara.

"High girl gets him," said Valeria.

Davis Bertram stood aside and waited.

He had the grace to blush.

Although Davis caused a small war, the benefits of his incursion far outweighed the drawbacks. For bringing Minos into the Stellar Union, history reveres him as a hero.

The same cannot be said of every outside visitor to a primitive world. Interstellar crime did not exist in the days of STL travel, but hyperdrive opened the starlanes to brigands of every sort. Yet those who would profit from the ignorance of others never consider the penalties for ignorance in themselves.

TEUCAN

Sometimes a nuclear-conversion engine develops an ulcer. The containing fields weaken long enough—a few microseconds, perhaps for the machine to start devouring itself. It doesn't happen often, but neither is it unheard of, and it will continue to happen until somebody abolishes the Uncertainty Principle. In the event of an ulcer, the only thing to do is to get out of the neighborhood—fast.

Weber considered himself lucky to be near a planet when his engine broke loose. He had, in fact, been coming in for a landing, and it was a moment's scrambling to get into a spacesuit. He grabbed for the chest where he kept his weapons, and a blue electric bolt sizzled to his hand and limned his insulated suit in ghostly fire. Cursing, he reached again, but the chest was already glowing red-hot and the white-blazing bulkhead aft was slumping into molten ruin. No time—when it went down, he'd get a radiation blast which would finish him. He dove for the airlock, awkward in free fall now that the gravity unit was gone.

Just in time! His impellers whirled him away.
The boat was a nova against the bitter stars of
space. Alone—weaponless—supplyless save for
the suit's little emergency pack — well, that planet
had better be habitable!

It was a great cottony ball of cloud below him,
blinding in the harsh spatial sunlight. Below
him—yes, he was close enough, well within the region of perceptible gravitation. He turned off his
impeller and let himself fall. A few hours—

The silence and loneliness oppressed him. As the
thunder of his heart and blood eased, he considered the years ahead, a liftime of separation from
humankind and all he had known. The lifetime
would be short unless he was lucky. His name
would be bandied among the Traders for perhaps a
decade, and then his very memory would be dust.

Well—not much he could do about it. At least his
instruments had told him the planet was Terra-
type: about the same size and mass, pretty similar
atmosphere. That meant green plants, which in
turn meant animals with high probability, which
might mean intelligent natives; but of course
everything might be poisonous to his metabolism.
He didn't think the natives would be very far advanced, technologically; the planet was rather
close to its sun, an obscure G6 dwarf, steamy and
tropical and perpetually cloudy—so it was unlikely that its dwellers would have much concept
of astronomy, the father of the sciences. Still, you
never knew.

First there was the problem of getting down. He
gave himself a northward velocity—the subarctic
regions would be most comfortable for a human. It
was necessary to be careful with energy; his
powerpack had barely enough to land him and

maybe fly around a bit, without wasting any.

The slow hours passed.

When he came below the high permanent clouds it was raining. He swung into the wind, the strong heavy flow of water sluicing over his helmet and blurring vision, lightning savage above him. By the time he was out of the storm, his energy meter was flickering near zero. He slanted groundward, studying the terrain with wary eyes.

It was a rolling land of hills and broad valleys, green with a sweeping stretch of jungle, snaked through by long rivers. But he was on the fringe of the wilds. Beyond were cultivated fields, stone huts scattered like grain seeds over the mighty planetscape, wide highways of beaten earth converging on the distant walls of a city. Quite a size-able city, too, there in the middle of its huge domain; it might well have twenty or thirty thousand inhabitants if they were humanoid. Weber's brain began to calculate.

You could never tell in advance how primitives were going to react. There were the unpredictable inherent differences, due to climate and ecology and physiology and the very external appearance; and then within the same species you could get fantastic variations of thought and behavior patterns from culture to culture. But his best chances lay in a sort of polite boldness, at least till he knew his way around a little better.

He landed with a jarring thump as his powerpack finally sputtered to extinction. Not far off, behind a grove of trees, stood a hamlet of some ten buildings. Dismissing thoughts of bacteria, molds, and other forms of slow or sudden death, Weber got to his feet, threw back his helmet and breathed deeply.

It was a warm, moist, pleasant air, pungent with the aroma of earth and forest and life, heady after the staleness of his suit. The clouds made a featureless gray sky overhead, and there were no visible shadows in that diffused light, but vision was clear enough. A brilliantly feathered bird flew squawking above him. He crossed the field in which he'd landed, set his boots on the road, and started walking toward the village.

The natives came out of it, and others ran from the distant farm huts, converging on him with shrill whoops. He stopped, folded his arms, and waited.

Humanoid—yes, very. If he survived, his shipwreck might prove quite tolerable. They were a slightly built folk, several centimeters shorter than the average Terran, six fingers to a hand and six toes to a sandaled foot, pointed ears, pale bluish skins, hair and eyes of deep purple, the males beardless as the females—but with handsome features not unlike the Caucasian, wiry and graceful of body. Both sexes wore little more than a loincloth, but the males had all the color and most of the shell, tooth, and hammered copper ornaments, feathers in their long hair, tattooing on their breasts. They brandished obsidian spears and axes, and some had wicked-looking wooden swords saw-toothed with chips of flint. They stood and stared at him.

Weber, who was a big blond man, lifted one arm with all the solemnity he could muster. The natives slowed their prancing approach, women huddling behind the ranked men, children screaming, a pack of lithe, long-bodied, blue-furred animals yowling. The peasants coming near, hoes and spades still clutched in their grimy hands, were almost as gaudily equipped as the villagers. Since it was unlikely that he had arrived precisely at a festival moment, Weber decided that the natives simply liked color. Well—the plain, burnished metal of his spacesuit stood out among them. He waited, taut as a drawn wire, holding his face impassive with a straining effort.

They converged again, closing warily in on all sides, muttering to each other. Weber caught one repeated word. *"Teucan."* It could mean stranger, god, demon, amazement, metal, or maybe just plain to hell with it—no way of knowing.

An old one finally stood forth—bigger than the rest, his face hard and seamed by ancient wounds. *"Teucan quituhiulat shu?"* he snapped. *"Baldemo azunabriun tzi?"*

"Sorry," said Weber. "No savvy." He read fright and a savage will in the narrowed purple eyes. The other blueskins had fallen silent; they were watching with an enormous anticipation.

Suddenly the native lifted his ax and whirled it down. Weber threw up his metal-clad arm just in time to save his skull. The native screeched and sprang like a wildcat, hacking again, raking the Trader's cheekbone. Weber struck at him, the armored fist glancing off the dodging native's shoulder and sending him spinning.

He stood panting, glaring at the Terran. Another native prodded him with a spear. Before Cosmos—they were egging him on!

He gathered his muscles and leaped again. This time Weber was prepared. He caught the blow once more on his arm, and his other fist slammed into the attacker's nose. He felt bone crunch and saw the blood spurt—red as his own, that blood. The native staggered, and Weber wrenched the ax from him.

Some of the watchers shouted, lifting their

weapons to the gray heaven. The assailant looked around him, eyes wild with despair through the blood that masked his broken face. There was no friendliness in the answering stares. With something like a groan, he drew an obsidian knife from his belt and charged afresh. Weber swung the ax, and the keen blade clove his skull.

The Trader stood panting over the body, looking around and raising the bloody weapon. "All right," he said hoarsely. "All right. Who else wants the same treatment?"

There was a long minute's silence, and then the cheers nearly split his eardrums. He was escorted into the village by a crowd that capered and yelled and brought forth flutes and drums to serenade him in. Only the peasants stayed behind, eagerly carving the body of the fallen into chunks, squabbling over the pieces and finally hastening back with their trophies.

Before Cosmos, thought Weber dazedly, *they* expected *a finish fight!*

He was shown to a good-sized hut well furnished with stools, mats, furs, and the other items of primitive wealth. Four nice-looking women came in with him, smiling somewhat timorously. Apparently he had inherited his enemy's possessions along with his rank—whatever that had been.

It might be duplicity, but he doubted it. The attempt to murder him had been honest enough, and the awe which he now received seemed honest, too. It was not the formal and silent respect of more civilized races—these people were whooping things up as much as they could—but it was there nonetheless. In the long blue twilight of the planet's day—he estimated it at thirty hours—they gave him a feast. Meats, vegetables, fruits, and a potent sort of beer—it was fun, and he staggered back to his new wives in the middle-sized hours of morning.

By Sirius, if he couldn't make a good thing out of this he didn't deserve the name of Trader!

Without making claims to brilliance or to any outstanding intellectual interests, beyond the making and spending of as much money as possible, Weber Franz had a sharp brain and knew how to use it. The first thing was to learn the language and find out what the devil he'd gotten himself into.

He held the most intelligent-looking of his wives back from work in his fields and drafted her as his instructor. There was little danger of upsetting his godhead, it any, by asking to be taught something—one very general rule about primitives is that they don't worry about consistency and a god who doesn't know the language is not a contradiction. He wasn't much disturbed in the next few days—his wives did the farming and household chores and except for the gaping children the villagers left him pretty much alone—so he could devote his full time to study. His tutor was only too pleased to be free of manual labor, and the primary trouble was the attempt of a couple of the others, jealous of her privilege, to kill her. Weber knocked a few teeth out and had no difficulties thereafter. He was beginning to realize that brutality was an accepted feature of this society. The men swaggered and fought, the villagers brow-beat the peasants, the children abused the animals—and still there seemed to be as much laughter here as anywhere else. *They must like it*, he thought.

Traders generally didn't have too much to do with races as backward as this one. The ideal was a people far enough advanced to have something worth buying or bilking them out of. Thus Weber's knowledge of the present level of society was scant, a fact which caused him considerable grief later on. But he had had mind training, and he understood linguistic principles, so he learned fast now. The names of simple objects and actions—more abstract words derived by indirection or from context—and the language was agglutinative, which helped a lot. It wasn't many days before he could understand and make himself understood.

This, it seemed, was the village of Tubarro, part of the domain of Azunica, to which it paid tribute in the form of food-stuffs and slaves. He—Beber, as they rendered it—was now the Teucan of Tubarro, having killed the old one. He didn't dare ask directly what the Teucan was—that might be going too far—and said merely that he had come from the far land of Terra.

Once a levy of soldiers marched down the road toward Azunica, gay with feathers and shields and flowing cloaks, drums and flutes and gongs, leading a hundred miserable-looking captives roped together. And there was a lot of traffic, runners speeding up and down the highway, porters moving under fantastic loads, nobles borne in litters and commoners trudging with goods bought or to sell. The life of this culture seemed to be in Azunica; Tubarro was only a sleepy fuel station and supply store. Weber decided that he would have to visit the city.

But as it happened, the city came to him.

They arrived toward evening, about two weeks after Weber's arrival—though he had lost count of time in the monotonous round of days. There was quite a procession—a squad of soldiers, a company of slaves, even a group of musicians—and they pushed arrogantly down the one street of Tubarro and halted before Weber's dwelling. The Terran, who was becoming aware of the importance of haughtiness, did not look up. He sat in front of his house, wearing the native dress, which showed his size and blondness to spectacular advantage, playing solitaire with the pack of cards he had had in his pocket at the time of the wreck.

"Are you, sir, the Teucan of Tubarro?"

Weber lifted heavy-lidded eyes. A tall old man had gotten from his litter—gaudily painted and ornamented, with a feather cloak swung from his shoulders and an elaborately carved staff in one hand. Weber, whose eyes missed little, noticed that his visitor and everyone in the troop had had the first joint of the little finger removed. He spread his five-fingered hands into plain sight.

"Yes, sir, I am," he replied, with the cold courtesy of formal occasions. Idly, he shuffled the cards and snatched one out of the air. Sleight-of-hand could be useful. "Would you like to come inside and take refreshment?"

"Thank you, sir, I would." The old—priest?—followed him into the house. Was it polite to go in before or after or arm-in-arm with your guest? Weber didn't know. He signaled a wife for food and drink.

"Word of you has come to Azunica, sir," said the visitor after due formalities. "It is said you came from a remote land, and most strangely attired."

"That is true, sir." Weber nodded his head very slightly to the polished spacesuit, standing in a corner. "Weaponless I overcame the old Teucan and gave his body to the earth. I did not choose to use my weapons against a single man."

"I see, sir." The priest made a bridge of his fingers and peered shrewdly at the Terran. "It is plain that you are from far away, and that the *teucans* have placed the holy sign on your hands themselves."

There was that word again—*teucan!* In this context it seemed to mean god; but as used by the villagers, and in view of Weber's daily life, it seemed to mean little more than battle-ax champion. The ins and outs of the primitive mind—they don't *think* like civilized people—

"What I wondered, sir," went on the native, "is why you chose to come to this little wallow, rather than to Azunica the great and sacred. You could, being plainly marked as holy yourself, have had the *teucanno* for the asking now that the old one has returned to the earth."

"I had my reasons, sir."

"So you did, sir, and I do not question them. But I am the Chief Servant of Azunica, and it is my duty to select the next Teucan of the city and the whole domain. I do not know how they do it in your land, sir, but in Azunica we determine the will of the *teucans* by drawing lots among all qualified young men. However, you yourself are so clearly the designated one that when word of you came I hastened to find you. It is past time for the choosing—the *banyaquil* must be planted soon or not at all. The people grow restless."

Weber reflected that most of the fields were still being cultivated, and that the crops in the planted ones were young. He must have arrived just in the sowing time, and apparently they needed someone to preside over fertility ceremonies and whatnot. If the old Teucan had lately died—

Hmmm—this, my boy, looks like the luck of the Webers. If you play it right—

"I am content here, sir," he said. "I have my house and my fields and my wives. Why should I move?"

"But reflect, sir. You will grow old and weak—or perhaps, even before that time, there will be a lucky challenger. There are many restless young men who seek a *teucanno* to make their fortune. You will have to fight many times a year. And all for this little village!"

"But there would be even more challangers in Azunica, would there not?"

For an instant the old man looked astonished, and then the mask clamped down again and the eyes were shrewd. There was a good brain under that grey-streaked purple hair. By betraying his ignorance, Weber had started the brain thinking. The Terran looked nervously at the door, but none of the soldiers shifted from the post of attention.

"You jest, sir," said the priest. "Unless it is indeed that they do matters very differently in your homeland. No, who would dare lift a hand against the Teucan of Azunica? He is—he is the *Teucan!* What he would have is his for the asking. Should he tell a man to slay himself, that man would plunge the knife in his own belly on the instant."

Hmmm—yes, apparently the Teucan of Azunica—which, after all, was the capital of a fairsized theocratic empire—was something different from the Teucan of a village. The latter were—what? Symbols of some kind, no more. The former might well be an incarnate god.

"The homes of Azunica are stuffed with gold and feathers, sir," said the priest persuasively. "The meats are tender, the fruits are sweet, the beer is a singing in the blood. The maidens are young and lovely. The lords of the realm are glad to wait on the Teucan as his slaves." He sighed. "It is clear to

me that you are the intended one, and there will be
an evil year if the wrong man should be raised to
the golden seat. That, sir, is why I am so anxious to
give you all this."

"Hmmm—and what must I do myself?"

"What you will, my lord. There are the ceremonies, of course, and appearances to keep up, but it
is not arduous. And every creature in the realm is
your chattel."

"I will consider it, sir. You shall have my answer
tomorrow."

He'd have to make a few discreet inquiries, con-
firm what had been said. He couldn't inquire too
much, of course, without giving himself away to a
dangerous extent—but he could at least find out if
the Teucan of Azunica had all that power. And if
so—*If so, Weber my boy, you'll take another step to
success. From Trader to god—not bad!*

Azunica was a big and well-built city, the heart
of a high-level barbarism. Large houses of stone
and rammed earth set well back from broad paved
streets; rows of painted, fang-mouthed idols leading toward a great central pyramid; parks where
flowers were a riot of color and the nobles sailed
their barges on artificial lakes to the soft music of
slave attendants; crowded, jostling marketplaces,
men and women yelling around the booths where
everything from rugs and pottery to slave girls
bred through many generations for beauty and
meekness were sold; workshops and factories—it
was a gay and colorful scene, and, as Weber saw it
from the litter that bore him to the Temple, he was
glad he had come. Whatever hapened, life on this
planet wasn't going to be dull.

The city, like the villages through which he had
passed, was clean, and there seemed to be no beg-

gars, slums, or cripples. It was a culture of priests, warriors, artisans, and slaves, but a healthy vigorous one resting on the sturdy foundation of an independent peasantry and nourished from a rich, deep soil. In centuries to come, its nastier features might die out, it could perhaps accomplish great things, but Weber had to live in its present. He was not an altruist and did not intend to make any changes which wouldn't be of direct personal benefit.

Careful questioning of the Chief Servant, the old high priest Zacalli, had already given him some notion of the social structure. The government was in the hands of the priesthood, who in the various ranks fulfilled not only religious but all important civil and military functions; theoretically, at least, everything was the personal property of the Tcucan and everyone his personal slave. A rather moderate tax, as such things go at this level of culture, supported the government and the army. The latter was enormous, every man putting in some time of service and a large cadre of professionals raised to arms from birth. Azunica was in a state of perpetual war with all surrounding nations—which all seemed to have a similar society—and the outer provinces, loosely held, were incessantly rebelling. This yielded slaves and tribute. Pretty rough on the borderland peoples, thought Weber, but it enriched the central domain, and the high soil-fertility and birth rate made it economically feasible. Cripples, the senile, and the hopelessly diseased were killed out of hand, brawls and duels were a casually accepted feature of daily life even among the lower classes; only slaves and low-born women were expected to be humble. The whole setup would have revolted an ordinary Galactic, but Weber had spent most of his life on the frontier and accepted it without too many qualms. The thing to do was to adapt; afterward he could see about steering events in what direction he might choose.

Temple headquarters were in a series of gaudily ornamented one-story palaces sprawling around the great pyramid. Weber was escorted past hundreds of prostrated slaves, servants, priests, and soldiers to a suite which was furnished with a barbaric magnificence that took even his breath away. There were a dozen virgins waiting for him, with the promise of as many more as he desired, and he was left to rest and prepare himself for the inaugural ceremonies.

Those took place that night, an awesome torchlit festival with all the city turned out to watch the dancers and musicians and wildly chanting priests. Weber had little to do but sit under his weight of gold and jewels and furs—until at dawn Zacalli gave him a knife and led him slowly up the stairway to the height of the great pyramid.

There was an interminable line of bound captives coming up the other side, toward the altar and the monstrous idol which loomed in the vague gray light. As Weber stared, four burly priests grabbed the first one and stretched him over the stone. "Now, my lord," said the old priest, "give back to the earth the life that came from it."

"Human sacrifice—no!"

"My lord, the *teucans* stoop low, they are waiting."

Weber looked at the prisoner's tightly drawn face, and back to the knife in his hand, and there was a sickness in his throat. "I can't do it," he whispered. "I can't."

"Hurry, my lord, the light is coming and the earth is hungry."

Weber caught at his sanity with both hands. *If I don't, someone else will—after I'm dead.*

He walked slowly forward. "The liver lies here, my lord," pointed Zacalli.

The knife was sharp, but there were many prisoners. Weber had to stop now and again to vomit. The priests' faces were like carven masks.

It was done—the earth had been fed—and Weber went down again to the orgiastic multitude and slowly back to his dwelling. Even after the blood had been washed off and his concubines had anointed him, he felt it red and wet on his skin, soaking through.

There is a certain type of man, energetic, adaptable, and possessed of a hard common sense rather than any great intellect, who goes where the most money is to be gotten and moves the world to get at it. Afterward he becomes a figure of legend and romance, but in his own time he is merely a practical, if adventurous, businessman, not a brute but not especially tender-minded, willing to take risks but not foolhardy. The glamor is added by others. In the so-called First Dark Age it was the viking. In the Second Dark Age it was the Martian war lord. Now, when man has reached the stars, it is the Trader.

He fulfills little economic purpose—civilization just doesn't need him—but by juggling goods from one planet to another he can often accumulate a tidy fortune for himself. He is, usually, cordially disliked by everyone else, for his practices are sharp at best and piratical at worst. He is apt to break the law and sneak beyond the frontier to find worlds never visited before, and there is little which the Co-ordination Service can do about it except hope that he doesn't work too much harm.

The Galaxy is just too big, and too little of it is known, for control. To the average Sol-bound Terran he is a swashbuckling hero, flitting from planet to wild new planet. To himself, he is merely a hard-working entrepreneur is a business which consists mostly of monotonous waiting, and he dreams only of the big strike and the fortune large enough to retire on—before he can spend it.

Weber was a Trader. He had gone into the uncharted Bucyrus region to find what he could find. If the Service had known where he was bound, they would have stopped him; if any of his fellows had known, they would have tried to get in ahead of him; so he went off in silence, and now there would be none to look for him and he would remain on this planet for the rest of his life. Wherefore it behooved him, first, to adapt his mind, and second, to make something of his situation.

At least, he thought, he'd been lucky in this planet. The food was nourishing to him, the natives were so humanoid that he wouldn't miss his own species, and he seemed immune to the local diseases. It could be worse. Much worse.

Only—well—he'd almost immediately reached the top. Without effort he'd become the adored god and absolute owner of his environment. It didn't take long for his restless nature to demand action. What to *do?*

The fertility rites attending the planting of the staple *banyaquil* had been exhausting, though—he grinned—fun. His officiation in daily ritual wasn't needed, and there wouldn't be another big ceremony till midsummer. Then another in the mid-rainy season, and then it would be spring again. The planet's year was shorter than Terra's, though not very accurately known in the absence of astronomy, and that swift crop cycle accounted in part for the food surplus which enabled the culture to support its permanent warfare. The prospect of a lifetime of the same round looked boring.

Well—he'd make changes. He could do it, being a god, *the* Teucan. First, though, he'd better learn a few more details.

He summoned Zacalli, who entered and prostrated himself. The old man lay there in silence for a long time before it occurred to Weber that he wouldn't speak or move without being told. "Rise," said the Terran. "Sis down over there." He lowered his own bulk to a cushioned stool. "I want to talk to you."

"As my lord commands."

"I want to ask some questions. Answer me truthfully, but otherwise as you would answer any other man. For I am a man and you know it, in spite of my being Teucan."

"Yes, my lord. The man is the Teucan and the Teucan is the man. The *teucanno* of the old one has entered you, as it will enter your successor, at the time when your own life returns to the earth."

"But a village Teucan is something different. He is but a man among men, and anyone who kills him may have his post. Why?"

Zacalli's eyes rested on Weber with an indrawn thoughtfulness. "My lord has come from far away indeed."

"I know. I admit to being ignorant of much about Azunica. Though—" Weber tried to look faintly ominous— "I know much of which you here have no inkling."

"Yes, my lord. They saw you come from the heavens. I have seen your clothing of unknown metal. I have seen your own self."

"Very well, then. Answer my question. Why may a village Teucan be challenged and *the* Teucan can not?"

"My lord, a Teucan is the life of his people. While he lives, he holds their life and the life of the land within him. Yet he must not sicken or die alone, for then the life of the land would die with him, the crops would fail and the women would grow barren. So he is slain by someone else, someone younger and stronger who can better hold the life. And the man-life of the old Teucan goes back to the earth."

Hmmm—a fertility cult, yes. Sympathetic magic—as the Teucan went, so went the village, and to avoid his wasting away the people had hit on the not unintelligent idea of cutting him off in his prime. And the body, the life of the body, went back to the soil—magic again—yes, that was why those peasants had divided up the corpse . . . In similar manner, the human sacrifices were made for the whole realm, to give the life of the captives to the land of the empire.

"But what then of me? What is the function of *the* Teucan?"

"My lord, you hold the life not of one small village but of the world. Yours is not the chance flux of rain or wind or drouth or heat at one place, it is the great cycle of the seasons all over the lands of man. The little Teucans are chance; you are the great overall harmony of the world and the seasons. Thus no one could challenge you; the power is too great to be poured from one vessel to another without due magical ceremony."

"I see. Yet you speak of the *teucans* sometimes as if they were—well—not men. Beings higher than men."

"Certainly, my lord. Are they not the *teucans*?

You yourself are now one of them, the *teucan* of the earth and of growth, rainy Mazotuca."

Weber shook his yellow head and gave up trying to follow a thought-pattern which, by civilized standards, just didn't make sense. It would have been well for him had he known more about primitive peoples; he would have realized that while their logic has a different basis it is quite rigorous, often fantastically so. A civilized man usually compromises with his postulates; a primitive does not, but carries them through to their ultimate logical conclusions.

And because the logic was not his own, he was also led to the assumption that the Azunicans, if not inherently stupid, were at least effectually so. That was another mistake. Zacalli and his cohorts could not have been the real rulers of a large and complex empire for the better part of a lifetime without developing a very practical intelligence.

Their new god was strange, he undoubtedly had remarkable powers and there was no guessing the extent of these. He was ignorant, and one could not tell how he would react to sudden new knowledge—he had certainly been revolted enough by the absolute necessities of the sacrifice. So the thing to do was to keep him in ignorance, and play on him as one plays on a powerful instrument, until—

Previous Teucans had been easy to handle. Sate them with every kind of luxury and it was enough. This one seemed to desire something more. Well, it might be possible to obtain it for him. The law was that the Teucan must have everything he wanted.

Weber was discovering that a god can be very lonely. His associates could not speak to him except in the most elaborately unctuous terms of flattery. A few times he summoned others to him, soldiers, artisans, commoners hailed in the streets as he went by, but they were too awed for coherence. With his harem he could relax, they laughed and frolicked with their master, but they were all featherheads who had never seen the real life of the world, born and bred merely to please a man's body. When he complained of this latter fact once to Zacalli, the Chief Servant hurried off and brought him the most intelligent woman in Azunica, wife of a petty noble, and she proved as evasive in her talk as the high priest himself. Coached in advance?

Yes—a conspiracy of some kind. Weber investigated, making surprise visits to all sections of the palaces, snapping questions at underlings who were too frightened to do more than stammer the truth. Such as it was—they weren't aware of a plot, they merely did their jobs, but the fact emerged and when he had it Weber laughed. This, at least, was something he could understand. And it was merely that the Teucan was an elaborate figurehead and the Temple bureaucracy did everything which counted.

Well—he'd see about that!

Easy, though, easy. He'd been thinking of a way to eliminate the human sacrifices, but it would be a long, difficult job. He couldn't merely order them discontinued—most likely the people wouldn't stand for that, and if somehow he did succeed it would be destroying the fertility cult which was the very basis of his power. No, changes would have to be slow, and he'd just have to rid himself of squeamishness.

But he learned there was to be a staff meeting to plan the summer campaign, and insisted on being there. It was an odd conference, the feathered and painted priest-officers discussing strategy and tactics with a cool calculation that would not have been amiss in the Coordination Patrol. He kept himself in the background at first, giving the men a chance to forget their awkwardness in his presence.

There was to be a battle with the neighbor state of Culacanni, and it was thought that a successful raid could be made far into their territory, stealing much treasure and taking many prisoners. Then the army would swing homeward through Azunica's own province of Onegar. "By then, sirs," promised Zacalli, "the revolt will be well under way, but not far enough so that their armies can stand us off."

"The revolt!" exploded Weber. "I never heard of a revolt there."

The impassive blue faces swung around to look at him. "Certainly not, my lord," said Zacalli. "It has not begun yct."

"But how do you know—"

"Why, our agents will start it themselves, of course, my lord. The Onegarans will expect help from Culacanni, but we will already have put those to flight and can crush the uprising without too much trouble."

"But—start a revolt—*why?*"

"My lord jests. We need prisoners for the harvest sacrifice. How could we get them save through war or the suppression of rebels?"

"Hm." Weber relapsed, grunting. The very basis of this culture seemed to be human sacrifice, and everything else followed logically from that. No sacrifices, no crops next year.

Well, he'd heard of stranger basics, here and there throughout the Galaxy. Even Terra's history would supply plenty of odd ones—there had, for instance, been the fantastic statist arrangements previously to the Second Dark Age, where everything was subordinated to the aggrandizement of the nation, which was somehow thought of as having a real and independent existence—

"I'll go along," he said.

"My lord!" gasped an officer. "You cannot—it is unheard of—"

Weber got up and hit the man in the face, hard. As he fell from his seat, Weber kicked him in the belly. "I go," he said.

He thought there was approval in the eyes of the rest. If their own society was brutal, their god, their ideal, ought to be a perfect bastard. Well, he'd give them their wish!

The campaign lasted through the whole short summer. Weber found himself enjoying most of it, since physical action could veil the fact that he was set apart and lonely. There was little danger to him personally; he could not risk his priceless life in battle and a large cordon of guards was assigned him. The bloodshed didn't worry him anymore. His environment was making him calloused.

They marched down the roads of the empire and up into hill country, through rain and heat, quiet fields and tangled colorful jungles and bare windy heights, hunting or stealing for their provisions, chanting as they went. In the long lightless dark there were rings of flickering campfires, wailing songs, harsh barking laughter. When they took an enemy village, they sacked it thoroughly, and Weber could have his pick of loot and captives. There were pitched battles, but no guerrilla harassment—after all, the war was fought not for possession of the country but of its inhabitants. He'd change that, thought Weber—he'd make something out of this drive to war and turn Azunica into the seat of a real empire. Since there was nothing else for him to do, he'd turn conqueror—next year, maybe, or the year after. It no longer occurred to him to worry about the need or justice of it. Sufficient that he, the Teucan, wanted it so.

They came back through Onegar and scattered the rebels and took prisoners by the hundreds. It was a triumphant return for them.

The harvest ceremonies came, and the grain was stored, and the long rains began.

Weber sat moodily in his palace, looking out at the endless flow of water from a lowering sky, drinking deep of the bowl which a slave kept filled for him. It wasn't right, he thought self-pityingly, that he should be so cut off from the life of the people, that they should all be obsequious masks. He suspected the hand of Zacalli in the constant frustration of his attempts to learn more. He'd have the Chief Servant killed soon. But right now he needed the old thus-and-so, and Zacalli was the only one who did talk intelligently with him. He realized that he was being drawn out—but what of that? Zacalli couldn't use the knowledge.

It was like trying to grasp a smooth sphere too big for the hand. He slipped away, unable to get a grip, unable to penetrate and understand. Damn! If only he'd known some primitive psychology—but he'd always despised the xenologists, it was their influence in Coordination, their eternal jabber about culture traits and the preservation of autochthonous developments, which had made so much grief for the Traders. Cosmos! Would not it ever stop raining?

He gulped down another mouthful of beer.

Wasn't much he could do now. Azunica was huddled into itself, waiting for spring, and the world lay dark and sodden beyond. His energy, baffled by its initial attempts, gave up the fight and turned to the pleasures which were given him in such unceasing abundance and variety. Now and then he thought dimly that it was bad to stop thinking, that there were implications which he should reason out for his own safety, but the very air seemed to cloud his brain. Some other time. There was time enough; he'd be here till he died.

A drum was beating, somewhere far off, it had been going every day for quite a while now. Zacalli said that it was the first faint rite of spring. When they had three clear days in a row, then it was time for the *banyaquil*.

Weber looked out again. By Cosmos, the rain was slackening. Night swirled slowly out of the streets, up toward the hidden sky, and a thick white mist rose with it. The rain grew thinner. Maybe there wouldn't be any tomorrow.

There wasn't, except for a brief shower which didn't count. Nor the next day. The drums were loud now, thuttering an insistent summons, and the Temple buildings were suddenly alive with softfooted priests hurrying on their errands. From the top of the pyramid, Weber could see that the peasants were already out, scratching up their fields, sowing grain. He'd have to give them a proper plow this year.

This year! Had it been a year? Well, the cycle was shorter on this planet. He wondered if it was springtime on Terra.

There was a feast that night—orgy might better describe it—over which he was expected to preside. Which he did, hilariously. The rains were ending! He slept most of the following day, which was quiet and sultry, and did not see the preparations that were made and the slow gathering of the throngs.

"Tonight, my lord," said Zacalli at dusk, "is yours to do as you will."

"Certainly it is," said Weber. "I'm the Teucan, am I not?" He threw another party.

Morning came with fresh rain clouds, sweeping low and black over the land on a hot wet wind. But that didn't matter. The rainy season was officially over.

Weber was shaken gently awake. It was Zacalli, robed and feathered and painted as never before, and a train of priests no less gaudy stood behind him. "Go away," mumbled the Terran.

"My lord, you must arise. It is the time of the festival's beginning."

"I said go away!" Weber sat up on his couch, holding one hand to his throbbing head. "It is my order. I am the Teucan."

"Hail the Teucan," murmured the deep voices. Thunder growled in the sky.

"My lord, you must. It is the law of the *teucans*."

Weber was half lifted to his feet. His mouth tasted vile. Well, if he must, then he must —couldn't be too unconventional at this stage of the game. What ceremony was it? Not the sacrifice—he knew it wasn't scheduled for several days yet. Odd that Zacalli hadn't coached him on the details of this performance, as he had of all others. *I suppose I just have to sit and look divine. Maybe I can catch a nap there.*

"Very well, I am coming, I am coming."

Slaves were there, bathing him, anointing him, painting his body and adorning it with the most gorgeous finery in the empire. He was so used to thinking of the attendants as faceless nonentities that he didn't notice anything special in their manner. He ate a large breakfast to the accompaniment of a wild religious chant whose words he only half caught. *"Now the Teucan, rainy Mazotuca, sinks into the earth and gives it his life, to arise gloriously renewed. . . . Hail the Teucan, dead and yet arisen, hail Mazotuca, who makes the earth to flower. . . ."*

Some kind of symbolism, he thought fuzzily. Hadn't that xenologist once said something about the death and resurrection of the fertility god in many primitive cultures throughout the Galaxy? Symbol of the grain, buried and rising anew, of old generations dying and the young springing from their loins, of summer which dies and is buried under winter and rises again in spring. . . . *So I am to be resurrected today, eh? Cosmos, I need it—ouch, my head—*

The priests had waited unmoving for him to finish. As he rose, they bowed to the floor, and Zacalli took his arm and led him into the hall.

There was a sudden curious, almost wistful note in the old priest's voice as he murmured: "My lord, you came from very far away indeed. I would I might have learned more of your country." And with a flicker of malice, "Perhaps you should have learned more of ours."

"Hm?" asked Weber.

They came out on the palace stairs at that moment, and the throng in the streets, surging and roaring behind the lines of guardsmen like a rainbow maelstrom, began to cheer, thunder of noise lifting into the thick dark sky and drowning the whine of wind. Weber shuddered as his head thumped.

Slowly down the avenue between the lines of the

army, leading the chanting priests and the skirling music, past the massive stone buildings to the pyramid. It loomed mountainous overhead, gray in the sulfurous storm-light, lightnings flickering about the idol on its summit. Thunder boomed and crashed; the gods were drumming up there.

Slowly they mounted the steps, up and up while the people of Azunica yelled at the base. The wind was strong, whipping cloaks, throwing the first heavy raindrops stingingly into Weber's face. Black overhead, streaked with an incessant fire of lightning, a hazy wall of rain marching down from the north, thunder and darkness and the idol grinning above him. Weber looked back, down the long slope and the barbaric procession winding at his heels, over the human sea and the heavy old buildings and out to the whole vast sweep of land. *His* land, by Cosmos, his earth lying rich and open for the rain's divine embrace, his valleys and rivers and sky-storming mountains, brawling, pulsing fury of life—standing here with the air blowing wild and the thunder a steady salute, crowned with lightnings, he *was* the Teucan and a sudden drunkenness of power sang in his blood. To be a god—

The priests formed a half-circle about the great idol, and their chants rose loud against the hooting wind. Zacalli prostrated himself once more in front of Weber. Then he stood up, and the knife gleamed in his hand, and four huge priests grabbed the Terran and threw him across the altar stone.

The god of life is reborn each year—but first, he must die.

Luckily, the damage done by Weber was petty and short-lived. Some Traders ravaged entire societies to satisfy their greed, driving some nameless victim to remark: "Commerce is piracy by other means."

Restraining interstellar predators was one responsibility of the Stellar Union's Coordination Service. The Cordys' goal was to maximize harmony and minimize discord among the stars. Like the Psychotechnic Institue before it, the Service trusted in the power of reason to create order.

But the cosmos is a chaotic place.

THE PIRATE

We guard the great Pact: but the young generations, the folk of the star frontier, so often do not
understand.

They avail themselves of our ordinary work.
(Ship Harpsong *of* Nerthus, *out of Highsky for
David's Landing, is long overdue . . . Please fore-
cast the competition which a cybernation venture
on Oasis would probably face after the older firms
elsewhere learned that a market had been established. . . . Bandits reported. . . . How shall we deal
with this wholly strange race of beings we have
come upon?)* But then we step in their own paths
and say, "Thou shalt not." And suddenly we are the
Cordys, the enemy.

The case of the slain world named Good Luck is
typical. Now that the Service is ready, after a generation, to let the truth be known, I can tell you
about Trevelyan Micah, Murdoch Juan,
Smokesmith, red Faustina, and the rest, that you
may judge the rights or wrongs for yourself.

In those days Trevelyan spent his furloughs on

Earth. He said its quiet, its intellectuality, were downright refreshing, and he could get all the rowdiness he wanted elsewhere. But of course his custom put him at the nerve center of the Service, insofar as an organization operating across a fraction of the galaxy can have one. He got a larger picture than most of his colleagues of how it fared with the Pact. This made him more effective. He was a dedicated man.

I suspect he also wanted to renew his humanity at the wellspring of humankind, he who spent most of his life amidst otherness. Thus he was strengthened in his will to be a faithful guardian.

Not that he was a prig. He was large and dark, with aquiline features and hard aquamarine eyes. But his smile was ready, his humor was dry, his tunic and culottes were always in the latest mode, he enjoyed every aspect of life from Bach to beer.

When the machine summoned him to the Good Luck affair, he had been living for a while at Laugerie Haute, which is in the heart of the steep, green, altogether beautiful Dordogne country. His girl of the moment had a stone house that was built in the Middle Ages against an overhanging cliff. Its interior renovation did not change its exterior ancientness, which made it seem a part of the hills or they a part of it. But in front grew bushes, covering a site excavated centuries ago, where flint-working reindeer hunters lived for millennia while the glacier covered North Europe. And daily overhead through the bright sky glided a spear that was the Greenland-Algeria carrier; and at night, across the stars where men now traveled, moved sparks that were spaceships lifting out of Earth's shadow. In few other parts of the planet could you be more fully in the oneness of time.

"You don't have to go, not yet," Braganza Diane

said, a little desperately because she cared for him
and our trumpeter blows too many Farewells each
year.

" 'Fraid I do," he said. "The computer didn't ring
me up for fun. In fact, it's a notoriously sober-
sided machine." When she didn't answer his grin,
he explained: "The data banks show I'm the only
person available who's dealt with, uh, a certain individual before. He's a slippery beast, with sharp
teeth, and experience might make the critical
quantum of difference."

"It better!" She curbed the tears that could have
caused him to think her immature and bent her
lips upward. "You will add . . . the rest of this
leave . . . to your next, and spend it with me. Won't
you?"

"I'd love to," he said, carefully making no prom-
ises. He kissed her, where they stood in the hay
scent of summer. They went back to the house for
a while.

After he packed his kit and phoned good-bye to
some neighbors—landholders, friendly folk whose
ancestors had dwelt here for generations beyond
counting—she flew him to Aerogare Bordeaux.
Thence he took a carrier to Port Nevada. The computer had briefed him so well that he could go
straight to work, and he wanted to catch Murdoch
Juan at ease if possible.

His timing was good. Sunset was slanting across
western North America and turning the mountains
purple when he arrived. The city walled him off
from that serenity as he entered. It shouldered big
square buildings above streets in which traffic
clamored; the growl of machines perpetually un-
derlay the shrill of voices; frantically flickering
signs drowned out the stars; humans and
nonhumans hustled, jostled, chiseled, brawled,

clashed, stole, evangelized, grew rich, grew poor, came, went, and were forgotten, beneath a tawdry front was that heedless vigor which the cargo ships bring from their homes to enclaves like this. Trevelyan allowed himself a brief "Phew!" when the stinks rolled around him.

He knew this town, on a hundred different worlds. He knew how to make inquiries of chance-met drinking companions. Eventually he found one of Murdoch's crew who could tell him where the boss was this evening. It turned out to be no dive, with the smoke of a dozen drugs stinging the eyes, but the discreet and expensive Altair House.

There a headwaiter, live though extraterrestrial, would not conduct him to his man. Captain Murdoch had requested privacy for a conference. Captain Murdoch was entitled to— Trevelyan showed his identification. It gave no legal prerogative; but a while ago the Service had forestalled a war on the headwaiter's native planet.

Upstairs, he chimed for admittance to the room. He had been told that Captain Murdoch's dinner guest had left, seemingly well pleased, while Captain Murdoch and his female companion stayed behind with a fresh order of champagne, vigorator, and other aids to celebration. "Come in, come in!" boomed the remembered hearty voice. The door dilated and Trevelyan trod through.

"Huh? I thought you were— Sunblaze! You again!" Murdoch surged to his feet. Briefly he stood motionless, among drapes and paintings, sparkling glassware, drift of music and incense. Then, tiger softly, he came around the table to a fist's reach of Trevelyan.

He was as tall, and broader in the shoulders. His features were rugged, deeply weathered, blond hair and a sweeping blond moustache. His clothes were too colorful to be stylish on Earth, but he wore them with such panache that you didn't notice.

The woman remained seated. She was as vivid in her way as he in his, superbly formed, the classicism of her face brought to life by the nearly Asian cheekbones; and she owned the rare combination of pure white skin and fox-red hair. Yet she was no toy. When she saw Murdoch thus taken aback, Trevelyan read shock upon her. It was followed by unflinching enmity.

He bowed to her. "Forgive me if I intrude," he said.

Murdoch relaxed in a gust of laughter. "Oh, sure, sure, Mike, you're forgiven. If you don't stay too mugthundering long." He clapped hands on the agent's shoulders. "How've you been, anyway? How many years since last?"

"Five or six." Trevelyan tried to smile back. "I'm sorry to bother you, but I understand you're shipping out day after tomorrow, which no doubt means you'll be busy for the prior twenty-four hours."

"Right, buck," Murdoch said. "This here tonight is our lift-off party. However, it began with business—lining up a financial backer for later on—so it may as well continue that way a few micro-seconds." The tone stayed genial, but the gaze was pale and very steady. "Got to be business, don't it? You didn't track me down just to wish an old sparring partner a bony voyage."

"Not really," Trevelyan admitted.

Murdoch took his arm and led him to the table. "Well, sit yourself and have a glug with us. Faustina, meet Trevelyan Micah of the Stellar

Union Co-ordination Service."

"Juan has spoken of you," the woman said distantly.

Trevelyan eased into a chair. His muscles relaxed, one by one, that his brain might be undistracted in the coming duel. "I hope he used language suitable to a lady," he said.

"I'm from New Mars," she snapped. "We don't have time for sex distinctions in our manners."

I might have guessed, he thought. There aren't as many unclaimed planets habitable by man as is popularly believed; so the marginal ones get settled too. He could imagine scarring poverty in her background, and Murdoch Juan as the great merry beloved knight who took her from it and would bear her on his saddlebow to the castle he meant to conquer for them.

"I did my duty as I saw it, which happened to conflict with Captain Murdoch's rights as he saw them," Trevelyan said.

"I was making a fortune off fur and lumber on Vanaheim," the other man said.

"And disrupting the ecology of a continent," Trevelyan replied.

"You didn't have to come in and talk them into changing the laws on me," Murdoch said without rancor. He rinsed a glass from the water carafe and filled it with champagne. "Hope you don't mind this being used first by a financier."

"No. Thank you." Trevelyan accepted.

"And then, when he was honorably engaged as a mercenary—" Faustina's tone held venom.

"Bringing modern weapons in against primitives who were no menace," Trevelyan said. "That's universally illegal. Almost as illegal as dispossessing autochthons or prior colonists."

"Does your precious Union actually claim jurisdiction over the entire cosmos?"

"Ease off, Faustina," Murdoch said.

"The Union is not a government, although many governments support it," Trevelyan said to the woman. "This galaxy alone is too big for any power to control. But we do claim the right to prevent matters from getting out of hand, as far as we're able. That includes wrongdoing by our own citizens anywhere."

"The Cordys never jailed me," Murdoch said. "They only scuppered my operation. I got away in time and left no usable evidence. No hard feelings." He raised his glass. Unwillingly, Trevelyan clinked rims with him and drank. "In fact," Murdoch added, "I'm grateful to you, friend. You showed me the error of my ways. Now I've organized a thing that'll not only make me rich, but so respectable that nobody can belch in my presence without a permit."

Faustina ignited a cigarette and smoked in hard puffs.

"I've been asked to verify that," Trevelyan said.

"Why, everything's open and honest," Murdoch said. "You know it already. I got me a ship, never mind how, and went exploring out Eridanus way. I found a planet, uninhabited but colonizable, and filed for a discoverer's patent. The Service inspection team verified that Good Luck, as I'm calling it, is a lawfully exploitable world. Here I am on Earth, collecting men and equipment for the preliminary work of making a defined area safe for humans. You remember." His manner grew deliberately patronizing. "Check for dangerous organisms and substances in the environment, establish the weather and seismic patterns, et cetera. When we're finished, I'll advertise my real estate and my ferry service to it. For the duration of my patent, I can set the terms of immigration, within limits. Most discoverers just charge a fee. But I aim to supply everything—transportation there, a functioning physical community built in advance, whatever people need to make a good start. That's why I've been discussing financial backing."

"Your approach has been tried," Trevelyan warned, "but never paid off. The cost per capita of a prefabricated settlement is more than the average would-be immigrant can afford. So he stays home, and puff goes the profit. Eventually, the entrepreneur is glad to sell out for a millo on the credit."

"Not this one," Murdoch said. "I'll be charging irrestibly little—about half what it'd cost 'em to buy unimproved land and make their own homes and highways and such out of local materials. They'll come." He tossed off the rest of his glass and refilled it. "But why are you curious, you Cordys? I haven't told you anything that isn't on file. If you wanted to snoop, why didn't you come see me earlier?"

"Because we have too much else on file," Trevelyan said bitterly. "Our computer didn't get around to correlating certain facts until yesterday. We're trying to keep the galaxy livable, but it's too much for us, too diverse—"

"Good!" Faustina said.

He gave her a grave look. "Be careful, my lady," he said, "or one day a piece of that diversity may kill you."

Murdoch scowled. "That'll do," he said. "I've been nice, but this is my evening out with my girl and you're obviously on a fishing expedition. You haven't got a thing against me, legally, have you? Very well, get out."

Trevelyan tensed where he sat.

"Or good night, if you prefer," Murdoch said in friendlier wise.

Trevelyan rose, bowed, murmured the polite formulas, and left. Inwardly he felt cold. There had been more than a gloat in his enemy's manner; there had been the expectation of revenge.

It looks as if I'd better take direct action, he thought.

The *Campesino* cleared from orbit, ran out of the Solar System on gravs, and went into hyperdrive in the usual fashion. She was a long-range cruiser with boats and gear for a variety of conditions. Aboard were Murdoch, Faustina, half a dozen spacemen, and a score of technicians.

The service speedster *Genji* followed, manned by Trevelyan and that being whose humanly unpronounceable name was believed to mean something like Smokesmith. To shadow another vessel is more art than science and more witchcraft than either. *Campesino* could easily be tracked while in the normal mode—by amplied sight, thermal radiation, radar, neutrinos from the powerplant. But once she went over to the tachyon mode, only a weak emission of super-light particles was available. And Murdoch also had detectors, surely kept wide open.

With skill and luck, *Genji* could stay at the effective edge of the field she was observing, while it masked her own. For this to be possible, however, she must be much smaller as well as much faster than the other craft. Therefore nothing more formidable than her could be used. She did have a blast cannon, a couple of heavy slugthrowers, and several one-meter dirigible missiles with low-yield nuclear warheads. But Trevelyan would have been surprised if Murdoch's people didn't build themselves huskier weapons en route.

He sat for hours at the conn, staring into the jeweled blackness of its star simulacrum, while the ship murmured around him and the subliminal beat of drive energies wove into his bones. At last he said, "I think we've done it." He pointed to the instruments. A hunter's exultation lifted within him. "They are defintely sheering off the Eridanus course."

"They may have become aware of us, or they may do so later, and attack," replied the flat artificial voice of Smokesmith.

"We take that chance," Trevelyan agreed. "I can't quite belive it of Murdoch, though. He plays rough, but I don't know about any cold-blooded murders he's done."

"Our information concerning his world line is fragmentary, and zero about its future segment. Futhermore, available data indicate that his companions are quite unintegrate."

"M-m-m, yes, hard cases, none Earth-born, several nonhumans from raptor cultures among them. That was one fact which alerted us."

"What else? We departed too hurriedly for me to obtain entire background, I being ignorant of the biological and social nuances among your species."

Trevelyan considered his shipmate. Chief Rodionov had had to assign the first and presumably best agent he could, and there were never many nonhumans at Australia Center. Homo Sapiens is a wolfish creature; two of him can end with ripping each other apart, on an indefinitely long voyage in as cramped a shell as this. But even when our agents have gentler instincts, we try to make up teams out of diverse breeds. The members must be compatible in their physical requirements but, preferably, different enough in psychologies and abilities that they form a whole which is more than its parts.

The trouble was, Trevelyan had never before encountered a being from the planet men called Reardon's. He had heard of them, but space is too full of life for us to remember it all, let alone meet it.

Smokesmith's barrel-like body stood about 140 centimeters high on four stumpy, claw-footed legs. Four tentacles ringed the top of it, each ending in three boneless fingers whose grip was astonishing. The head was more like a clump of fleshy blue petals than anything else; patterns upon them were the outward signs of sense organs, though Trevelyan didn't know how these worked. Withal, Smokesmith was handsome in his (?) fashion. Indeed, the mother-of-pearl iridescence on his rugose torso was lovely to watch.

The man decided on a straightforward approach. "Well," he said, "the fact that Murdoch is involved was in itself suspicious. He probably came to Earth to outfit, rather than some colonial world where he isn't known, because he wouldn't attract attention."

"I should extrapolate otherwise, when few commercial ventures originate on Earth."

"But the average Terrestrial hasn't got the average colonist's lively interest in such matters. The port cities are mostly ignored by the rest of the planet, a regrettable necessity to be kept within proper bounds. Then, too, Murdoch would have a better chance of getting substantial but close-mouthed—uh, that means secretive—money help on Earth, which is still the primary banker of the human species. And finally, though it's true that Service reports from everywhere go to the molecular file at Center . . . that fact makes the data flow so huge that Murdoch might well have completed his business and departed before the continuous search-and-correlation noticed him."

"What was smelled, then, to excite suspicion? I do no hypothesize that the initial stimulus was the composition of his crew."

"No. We checked that out later. Nor did the economics of his project look especially interesting. Doubtless his ready-built community will be a wretched clutter of hovels; but *caveat emptor,* he'll be within the law, and word will soon get around not to buy from him.

"No, the real anomaly is the equipment he ordered. The report on this Good Luck of his is complete enough that you can fairly well predict what a ground-preparation gang will need. The planet's smaller than Earth, relatively cold and arid, relatively thin atmosphere. But it has a magnetic field and a weak sun; hence the radiation background is low."

"What is required would depend on what race is to colonize."

"Sure. Murdoch will sell to humans. Not Earth humans, naturally. Colonial ones, from all over. We won't be able to monitor every embarkation and debarkation, any except a tiny fraction. Not when we are as few as we are, with so much else to do. And local authorities won't care. They'll be too glad to get rid of excess population. Besides, most colonials are anarchic oriented; they won't stand for official inquiries into their business." Trevelyan blinked in surprise. "What started me off on that?" .

"Conceivably an element of your mentation has

sensed a thought."

"If so, it's a hunch too faint to identify. Well. Why doesn't he have water-finding gear with him, drills and explosives to start forming lakes, that kind of stuff? Why does he have a full line of radiation spotters and protective suits? The biological laboratory he's assembled isn't right for Good Luck either; it's meant to study life forms a lot more terrestroid. I could go on, but you get the idea."

"And now he has changed course." Smokesmith considered the indicators with whatever he used to see. "A geodesic, which will bring him in the direction of Scorpius."

"Huh? You don't have to ask the computer? . . . Trouble is, no law says he must go to his announced destination, or tell us why he didn't." Trevelyan smiled with shut lips. "Nor does any law say we can't tail along."

A keening broke from Smokesmith, made not with his vocoder but with his own tympani. It wavered up and down the scale; a brief shakenness in his nerves told Trevelyan it entered the subsonic. Odors rolled upon the air, pungencies like blood and burnt sulfur and others men do not know.

"Good Cosmos, what're you doing?" he exclaimed.

"It is an old communication of my infraculture. Of whetted winds, frost, a mountain that is a torch, beneath iron moons, a broken night, and the will to pursue that which has poison fangs. . . . Enough."

Five hundred and twenty-eight light-years from Sol, the sky ahead suddenly blazed.

Trevelyan had been meditating upon his philosophy. That, and reading, and listening to music tapes, and tinkering with handicrafts, and physical exercises, had been his refuge from the weary weeks. Smokesmith was a decent being in his way, but too alien for games or conversation. When asked how he passed the time, with no apparent motion save of his endlessly interweaving arms, he replied: "I make my alternate life. Your language lacks the necessary concepts."

The blossoming of what had been merely another, slowly waxing blue star, jerked Trevelyan to alertness. He sat up, clenched hands on chair arms, and stared at the simulacrum until his vision seemed to drown in those glittering dark depths. The star climbed in brilliance even as he watched, for *Genji* passed the wave front of the initial explosion and entered that which had come later. It dominated the whole sky before Trevelyan could shout:

"Supernova!"

And still it flamed higher, until its one searing point gave fifty times the light that full Luna does to Earth, ten million times the light of the next most luminous—and nearby—sun. Although the screens throttled down that terrible whiteness, Trevelyan could not look close to it, and his vision was fogged with shining spots for minutes after the glimpse he had first gotten.

Smokesmith's claws clicked on the deck of the conn section as the Reardonite entered. Trevelyan caught a hackle-raising whiff from him and knew he was equally awed. Perhaps his expressionless phrasing was a defense:

"Yes, a supernova of Type II, if the theoretical accounts I have witnessed are correct. They are estimated to occur at the rate of one every fifty-odd years in the galaxy. The remnants of some have been investigated, but to date no outburst has been observed within the range of recorded explorations."

"We've gone beyond that range already," the man whispered. He shook himself. "Is Murdoch headed toward it?"

"Approximately. No change in course."

"Can't be coincidence. He must have traveled far, looking for game the Cordys wouldn't take from him, and—" Roughly: "Let's get some readings."

Instruments, astrophysical files carried on every Service vessel, and computation produced a few answers. The star was about 150 parsecs away, which meant it had died five centuries ago. It had been a blue giant, with a mass of some ten Sols, an intrinsic luminosity of perhaps 50,000; but the Scorpian clouds had hidden it from early Terrestrial astronomers, and modern scientists were as yet too busy to come this far afield.

So wild a burning could not go on for many million years. Instabilities built up until the great star shattered itself. At the peak of its explosion, it flooded forth energy equal to the output of the rest of the galaxy.

That could last for no more than days, of course. Racing down the light-years, Trevelyan saw the lurid splendor fade. A mistiness began to grow, a nebula born of escaped gases, rich in new nuclei of the heavier elements, destined at last to enter into the formation of new suns and planets. Insturments picked out the core of the star: whitely shining, fiercer still in the X-ray spectrum, lethal to come near. But it collapsed rapidly beneath its own monstrous gravitation, to the size of a dwarf, a Jupiter, an Earth. At the end it would be so dense that nothing, not even light, could leave;

and it would have vanished from the universe.

Trevelyan said with bleak anger: "He didn't report it. The information that's already been lost as the wave front swelled—"

"Shall we return at once?" the Reardonite asked.

"Well . . . no, I suppose not. If we let Murdoch go, Cosmos knows what deviltry might happen. There'll be other supernovas, but a dead sentience doesn't come back."

"We have a strong indication of his goal."

"What?" Trevelyan set down the pipe he had been nervously loading.

"Examine the photomultiplier screen, and next these." Fingertendrils snaked across dial faces. "The star to which I point is an ordianry G3 sun within a hundred light-years of the supernova. Proper motions show that it was somewhat closer at the time of the eruption. Our study object is on an unmistakable intercept track. It is plausible that this is meant to terminate there."

"But— No!" Trevelyan protested. "What can he want?"

"The dosage received by any planet of the lesser sun, through the cosmic rays given off by the larger at its maximum, was in the thousands of roentgens, delivered in a period of days. Atmosphere and magnetic field would have provided some shielding, but the effect must nonetheless have been biologically catastrophic. Presumably, though, most lower forms of life would survive, especially vegetable and marine species. A new ecological balance would soon be struck, doubtless unstable and plagued by a high mutation rate but converging upon stability. Probably the infall of radionuclides, concentrated in certain areas by natural processes, would make caution advisable to the present time. But on the whole, this hypothetical planet could now be salubrious for your race or mine, if it otherwise resembles our homes sufficiently. I might add that it has been conjectured that accidents of this sort were responsible for periods of massive extinction on numerous worlds, including, I have absorbed, your own home sphere."

Trevelyan scarcely heard the flat words. All at once he was confronting horror.

When the yellow sun was a disk, too lightful for bare eyes but softly winged with corona and zodiacal glow in a step-down screen: then the supernova nebula, thirty parsecs off, was only an irregular blur, a few minutes across, among the constellations opposite, as if a bit of the Milky Way had drifted free. One had trouble imagining how it had raged in these skies four hundred years ago. Nor did interplanetary space any longer have an unusual background count; nor did the seven attendant worlds that *Genji's* cameras identified seem in any way extraordinary.

That was a false impression, Trevelyan knew. Every world is a wilderness of uncountably many uniquenesses. But the third one out, on which his attention focused, resembled Earth.

He was confident to optical means of study. Beams and probes might be detected aboard *Campesino*. Murdoch had gone out of hyper into normal mode several millions of kiolmeters back. His shadowers necessarily followed suit. Then—lest he spot their neutrino emission, as they were now tracking him by his—they stopped the fusion generators and orbited free at their considerable distance, drawing power from the accumulators.

"The study object is in the final phase of approach to atmosphere of the terrestroid planet," Smokesmith announced.

"I'm scarcely surprised," Trevelyan answered. He looked up from his meters and notes. "Apparently it is as terrestroid as any you'll ever find, too. Air, irradiation, size, mass as gotten from the satellites—nearly identical. Those are two small, fairly close-in moons, by the way; so the tide patterns must be complicated, but the oceans will be kept from stagnation. Twenty-eight-hour spin, twelve-degree tilt. Mean temperature a touch higher than Earth's, no polar caps, somewhat less land area . . . an interglacial macroclimate, I'd guess. In short, aside from pockets of leftover radioactivity, idyllic."

"And possible ecological difficulites," the Reardonite said.

Trevelyan winced. "Damn, did you have to remind me?" He left off peering, leaned back in his chair, held his chin, and scowled. "Question is, what do we do about Murdoch? He doesn't seem to have committed any violation except failure to register a discovery. And we probably couldn't prove this isn't his own first time here, that he didn't come this way on impulse. Besides, the offense is trivial."

"Do methods not exist of compelling humans to speak truth?"

"Yes. Electronic brainphasing. Quite harmless. But our species has rules against involuntary self-incrimination. So it's mainly used to prove the honesty of prosecution withnesses. And as I said, I've no real case against him."

"Need we do more than report back? Authorized expeditions could then be dispatched."

" 'Back' " is a mighty long ways. What might he do here meanwhile? Of course—hm—if Murdoch doesn't suspect we're on to him, he may proceed leisurely with his preparations, giving us a chance to—"

"The study object has ceased to emit."

"What?" Trevelyan surged from his chair. He abraded his arm on his companion's integument, so fast did he brush by to look for himself. The indications were subtle, because the normal neutrino count is always high. But this tracer included a computer which identified engine sign amidst noise and put its volume on a single dial. That needle had fallen to zero.

Chilled, Trevelyan said: "He's going down on accumulators and aerodynamics. By the time we come in range for a different tracking method, he can be wherever on the surface."

Smokesmith's tone was unchanging, but an acrid odor jetted from him and the petals of his face stirred. "Apparently he does not fear detection from the ground. We observe no trace of atomic energy, hence doubtless no one capable of locating it. The probability is that he desires to remove us and none else from his trail."

"Yeh." Trevelyan began to pace, back and forth between the caging bulkheads. "We half expected he'd tag us somewhere along the line, when I'd already put him on the *qui vive* in Port Nevada. But why's he telling us unequivocally that he has?"

"In my race, messages are always intended as vectors on the world line of the percipient."

"In mine too, sort of." Trevelyan's strides lengthened. "What does Murdoch hope to get us to do by thumbing his nose at us? We have two alternatives. We can go straight back, or we can land first for a closer look."

"The latter would not add significantly to the interval before we can have returned."

"That's the black deuce of it, my friend. The very nearest Service base where we could originate any kind of investigatory expedition is, um, Lir, I suppose, if they aren't still too busy with the Storm Queen affair. There are frontier planets closer than that, full of men who'll gladly swarm here for a chance of striking it rich. And if they can also do the Cordys one in the eye, why, fine."

"Furthermore," Smokesmith pointed out, "we have no clear proof that anything is involved sufficiently important to justify a long-range mission. The supernova, yes. That is a scientific treasure. But here we have merely a seemingly uninhabited planet. Why should a base commander who does not know Murdoch's past —especially a nonhuman base commander who cannot ingest its significance—assume he has an unlawful purpose? Will he not expect Murdoch to request an inspection team, that a patent of discovery may be issued?"

Trevelyan nodded. We are scattered so thinly, we who guard the great Pact. Often we must pass by tracks that may well lead toward a hidden evil, because we *know* about another beast elsewhere. Or we learn of something that was wrong at the beginning and should have been stopped, but whose amendment now would be a worse wrong. We have Nerthus, for example, always before us: a human colony founded and flourishing, then learning that native intelligent life did exist. We are fortunate that in that case the interests of the two species are reconcilable, with endless difficulty.

"Does Murdoch wish us to return in alarm bearing data inadequate to provoke prompt official action?" Smokesmith queried. "That seems plausible. Coming as he lately did from the Union's Scorpian march, he must be better informed than we about current situations there. Thus, he might know we can get no help at Lir."

"We can—we can even commandeer civilian ships and personnel—if yonder planet has sentient beings on it. Clear and present danger of territorial conquest. Or Murdoch might simply be plundering them."

"It is improbable that such are alive."

"True. But if dead—"

Trevelyan stopped. He looked long outward. Unmagnified, the world was a point of light, a clear and lovely blue. But close in would be mapless immensity. The other crew would have had ample chance to conceal their vessel. They could be anywhere, preparing anything. They surely outnumbered ad outgunned him. He hated to imagine big, bluff Murdoch Juan as planning murder. On the other hand, Faustina might, and she had had this entire voyage in which to be the only human female. . . .

Resolution crystallized. "We're going in," he said.

They approached slowly, both to observe in detail and to make certain preparations. Circling in the fringes of atmosphere, they confirmed the thing they had guessed at.

His had been a peopled world. The people had been slain.

Were there survivors, there would be evidence of them. Civilization might well have gone under in mass death, panic, anarchy, and famine after crops perished in fields now brushland or desert.

But savage descendants of a city-building race would live in villages. *Genji's* sensors would register their very campfires. Besides, it was more reasonable that some comeback would have been made, however weak. For the sleet of cosmic radiation harmed no buildings, no tools or machines, no books, little, indeed, except what was alive.

Gazing into a viewscreen, where clouds panted briefly to show high towers by a lake, Trevelyan said: "Populous, which means they had efficient agriculture and transportation, at least in their most advanced regions. I can identify railway lines and the traces of roads. Early industrial, I'd guess, combustion engines, possible limited use of electricity. . . . But they had more aesthetic sense, or something, than most cultures at that technological level. They kept beauty around them." He hauled his thoughts away from what that implied. If he did not stay impersonal he must weep.

"Did they succumb to radiation effects alone?" Smokesmith wondered. He appeared to have no trouble maintaining detachment. But then, he did not feel humanlike emotions, as Trevelyan judged the dead beings had. "Shelter was available."

"Maybe they didn't know about radioactivity. Or maybe the escapers were too few, too scattered, too badly mutated. Anyhow, they're gone—Hold!"

Trevelyan's hands danced over the board. *Genji* swung about, backtracked, and came to hover.

Atmosphere blurred the magnified view, but beams, detectors, and computer analysis helped. A town stood on an island in a wide river. Thus, despite the bridges that soared from bank to bank, it was not thickly begrown by vegetation. What had entered was largely cleared away: recent work, the rawness identifiable. The job had been done by machines, a couple of which stood openly in a central plaza. Trevelyan couldn't spot details, but never doubted they were Earth-made robotic types. Several buildings had been blasted, either as too ruinous or as being in the way, and the rubble shoved aside. He got no indications of current activity, but strong electronic resonance suggested that a modern power network was partly completed.

"Murdoch," Trevelyan said like a curse.

"Can you obtain indictions of his ship?" the Reardonite asked.

"No. When he detected us approaching, he must have moved her, and screened as well as camouflaged the hull. Maybe he hoped we wouldn't chance to notice what he's been up to, or maybe this is another gibe. Certainly he must've gotten busy here the instant he landed, after choosing the site on his first visit."

Trevelyan put the speedster back into orbit. For a while the conn held only a humming silence. The planet filled half the sky with clouds, seas, sunrises and sunsets; the other half was stars.

"No autochthons left," Smokesmith mused at last. "Their relics are of limited scientific interest. Will this be adjudged grounds for sending armed craft, that are badly needed elsewhere, to make him stop?"

"Supposing it is—that's uncertain, as you say, but supposing it is—*can* they stop him?" Trevelyan seized the controls again. The power hum deepened. "Prepare for descent."

He chose a city near the edge of morning, that he might have a long daylight. A mole jutted from the waterfront into an emerald-and-sapphire bay. Sonic beams declared it to be of reinforced concrete, as firm as the day it was dedicated. He landed there, and presently walked forth. A grav sled would have taken him faster and easier, but part of his aim was to get to know somewhat about those who were departed. His ship, all systems on standby, fell behind him like a coppery cenotaph.

He didn't worry about the safety of the environment. Murdoch had proven that for him. What had still to be learned was mere detail: for instance, what imported crops would do well?"

Any number, Trevelyan felt sure. It was a rich and generous planet. No doubt it had been more so before the catastrophe, but it remained wonderful enough, and nature was fast healing the wounds.

The bay glittered and chuckled between golden-green hills. At its entrance began an ocean; coming down, he had identified fantastically big shoals of marine plants and animals. No wings rode the wind that rumpled his hair. Most, perhaps all vertebrates were extinct. But lower forms had survived the disaster. Insects, or their equivalent, swarmed on delicate membranes that often threw back the sunlight in rainbows. Silvery forms leaped from the water. The wind smelled of salt, iodine, and life.

Overhead wandered some clouds, blue-shadowed in a dazzlingly blue heaven. At this season, the supernova was aloft by day, invisible. Disaster, Trevelyan thought with a shudder. How little had Earth's ancient astrologers known of how terrible a word they were shaping!

But the day was sunny, cool, and peaceful. He walked shore-ward, looking.

The watercraft had sunk or drifted free of their rotted lines. However, the shallower water inshore was so clear that he could see a few where they lay, somewhat preserved. The gracious outlines of the sailboats did not astonish him; that demand was imposed by natural law. But his eyes stung to think that the dead had loved sloops and yawls as much as he did. And they had put bronze figure-heads on many, whose green-corroded remnants hinted at flowers, wings, flames, anything fair and free. A large ship had drifted aground. It had been iron-hulled and, judging from the stacks, steam-propelled. But it, no, she had also been designed to look like a dancer on the waves.

He neared the quay. A row of wooden ware-houses (?) was partly moldered away, partly buried under vines. Nevertheless he could make out how roofs once swept in high curves that the door-ways matched. A rusting machine, probably a crane, was decorated at the end of its lifting arm with a merry animal face.

He stood for some while before an arch at the head of the mole. Here the dwellers had repre-sented themselves.

Their art was not photographic. It had a swing of line and mass that woke a pulse in Trevelyan, it was not quite like anything he had ever seen be-fore. But the bipeds with their long slim six-fingered hands, long necks, and long-beaked heads, came through to him as if still alive. He al-most thought he could hear their stone cloaks flap in the wind.

Walking farther into the city, he began to find their bones.

Carrion eaters had seldom or never disturbed them. Dust blew in, settled on pavement, became soil; seeds followed, struck frail roots that gradu-ally crumbled brick and concrete; bushes and vines grew over that first carpet and up the walls; those kinds of trees that survived extended their range into the domains of trees that had not, and beyond into farm and town. But the invasion was slow. The wilderness had all the time in the world. It was in full occupation of the shoreward edges of this city, and reducing the next line, but as yet just a few forerunners and (Trevelyan thought with a hurtful smile) sappers had won this near the waterfront.

The buildings of granite, marble, and masonry rose tall, washed by rain and sunlight, little damaged by weather, only occasional creepers blurring their outlines. Like the relief sculpture on their walls, they leaped and soared, not as manbuilt skyscrapers do but in that peculiar rhythm which made their heights seem to fly. They were colonnaded, balustraded, many-windowed, and kept some of the coloring that once softened their austerity.

Trevelyan wondered at the absence of parks or gardens. His observations from altitude had suggested a deep-reaching love of landscape and care for it. And floral motifs were about the commonest decorations. Well, the dwellers had not been human; it would take long to get some insight to what their race psyche might have been. Maybe they enjoyed the contrast of art and openness. If this place was typical, every city was a delight to live in. At some economic sacrifice, the dwellers had avoided filling their air and water with noise, dirt, and poison. To be sure, they were lucky that no heating was required. But as far as Trevelyan had been able to ascertain, industrial plants were widely scattered outside urban limits, connected by railways. There were no automobiles, though that was probably within the technological capabilities. Instead, he found the depictions, and some bones, of large quadrupeds that served like horses; he also identified the hulks of what appeared to have been public vehicles with primitive electric motors. It was hard to tell after four hundred years, but he at least got the impression that, while theirs was a productive and prosperous civilization, the dwellers had not created overly much trash either. They could have foreseen the problem and taken steps. He'd like to know.

Not that they were saints. He came upon statues and dimmed murals which showed combat. Twice, above inscriptions he would never interpret, he saw a being dressed in rags bursting chains off himself; no doubt somebody put those chains on in the first place. But oftenest he found imagery which he read as of affection, gentleness, work, teaching, discovery, or the sheer splendor of being alive.

He entered courtyards, walked past dried pools and fountains, on into the buildings. Few had elevators, which was suggestive since the culture could have supplied them. He noted that the shafts of the wide circular staircases would easily accommodate grav lifts. The murals indoors were scarcely faded; their vividness took some of the grief off him. Nevertheless, and although he was not superstitious or even especially religious, he knocked on the first door he came to.

Every door was sliding or folding, none bore locks or latches, which again implied unusual traits. The majority of apartments had been deserted. Cloth had decayed, metal tarnished, plaster cracked, and dust fallen centimeters thick. But the furnishings remained usable by humans, who were formed quite like the dwellers. Clean and patch up; restore the water supply; make do with the airily shaped oil lanterns, if need be, and a camp stove since the original owners didn't seem to have cooked anything; throw padding over chairs, divans, beds, intricately grained floors: and you would be altogether comfortable. Soon power would become available, and you could change the place around at your leisure until it was ideal.

Early in the game, though, you'd better get rid of those pictures, papers, enigmatic tools, and shelves full of books. They could be disturbing to live with.

As the hours passed, Trevelyan did find skeletons in a few apartments. Either these individuals had died by surprise, like those he infrequently noticed in the streets, or they desired privacy for their final day. One lay in a kind of chaise longue, with a book upon what had been the lap. Twice he found small skeletons covered by a large one. Did the mother understand that death was coming from the sky? Yes, she could see it up there, a point of radiance to brilliant to look near, surrounded by the auroras it evoked in this atmosphere. Probably she knew the death was everywhere. But she was driven by the instinct of Niobe.

When he discovered the ossuary, Trevelyan decided there must be several, and this was how the average dweller had elected to go. It was in a large hall—theater? auditorium? temple? The most susceptible must already have died, and radiation sickness be upon the rest. In man it approaches its terminus with nausea, vomiting, hair coming out, internal bleeding, blood from the orifices and eyes, strengthlessness, fever, and delirium. Doubtless it was similar for the dwellers.

Outside were the remants of several improvised coal furnaces. Their pipes fed into the sealed hall, carbon monoxide generators. Bones and rusted weapons nearby suggested the operators had finished their task and then themselves. The door was the single tightly fastened one Trevelyan had encountered, but being wooden it yielded to his boot in a cloud of punk. Beyond lay the skeletons of adults, hundreds of them, and many more young, and toys, games, cups, banners, musical instruments—*I don't know what they did at that party*, Trevelyan thought, *but if we humans had the same guts, we'd tell the children that Carnival came early this year.*

He walked back out into the bright quiet. Something like a butterfly went past, though its wings were fairer than anything evolved on Earth. Being a little of an antiquarian, he said aloud: "The Lord giveth and the Lord taketh away; I will not bless the name of the Lord. But I will remember. Oh, yes, I will remember."

He had not gone much farther toward the middle of town when he heard a thunder rumble. Looking up past the towertops, he saw the great shining form of *Campesino* descent. She came between him and the sun and covered him with her shadow.

Reflexively, he took shelter in a doorway. One hand dropped to his pistol. With a sour grin at himself, he activated the tiny radio transceiver in his tunic pocket. On the standard band, he heard Murdoch's voice: "Cordy ahoy! Respond!"

The empty speedster made no reply. A drone and a quivering went through the air as *Campesino* balanced on her gravs. "You!" Murdoch barked. "We picked up your tachyons halfway to here. We followed you down by your neutrinos. Don't try bluffing us about having a friend in reserve. You're alone, and we've got a cyclic blast zeroed in, and I want to speak with you."

More silence in the receivers. Trevelyan felt the

sweat on his ribs, under his arms, and smelled it.
He could not foretell what would happen. At best,
he had sketched behavior patterns Murdoch might
adopt and responses he might make. His plan
amounted to creating a situation where he could
improvise . . . whether successfully or not.

A barely distinguishable background growl: "No
one inside, I'd guess. Exploring the city?"

"Could be," Murdoch said. "Odd they'd leave
their boat unguarded."

"A trap?"

"Well—maybe. Don't seem Cordy style, but
maybe we better keep clear."

Trevelyan did in fact wish *Camqpesino* to set
down elsewhere, making *Genji* less of a hostage.
He decided to push matters, trod forth, and shot a
flash from his gun into the air. It crackled. Ozone
touched his nostrils.

"Look! Below! You, d'you read us?"

Trevelyan saw no sense in giving away the fact
that he could listen. He might gain some slight advantage thereby; and Cosmos knew, with that
metal storm cloud hanging above him, he needed
whatever help he could get. He waved and jogged
off toward the city center, where he had noticed a
plaza from above.

After a conference he couldn't make out, the
others did what he would have done in their place.
Campesino opened a hatch and discharged a grav
sled with a man or two aboard. Not carrying
missles, she could give them no effective armament. But they would hover near *Genji* and cry
warning of anything suspicious. The ship herself
dropped behind the towers. When she landed, the
ground trembled and echoes boomed slowly from
wall to wall.

Trevelyan switched off his radio speaker, turned

on the transmitter, and hastened his trot. Once he accidentally kicked a skull. It rolled aside with a dry clatter. *I'm sorry,* he thought to it. That being not altogether alien to him had felt this street underfoot, sunwarmth reflected off cataract-like façades, muscle movement, heartbeat, breath. The city had lived around the being, with friends, loves, traffic, music, pleasure . . . did the race laugh? *I may be joining you soon,* he added, and scorned himself for the juvenilism.

He emerged not on a square but a golden rectangle. Grassy growth was thrusting up and apart those blocks which had paved it, but the rains of four centuries had not quite washed out the grooves worn by generations of feet. The enclosing buildings were lower here. Their lines bespoke tranquillity rather than excitement, though three of them held the fragments of dazzling stained-glass windows. Numerous skeletons lay prostrated before one. *Campesino* rose brutal from the plaza center.

Several men and not-men waited, guns at the ready. They were a hard-looking gang. Murdoch stood at ease, Faustina tensed beside him. Both wore black coveralls with silver ornamentation. Her hair glowed in the light. Trevelyan approached at a reduced pace, hands well away from his pistol.

"Mike!" the adventurer bawled. He threw back his head in laughter that made his moustaches vibrate. "Why the chaos didn't I expect you'd be the one?"

"Who else with you?" Faustina said.

Trevelyan shrugged. "Who with you?" he countered.

"You've seen our roster," Murdoch said. "I figured you'd refuse to board, afraid we'd grab you, so I came out." He jerked a thumb at the sheer hull behind. "Got a full complement inside at alert stations."

Trevelyan achieved a smile. "What makes you expect trouble, Juan?" he asked in his mildest voice.

Murdoch blinked. "Why . . . you dogged us clear from Earth—"

"No, think," Trevelyan said. "Space is free. The Co-ordination Service investigates where it can, but forbids violence to its agents except under extreme necessity. You know that as well as I do."

The guards around shifted stance, muttered among themselves, flicked eyes from side to side. Trevelyan virtually felt the unease in them.

"For example," he drawled, "you're breaking the law here, first by not reporting a discovery—"

"We've only just made it!" Faustina said. Red stained the white cheekbones. Her fists were clenched. He studied her for a moment, thinking with compassion: *She's afraid I'll take away her glory—her chance to rake in money until she can lose the fear of being poor that was ground into her,* and with caution: *In an aggressive human personality, fear begets ruthlessness.*

"Please let me finish," he said. "I'm not interested in lodging charges, nor would my superiors be. The offense probably occurs hundreds of times a year, and seldom matters. Out of necessity, the Service operates on the old principle that the law should not concern itself with trifles."

She stepped back, breathing hard, lips pulled away from teeth, but plainly bemused. Murdoch's massive features had grown immobile. "Continue," he said.

"You've committed a more important breach of law by tampering with and destroying material of

scientific value." Trevelyan kept his tone amiable
and a faint smile on his mouth. "I refer to that island city. But the planet is such an archaeological
and biological Golconda that we'll overlook your
indiscretion, we'll put it down to an amateur's for-
givable enthusiasm, in exchange for the service
you've done to civilization by bringing this world
to our knowledge. You'll remember an agent like
me has authority to issue pardons in minor cases.
I'll write you one today, if you wish, and recommend you for next year's Polaris Medal into the
bargain."

He offered his hand. "Stop worrying," he said.
"Let's have a drink and go home together."

Murdoch did not take the hand. The big man
stood for a while, staring, and the silence of the
dead grew and grew. He broke it with a whisper:
"Are you serious?"

Trevelyan dropped pretense. He said in a hard-
ened voice, while his nerves felt the surrounding
guns: "It's an honest offer. You already have Good
Luck to make your living off. Be content with
that."

"Good Luck?" Faustina cried. She swept one
arm in a taloned arc. "You incredible idiot! *This* is
Good Luck!"

"I kept hoping it wasn't," Trevelyan said low.

"What do you figure I had in mind?" Murdoch
demanded.

"Obvious," Trevelyan sighed. "Here was your
real discovery. But how to exploit it? You couldn't
get a patent, because the Union would forbid colonization until the scientists finished their re-
searches. Considering the distance, and the short-
age of personnel, and the vast amout there is to
study, that would take at least a hundred years,
probably longer. In fact, the odds are we'd put a se-

crecy seal on the co-ordinates for a decade or two, to keep unqualified visitors away until a big enough enterprise got started that the scientists could do their own guarding."

"Scientists!" Faustina nearly shrieked. Murdoch laid a warning grip on her arm. His predator's gaze stayed on Trevelyan.

"What a means to a fortune, though!" the Co-ordinator said. "You could offer an utterly desirable home, complete with every facility for hundreds of millions of people, at a price the ordinary colonial can afford. You stood to become one of the wealthiest humans that ever lived.

"Well, you went looking for a world we wouldn't disallow. What you turned up isn't particularly good. But it's no worse than some which have been settled, and at least doesn't have a population already squeezing its meager resources. People would buy your real estate there, if the preliminary work had been done for them and the cost was not beyond their means.

"Some you actually would take to the marginal planet—say when an agent like me happened to be around. You'd lose money on them. But it wouldn't matter, because most would be shipped here, where entire cities cost you practically nothing. They'd write home. Your ships would carry the overjoyed mail, maybe censoring it a wee bit to keep us Cordys from getting wind of your enterprise too soon. Not that we'd be likely to, when we're run off our feet with urgent cases, and when few people on those thousands of entire worlds give us any active co-operation. You could carry on for a number of years, I'm sure, before the discrepancies got so glaring that we investigated."

"What'd you do after you learned?" Murdoch asked.

"Nothing," Trevelyan said. "How could we displace tens of thousands, maybe millions of men, women, and children, who'd come in good faith, started a good new life, put down roots, begun bringing forth a new generation? It'd be a political impossibility, a moral one, maybe a physical one. They'd fight for their homes, and we couldn't bomb them, could we?

"You personally would be subject to—in theory, confiscation of your properties and imprisonment of your body. In practice, you'd have put both where we couldn't touch them without more effort and killing than it was worth. You'd have rigged the colonial government and its constitution early in the game to make you something like the Founding Father president of Good Luck. They'd fight for you too. So, rather than violate its own prohibition on conquest—for the sake of scientific and aesthetic values that'd already been ruined—the Union would accept what you'd done to it."

Trevelyan closed his mouth. He felt hoarse and tired and wanted a smoke, but didn't dare reach for his pipe under those guns.

Murdoch nodded. "You read me good." He chuckled. "Thanks for the Founding Father title. I hadn't thought of that. Sounds like what I need."

"I can't allow it, you know," Trevelyan said.

"Why not?" Murdoch grew curiously earnest. "What's here, really? A worldful of bones. I'm sorry it happened, but dead's dead. And they were, well, one more race among millions. What can we learn from them that matters? Oh, I suppose you can hope for a new technique or art form or whatever, that'll revolutionize civilization. But you prob'ly understand better than me how small that chance is. Meanwhile, yonder we've got people who're alive, and hurting, now."

"The planet will be opened for settlement, region by region, in due course."

"How long is due course? How many'll die during it, that could've lived happier?"

"Emigrants are always replaced at home by fresh births. In the long run, the exact time of migration makes no difference."

"Forget the long run and thick about flesh and blood."

Trevelyan's anger broke his control. "Don't hand me that guff, Murdoch," he snapped. "You're about as altruistic as a blast cannon."

"And you," Faustina spat, "you're a machine. I look forward to killing you—dismantling you!"

"Wait, wait, there," Murdoch said. "Ease off and let's talk sane."

He regarded the ground for a moment before he straightened, faced Trevelyan squarely, and said:

"I'll tell you how it lies. When we knew we were being dogged, we decided to lead you on, because once the supernova got reported, this sector 'ud be swarmed and somebody else might find our Good Luck.

"You could've skited for home without landing. If you'd done that, we'd've made for the nearest human planets to here. We'd've rallied a lot of men, transported 'em free, gotten well dug in before you could raise any action at headquarters. It might've been enough to stop you from doing anything."

"I assumed that was your plan," Trevelyan said. "On my way back, I'll visit every Scorpian world and announce, without specifying location too closely, that this planet is interdicted to preserve culturral values. To come here then, knowingly, will justify and require violence by the Service. We do have to maintain the precedent."

"What makes you think you're going back?" asked Faustina. She grinned with hatred.

"Ease off," Murdoch repeated. To Trevelyan: "I did hope you'd land, like you have. Waved a large red flag at you, didn't I? You see, I knew you must have less beef than my ship. Now I've got you."

"What will you do with me?" the Co-ordinator replied.

"Well, uh, I'll admit some of my mates got a little, uh, vehement," Murdoch said. "But I don't see any point in killing you. I sure don't want to. You're not a bad osco, Mike, for a Cordy. And they can't have any idea on Earth which way we headed. I'm not about to return there; I've done my credit arranging. If they ask me about you later on, why, I never had any notion you were trying to follow me. You must've come to grief somehow, and I'm awful sorry. Maybe I'll use your boat to fake some clues."

His mask of bashfulness fell away. He beamed. "Tell you what, Mike," he said. "Let's find you a nice island out in mid-ocean. We'll leave you tools and supplies and show you what's safe to eat. You Cordys are supposed to be philosophers. You should be glad of a few years for thinking. If you want, I'll try to get you a woman. And soon's I can, I'll fit you to our spaceport we'll've built. How's that for a fair proposition?"

Trevelyan savored the breath he drew, the light he saw, the will rising within him like a physical tide. "Let me be sure I understand you," he said. "Do you seriously intend to maroon me in order that I won't report the facts of this case?"

"Too good for you," Faustina said. "But if Juan's that tender-spirited, yes."

"Do you realize that this involves grave violaations of personal integrity?" Trevelyan asked. "Do you realize that it involves direct interference with an officer of the Union in the performance of his duty?"

Murdoch flushed. "Obscenity your duty!"

"I demand you let me go back to my spacecraft and depart unmolested," Trevelyan said.

Faustina snickered.

"You will not?" Trevelyan asked. He waited. A breeze whispered.

"Very well," he said. "I can now testify under brainphasing that you are guilty of attempted crimes sufficient to justify your arrest. Will you come quietly with me?"

"Have you lost your orbit?" Murdoch exclaimed.

"Since you resist arrest in addition," Trevelyan said, "the necessity of applying force becomes incontestable."

The guards jabbered, swore, and brought their weapons to bear. Faustina hissed. Murdoch's hand streaked to his own pistol.

Trevelyan ostentatiously folded his arms and said: "If my Service does not respect your rights, civilization is worthless. But civilization has rights of its own. I admit I led your thoughts away from my partner"—he heard a gasp and an oath—"but that scarcely constitutes entrapment. He's under a roof in this city, on an accumulator-powered grav sled, along with several nuclear missiles. Through a miniradio in my pocket, he's been listening to our conversation. If you don't surrender yourselves, he'll destroy you."

He paid scant attention to the uproar of the guards. His focus was entirely on their leaders.

Murdoch yanked a transceiver from his jacket to speak an order. "Give them a demonstration, Smokesmith," Trevelyan said.

No one saw the torpedo rise. It went too fast. Momentarily the sky was bedazzled with hell-colored flame. Concussion smote, not unduly hard from that altitude, but it shook men where they stood and bellowed in their ears. The bones before the temple shuddered.

"A bit close," Trevelyan said. He was aware that his own body quivered and went dry in the mouth. A remote part of him decided this was an unintegrate reaction and he needed more training. Speech and reasoning mind, though, were steel cool. "We may want antirad shots. I think you'll agree, Juan, the next can drop right here. Afterward my Reardonite friend won't have trouble picking off your watchmen."

"You'll be dead too," Murdoch groaned.

"I don't want to be," Trevelyan said, "but rather more is at stake than what I want."

Faustina whipped around behind Murdoch. She snatched his gun from the holster, flung herself forward, and rammed the muzzle into Trevelyan's belly. "Oof!" he choked. *I don't exactly cut a heroic figure, do I?* flashed through him. *But the beings here only had what dignity they could make for themselves, after heaven's meaningless anger fell on them.*

"I'll kill you myself!" she raved.

He knew tricks for knocking the weapon aside and taking it from her. But others were trained on him. He met her eyes, from which the tears went flooding, and said: "If you do, why should my partner not destroy you?"

Murdoch wrenched the gun from her. She raked at his face. He knocked her down. Panting, sweat a-river on his skin, he said: "What do you want?"

"If you know something about Reardonites," Trevelyan said, and saw that Murdoch did, "you'll

realize it won't bother Smokesmith to annihilate
me along with you. But he agrees it's undesirable.
So is the destruction of this beautiful plaza. Let's
compromise."

"I asked what do you want, you devil?"

"Safe conduct back to my vessel. Smokesmith
will monitor me by radio. Your ship will stay put.
At the first sign of any ill faith whatsoever, he
shoots. At worst, you see, he must eliminate both
ships and hope this world gets rediscovered by
someone who'll respect it. Once aloft, I'll quickly
drop down again and pick him up, too quickly for
you to rise. At that point you'll be helpless; but
have no fears. With a head start and a faster craft,
I'll be on the frontier planets before you, issuing
prohibitions. No one's going to follow you when he
knews it'll bring warships down on him. I suggest
you find an obscure place and lie low."

Murdoch beat fist into palm, again and again.
For a minute he looked old and hollowed out.

Then his mirth awoke. "You win this 'un too,
Mike," he said. "I'll escort you to your boat personal. Here." He offered his pistol. Trevelyan accepted it.

Faustina sat up. A bruise was spreading on her
slim jaw where her lover's fist had smitten. She
looked at them both, through tears and matted
locks, and was no longer anything except a bewildered beaten child.

"Why?" she pleaded. "Why can't we have a
patent—when w-w-we found the supernova for
you? You'd do this—wreck everything for . . . two,
three   hundred   s-s-specialists—and   their
curiosity?"

Trevelyan hunkered down before her. He took
both her hands in one of his. The other pointed
around, ending at the temple. "No," he said most

gently. "For these. Have they no rights? That someone shall come to know them, and they won't be lost from us."

But she did not understand. We guard the great Pact, which is the heart of civilization, of society, and ultimately of life itself: the unspoken Pact between the living, the dead, and the unborn, that to the best of poor mortal abilities they shall all be kept one in the oneness of time. Without it, nothing would have meaning and it may be that nothing would survive. But the young generations so often do not understand.

Trevelyan was never afterwards content in his work. The uncertainty of life in an uncaring universe mocked his pattern-making rationality. He knew that his civilization—even his race—could perish as completely as the beings the supernova slew.

A few years later, he took a Nomad wife and resigned from the Service to join her ship. He found the Nomads' closeknit, tradition-laden ways more satisfying than the atomized, cerebral existence considered normal on Earth. Even before becoming a clansman of the Peregrine, Trevelyan himself passed into legend for thwarting a plot by the antitechnic Alori to subvert human nature.

One—even many—foes without could be vanquished; against the enemy within there was no defense. Given the prevailing stage of psychodevelopment, the innate contradictions with individuals and societies could not be resolved. Critical data that needed to be gathered surpassed the capacity of any organization to comprehend, much less coordinate. The Stellar Union flew apart like an overwound spring.

But as Trevelyan had wisely foreseen, the self-sufficient, enterprising Nomads bore various seeds of knowledge safely through the Third Dark Ages. The antecedents of our own civilization were among those who reaped what the Nomads had sown.

By the uncertain dawn of the fifth millenium, Earth's farflung children had all but forgotten her. The cradle-world had become "less a planet and a population than a dream." But even dreams must have an ending.

THE CHAPTER ENDS

"No," said the old man.

"But you don't realize what it means," said Jorun. "You don't know what you're saying."

The old man, Kormt of Huerdar, Gerlaug's son, and Speaker for Solis Township, shook his head till the long, grizzled locks swirled around his wide shoulders. "I have thought it through," he said. His voice was deep and slow and implacable. "You gave me five years to think about it. And my answer is no."

Jorun felt a weariness rise within him. It had been like this for days now, weeks, and it was like trying to knock down a mountain. You beat on its rocky flanks till your hands were bloody, and still the mountain stood there, sunlight on its high snow fields and in the forests that rustled up its slopes, and it did not really notice you. You were a brief thin buzz between two long nights, but the mountain was forever.

"You haven't thought at all," he said with a rudeness born of exhaustion. "You've only reacted unthinkingly to a dead symbol. It's not a human re-action, even, it's a verbal reflex."

Kormt's eyes, meshed in crow's-feet, were se-rene and steady under the thick gray brows. He smiled a little in his long beard, but made no other reply. Had he simply let the insult glide off him, or had he not understood it at all? There was no real talking to these peasants; too many millennia lay between, and you couldn't shout across that gulf.

"Well," said Jorun, "the ships will be here to-morrow or the next day, and it'll take another day or so to get all your people aboard. You have that long to decide, but after that it'll be too late. Think about it, I beg of you. As for me, I'll be too busy to argue futher."

"You are a good man," said Kormt, "and a wise one in your fashion. But you are blind. There is something dead inside you."

He waved one huge gnarled hand. "Look around you, Jorun of Fulkhis. This is *Earth*. This is the old home of all humankind. You cannot go off and for-get it. Man cannot do so. It is in him, in his blood and bones and soul; he will carry Earth within him forever."

Jorun's eyes traveled along the arc of the hand. He stood on the edge of the town. Behind him were its houses—low, white, half-timbered, roofed with thatch or red tile, smoke rising from the chimneys; carved galleries overhung the narrow, cobbled, crazily twisting streets; he heard the noise of wheels and wooden clogs, the shouts of children at play. Beyond that were trees and the incredible ruined walls of Sol City. In front of him, the wooded hills were cleared and a gentle landscape of neat fields and orchards rolled down toward the distant glitter of the sea; scattered farm buildings, drowsy cattle, winding gravel roads, fence walls of ancient marble and granite, all dreaming under the sun.

He drew a deep breath. It was pungent in his nostrils. It smelled of leaf mold, plowed earth baking in the warmth, summery trees and gardens, a remote ocean odor of salt and kelp and fish. He thought that no two planets ever had quite the same smell, and that none was as rich as Terra's.

"This is a fair world," he said slowly.

"It is the only one," said Kormt. "Man came from here; and to this, in the end, he must return."

"I wonder—" Jorun sighed. "Take me; not one atom of my body was from this soil before I landed. My people lived on Fulkhis for ages, and changed to meet its conditions. They would not be happy on Terra."

"The atoms are nothing," said Kormt. "It is the form which matters, and that was given to you by Earth."

Jorun studied him for a moment. Kormt was like most of this planet's ten million or so people—a dark, stocky folk, though there were more blond and red-haired throwbacks here than in the rest of the Galaxy. He was old for a primitive untreated by medical science—he must be almost two hundred years old—but his back was straight, and his stride firm. The coarse, jut-nosed face held an odd strength. Jorun was nearing his thousandth birthday, but couldn't help feeling like a child in Kormt's presence.

That didn't make sense. These few dwellers on Terra were a backward and impoverished race of peasants and handicraftsmen; they were ignorant and unadventurous; they had been static for more thousands of years than anyone knew. What could they have to say to the ancient and mighty civilization which had almost forgotten their little planet?

Kormt looked at the declining sun. "I must go now," he said. "There are the evening chores to do. I will be in town tonight if you should wish to see me."

"I probably will," said Jorun. "There's a lot to do, readying the evacuation, and you're a big help."

The old man bowed with grave courtesy, turned, and walked off down the road. He wore the common costume of Terran men, as archaic in style as in its woven-fabric material: hat, jacket, loose trousers, a long staff in his hand. Contrasting the drab blue of Kormt's dress, Jorun's vivid tunic of shifting rainbow hues was like a flame.

The psychotechnician sighed again, watching him go. He liked the old fellow. It would be criminal to leave him here alone, but the law forbade force—physical or mental—and the Integrator on Corazuno wasn't going to care whether or not one aged man stayed behind. The job was to get the *race* off Terra.

A lovely world. Jorun's thin mobile features, pale-skinned and large-eyed, turned around the horizon. *A fair world we came from.*

There were more beautiful planets in the Galaxy's swarming myriads—the indigo world-ocean of Loa, jeweled with islands; the heaven-defying mountains of Sharang; the sky of Jareb, that seemed to drip light—oh, many and many, but there was only one earth.

Jorun remembered his first sight of this world, hanging free in space to watch it after the grueling ten-day run, thirty thousand light-years, from Corazuno. It was blue as it turned before his eyes, a burnished turquoise shield blazoned with the living green and brown of its lands, and the poles

were crowned with a glimmering haze of aurora.
The belts that streaked its face and blurred the
continents were cloud, wind and water and the
gray rush of rain, like a benediction from heaven.
Beyond the planet hung its moon, a scarred golden
crescent, and he had wondered how many generations of men had looked up to it, or watched its
light like a broken bridge across moving waters.
Against the enormous cold of the sky—utter black
out to the distant coils of the nebulae, thronging
with a million frosty points of diamond-hard blaze
that were the stars—Earth had stood as a sign of
haven. To Jorun, who came from Galactic center
and its uncountable hosts of suns, heaven was
bare, this was the outer fringe where the stars
thinned away toward hideous immensity. He had
shivered a little, drawn the envelope of air and
warmth closer about him, with a convulsive movement. The silence drummed in his head. Then he
streaked for the north-pole rendezvous of his
group.

Well, he thought now, *we have a pretty routine
job. The first expedition here, five years ago, prepared the natives for the fact they'd have to go. Our
party simply has to organize these docile peasants
in time for the ships.* But it had meant a lot of hard
work, and he was tired. It would be good to finish
the job and get back home.

Or would it?

He thought of flying with Zarek, his teammate,
from the rendezvous to this area assigned as
theirs. Plains like oceans of grass, wind-rippled,
darkened with the herds of wild cattle whose hoof-
beats were a thunder in the earth; forests, hundreds of kilometers of old and mighty trees, rivers
piercing them in a long steel gleam; lakes where
fish leaped; spilling sunshine like warm rain, radi-

ance so bright it hurt his eyes, cloud-shadows swift across the land. It had all been empty of man, but still there was a vitality here which was almost frightening to Jorun. His own grim world of moors and crags and spindrift seas was a niggard beside this; here life covered the earth, filled the oceans, and made the heavens clangorous around him. He wondered if the driving energy within man the force which had raised him to the stars, made him half-god and half-demon, if that was a legacy of Terra.

Well—man had changed; over the thousands of years, natural and controlled adaptation had fitted him to the worlds he had colonized, and most of his many races could not now feel at home here. Jorun thought of his own party: round, amber-skinned Chuli from a tropic world, complaining bitterly about the cold and dryness; gay young Cluthe, gangling and bulge-chested; sophisticated Taliuvenna of the flowing dark hair and the lustrous eyes—no, to them Earth was only one more planet, out of thousands they had seen in their long lives.

And I'm a sentimental fool.

He could have willed the vague regret out of his trained nervous system, but he didn't want to. This was the last time human eyes would ever look on Earth, and somehow Jorun felt that it should be more to him than just another psychotechnic job.

"Hello, good sir."

He turned at the voice and forced his tired lips into a friendly smile. "Hello, Julith," he said. It was a wise policy to learn the names of the townspeople, at least, and she was a great-great-granddaughter of the Speaker.

She was some thirteen or fourteen years old, a freckle-faced child with a shy smile, and steady green eyes. There was a certain awkward grace about her, and she seemed more imaginative than most of her stolid race. She curtsied quaintly for him, her bare foot reaching out under the long smock which was daily female dress here.

"Are you busy, good sir?" she asked.

"Well, not too much," said Jorun. He was glad of a chance to talk; it silenced his thoughts. "What can I do for you?"

"I wondered—" She hesitated, then, breathlessly: "I wonder if you could give me a lift down to the beach? Only for an hour or two. It's too far to walk there before I have to be home, and I can't borrow a car, or even a horse. If it won't be any trouble, sir."

"Mmmmm—shouldn't you be at home now? Isn't there milking and so on to do?"

"Oh, I don't live on a farm, good sir. My father is a baker."

"Yes, yes, so he is. I should have remembered." Jorun considered for an instant. There was enough to do in town, and it wasn't fair for him to play hooky while Zarek worked alone. "Why do you want to go to the beach, Julith?"

"We'll be busy packing up," she said. "Starting tomorrow, I guess. This is my last chance to see it."

Jorun's mouth twisted a little. "All right," he said; "I'll take you."

"You are very kind, good sir," she said gravely.

He didn't reply, but held out his arm, and she clasped it with one hand while her other arm gripped his waist. The generator inside his skull responded to his will, reaching out and clawing it-self to the fabric of forces and energies which was physical space. They rose quietly, and went so slowly seaward that he didn't have to raise a windscreen.

"Will we be able to fly like this when we get to the stars?" she asked.

"I'm afraid not, Julith," he said. "You see, the people of my civilization are born this way. Thousands of years ago, men learned how to control the great basic forces of the cosmos with only a small bit of energy. Finally they used artificial mutation—that is, they changed themselves, slowly, over many generations, until their brains grew a new part that could generate this controlling force. We can now, even, fly between the stars, by this power. But your people don't have that brain, so we had to build space ships to take you away."

"I see," she said.

"Your great-great-grandchildren can be like us, if your people want to be changed thus."

"They didn't want to change before," she answered. "I don't think they'll do it now, even in their new home." Her voice held no bitterness; it was an acceptance.

Privately, Jorun doubted it. The psychic shock of this uprooting would be bound to destroy the old traditions of the Terrans; it would not take many centuries before they were culturally assimilated by Galactic Civilization.

Assimilated—nice euphemism. Why not just say—eaten?

They landed on the beach. It was broad and white, running in dunes from the thin, harsh, salt-streaked grass to the roar and tumble of surf. The sun was low over the watery horizon, filling the damp, blowing air with gold. Jorun could almost look directly at its huge disc.

He sat down. The sand gritted tinily under him, and the wind rumpled this hair and filled his nostrils with its sharp wet smell. He picked up a conch and turned it over in his fingers, wondering at the intricate architecture of it.

"If you hold it to your ear," said Julith, "you can hear the sea." Her childish voice was curiously tender around the rough syllables of Earth's language.

He nodded and obeyed her hint. It was only the small pulse of blood within him—you heard the same thing out in the great hollow silence of space—but it did sing of restless immensities, wind and foam, and the long waves marching under the moon.

"I have two of them myself," said Julith. "I want them so I can always remember this beach. And my children and their children will hold them, too, and hear our sea talking." She folded his fingers around the shell. "You keep this one for yourself."

"Thank you," he said. "I will."

The combers rolled in, booming and spouting against the land. The Terrans called them the horses of God. A thin cloud in the west was turning rose and gold.

"Are there oceans on our new planet?" asked Julith.

"Yes," he said. "It's the most Earthlike world we could find that wasn't already inhabited. You'll be happy there."

But the trees and grasses, the soil and the fruits thereof, the beasts of the field and the birds of the air and the fish of the waters beneath, form and color, smell and sound, taste and texture, every-

thing is different. Is alien. The difference is small, subtle, but it is the abyss of two billion years of separate evolution, and no other world can ever quite be Earth.

Julith looked straight at him with solemn eyes. "Are you folk afraid of Hulduvians?" she asked.

"Why, no," he said. "Of course not."

"Then why are you giving Earth to them?" It was a soft question, but it trembled just a little.

"I thought all your people understood the reason by now," said Jorun. "Civilization—the civilization of man and his non-human allies—has moved inward, toward the great star-clusters of Galactic center. This part of space means nothing to us any more; it's almost a desert. You haven't seen starlight till you've been by Sagittarius. Now the Hulduvians are another civilization. They are not the least bit like us; they live on big, poisonous worlds like Jupiter and Saturn. I think they would seem like pretty nice monsters if they weren't so alien to us that neither side can really understand the other. They use the cosmic energies too, but in a different way—and their way interferes with ours just as ours interferes with theirs. Different brains, you see.

"Anyway, it was decided that the two civilizations would get along best by just staying away from each other. If they divided up the Galaxy between them, there would be no interference; it would be too far from one civilization to the other. The Hulduvians were, really, very nice about it. They're willing to take the outer rim, even if there are fewer stars, and let us have the center.

"So by the agreement, we've got to have all men and manlike beings out of their territory before they come to settle it, just as they'll move out of ours. Their colonists won't be coming to Jupiter and Saturn for centuries yet; but even so, we have to clear the Sirius Sector now, because there'll be a lot of work to do elsewhere. Fortunately, there are only a few people living in this whole part of space. The Sirius Sector has been an isolated, primi—ah—quiet region since the First Empire fell, fifty thousand years ago."

Julith's voice rose a little. "But those people are *us!*"

"And the folk of Alpha Centauri and Procyon and Sirius and—oh, hundreds of other stars. Yet all of you together are only one tiny drop in the quadrillions of the Galaxy. Don't you see, Julith, you have to move for the good of all of us?"

"Yes," she said. "Yes, I know all that."

She got us, shaking herself. "Let's go swimming."

Jorun smiled and shook his head. "No, I'll wait for you if you want to go."

She nodded and ran off down the beach, sheltering behind a dune to put on a bathing-suit. The Terrans had a nudity taboo, in spite of the mild interglacial climate; typical primitive irrationality. Jorun lay back, folding his arms behind his head, and looked up at the darkening sky. The evening star twinkled forth, low and white on the dusk-blue horizon. Venus—or was it Mercury? He wasn't sure. He wished he knew more about the early history of the Solar System, the first men to ride their thunderous rockets out to die on unknown hell-worlds—the first clumsy steps toward the stars. He could look it up in the archives of Corazuno, but he knew he never would. Too much else to do, too much to remember. Probably less than one per cent of mankind's throngs even knew where Earth was, today—though, for a while, it had been quite a tourist center. But that was perhaps thirty thousand years ago.

Because this world, out of all the billions, has certain physical characteristics, he thought, *my race has made them into standards. Our basic units of length and time and acceleration, our comparisons by which we classify the swarming planets of the Galaxy, they all go back ultimately to Earth. We bear that unspoken memorial to our birthplace within our whole civilization, and will bear it forever. But has she given us more than that? Are our own selves, bodies and minds and dreams, are they also the children of Earth?*

Now he was thinking like Kormt, stubborn old Kormt who clung with such a blind strength to this land simply because it was his. When you considered all the races of this wanderfooted species—how many of them there were, how many kinds of man between the stars! And yet they all walked upright; they all had two eyes and a nose between and a mouth below; they were all cells of that great and ancient culture which had begun here, eons past, with the first hairy half-man who kindled a fire against night. If Earth had not had darkness and cold and prowling beasts, oxygen and cellulose and flint, that culture might never had gestated.

I'm getting illogical. Too tired, nerves worn too thin, psychosomatic control slipping. Now Earth is becoming some obscure mother-symbol for me.

Or has she always been one, for the whole race of us?

A sea gull cried harshly overhead and soared from view.

The sunset was smoldering away and dusk rose like fog out of the ground. Julith came running back to him, her face indistinct in the gloom. She was breathing hard, and he couldn't tell if the catch in her voice was laughter or weeping.

"I'd better be getting home," she said.

They flew slowly back. The town was a yellow twinkle of lights, warmth gleaming from windows across many empty kilometers. Jorun set the girl down outside her home.

"Thank you, good sir," she said, curtseying. "Won't you come in to dinner?"

"Well—"

The door opened, etching the girl black against the ruddiness inside. Jorun's luminous tunic made him like a torch in the dark. "Why, it's the starman," said a woman's voice.

"I took your daughter for a swim," he explained. "I hope you don't mind."

"And if we did, what would it matter?" grumbled a bass tone. Jorun recognized Kormt; the old man must have come as a guest from his farm on the outskirts. "What could we do about it?"

"Now, Granther, that's no way to talk to the gentleman," said the woman. "He's been very kind. Won't you come eat with us, good sir?"

Jorun refused twice, in case they were only being polite, then accepted gladly enough. He was tired of cookery at the inn where he and Zarek boarded. "Thank you."

He entered, ducking under the low door. A single long, smoky-raftered room was kitchen, dining room, and parlor; doors led off to the sleeping quarters. It was furnished with a clumsy elegance, skin rugs, oak wainscoting, carved pillars, glowing ornaments of hammered copper. A radium clock, which must be incredibly old, stood on the stone mantel, above a snapping fire; a chemical-powered gun, obviously of local manufacture, hung over it. Julith's parents, a plain, quiet peasant couple, conducted him to the end of the wooden table, while half a dozen children watched him with large eyes. The younger children were the only Terrans who seemed to find this removal an adventure.

The meal was good and plentiful: meat, vegetables, bread, beer, milk, ice cream, coffee, all of it from the farms hereabouts. There wasn't much trade between the few thousand communities of Earth; they were practically self-sufficient. The company ate in silence, as was the custom here. When they were finished, Jorun wanted to go, but it would have been rude to leave immediately. He went over to a chair by the fireplace, across from one in which Kormt sprawled.

The old man took out a big-bowled pipe and began stuffing it. Shadows wove across his seamed brown face, his eyes were a gleam out of darkness. "I'll go down to City Hall with you soon," he said. "I imagine that's where the work is going on."

"Yes," said Jorun. "I can relieve Zarek at it. I'd appreciate it if you did come, good sir. Your influence is very steadying on these people."

"It should be," said Kormt. "I've been their Speaker for almost a hundred years. And my father Gerlaug was before me, and his father Kormt was before him." He took a brand from the fire and held it over his pipe, puffing hard, looking up at Jorun through tangled brows. "Who was your great-grandfather?"

"Why—I don't know. I imagine he's still alive somewhere, but—"

"I thought so. No marriage. No family. No home.

No tradition." Kormt shook his massive head, slowly. "I pity you Galactics!"

"Now please, good sir—" Damn it all, the old clodhopper could get as irritating as a faulty computer. "We have records that go back to before man left this planet. Records of everything. It is you who have forgotten."

Kormt smiled and puffed blue clouds at him. "That's not what I meant."

"Do you mean you think it is good for men to live a life that is unchanging, that is just the same from century to century—no new dreams, no new triumphs, always the same grubbling rounds of days? I cannot agree."

Jorun's mind flickered over history, trying to evaluate the basic motivations of his opponent. Partly cultural, partly biological, that must be it. Once Terra had been the center of the civilized universe. But the long migration starward, especially after the fall of the First Empire, drained off the most venturesome elements of the population. That drain went on for thousands of years.

You couldn't call them stagnant. Their life was too healthy, their civilization too rich in its own way—folk art, folk music, ceremony, religion, the intimacy of family life which the Galactics had lost—for that term. But to one who flew between the streaming suns, it was a small existence.

Kormt's voice broke in on his reverie. "Dreams, triumphs, work, deeds, love and life and finally death and the long sleep in the earth," he said. "Why should we want to change them? They never grow old; they are new for each child that is born."

"Well," said Jorun, and stopped. You couldn't really answer that kind of logic. It wasn't logic at all, but something deeper.

"Well," he started over, after a while, "as you

know, this evacuation was forced on us, too. We don't want to move you, but we must."

"Oh, yes," said Kormt. "You have been very nice about it. It would have been easier, in a way, if you'd come with fire and gun and chains for us, like the barbarians did long ago. We could have understood you better then."

"At best, it will be hard for your people," said Jorun. "It will be a shock, and they'll need leaders to guide them through it. You have a duty to help them out there, good sir."

"Maybe." Kormt blew a series of smoke rings at his youngest descendant, three years old, who crowed with laughter and climbed up on his knee. "But they'll manage."

"You can't seem to realize," said Jorun, "that you are the *last man on Earth* who refuses to go. You will be *alone*. For the rest of your life! We couldn't come back for you later under any circumstances, because there'll be Hulduvian colonies between Sol and Sagittarius which we would disturb in passage. You'll be alone, I say!"

Kormt shrugged. "I'm too old to change my ways; there can't be many years left me, anyway. I can live well, just off the food-stores that'll be left here." He ruffled the child's hair, but his face drew into a scowl. "Now, no more of that, good sir, if you please; I'm tired of this argument."

Jorun nodded and fell into the silence that held the rest. Terrans would sometimes sit for hours without talking, content to be in each other's nearness. He thought of Kormt, Gerlaug's son, last man on Earth, altogether alone, living alone and dying alone; and yet, he reflected, was that solitude any greater than the one in which all men dwelt all their days?

Presently the Speaker set the child down, knocked out his pipe and rose. "Come, good sir," he said, reaching for his staff. "Let us go."

They walked side by side down the street, under the dim lamps and past the yellow windows. The cobbles gave back their footfalls in a dull clatter. Once in a while they passed someone else, a vague figure which bowed to Kormt. Only one did not notice them, an old woman who walked crying between the high walls.

"They say it is never night on your worlds," said Kormt.

Jorun threw him a sidelong glance. His face was a strong jutting of highlights from sliding shadow. "Some planets have been given luminous skies," said the technician," and a few still have cities, too, where it is always light. But when every man can control the cosmic energies, there is no real reason for us to live together; most of us dwell far apart. There are very dark nights on my own world, and I cannot see any other home from my own—just the moors."

"It must be a strange life," said Kormt. "Belonging to no one."

They came out on the market-square, a broad paved space walled in by houses. There was a fountain in its middle, and a statue dug out of the ruins had been placed there. It was broken, one arm gone—but still the white slim figure of the dancing girl stood with youth and laughter, forever under the sky of Earth. Jorun knew that lovers were wont to meet here, and briefly, irrationally, he wondered how lonely the girl would be in all the millions of years to come.

The City Hall lay at the farther end of the square, big and dark, its eaves carved with dragons, and the gables topped with wing-spreading birds. It was an old building; nobody knew how many generations of men had gathered here. A long, patient line of folk stood outside it, shuffling in one by one to the registry desk; emerging, they went off quietly into the darkness, toward the temporary shelters erected for them.

Walking by the line, Jorun picked faces out of the shadows. There was a young mother holding a crying child, her head bent over it in a timeless pose, murmuring to soothe it. There was a mechanic, still sooty from his work, smiling wearily at some tired joke of the man behind him. There was a scowling, black-browed peasant who muttered a curse as Jorun went by; the rest seemed to accept their fate meekly enough. There was a priest, his head bowed, alone with his God. There was a younger man, his hands clenching and unclenching, big helpless hands, and Jorun heard him saying to someone else: "—if they could have waited till after harvest. I hate to let good grain stand in the field."

Jorun went into the main room, toward the desk at the head of the line. Hulking hairless Zarek was patiently questioning each of the hundreds who came, hat in hand, before him: name, age, sex, occupation, dependents, special needs or desires. He punched the answers out on the recorder machine, half a million lives were held in its electronic memory.

"Oh, there you are," his bass rumbled. "Where have you been?"

I had to do some concy work," said Jorun. That was a private code term, among others: concy, conciliation, anything to make the evacuation go smoothly. "Sorry to be so late. I'll take over now."

"All right. I think we can wind the whole thing

up by midnight." Zarek smiled and clapped him on
the back to go out for supper and sleep. Jorun
beckoned to the next Terran and settled down to
the long, almost mindless routine of registration.
He was interrupted once by Kormt, who yawned
mightily and bade him good night; otherwise it
was a steady, half-conscious interval in which one
anonymous face after another passed by. He was
dimly surprised when the last one came up. This
was a plump, cheerful, middle-aged fellow with
small shrewd eyes, a little more colorfully dressed
than the others. He gave his occupation as
merchant—a minor tradesman, he explained, deal-
ing in the little things it was more convenient for
the peasants to buy than to manufacture
themselves.

"I hope you haven't been waiting too long," said
Jorun. Concy statement.

"Oh, no." The merchant grinned. "I knew those
dumb farmers would be here for hours, so I just
went to bed and got up half an hour ago, when it
was about over."

"Clever," Jorun rose, sighed, and stretched. The
big room was cavernously empty, its lights a harsh
glare. It was very quiet here.

"Well, sir, I'm a middling smart chap, if I say it
as shouldn't. And you know, I'd like to express my
appreciation for all you're doing for us."

"Can't say we're doing much." Jorun locked the
machine.

"Oh, the apple-knockers may not like it, but
really, good sir, this hasn't been any place for a
man of enterprise. It's dead. I'd have got out long
ago if there'd been any transportation. Now, when
we're getting back into civilization, there'll be
some real opportunities. I'll make my pile inside of
five years, you bet."

Jorun smiled, but there was a bleakness in him. What chance would this barbarian have even to get near the gigantic work of civilization—let alone comprehend it or take part in it. He hoped the little fellow wouldn't break his heart trying.

"Well," he said "good night, and good luck to you."

"Good night, sir. We'll meet again, I trust."

Jorun switched off the lights and went out into the square. It was completely deserted. The moon was up now, almost full, and its cold radiance dimmed the lamps. He heard a dog howling far off. The dogs of Earth—such as weren't taken along—would be lonely, too.

Well, he thought, *the job's over. Tomorrow, or the next day, the ships come.*

He felt very tired, but didn't want to sleep, and willed himself back to alertness. There hadn't been much chance to inspect the ruins, and he felt it would be appropriate to see them by moonlight.

Rising into the air, he ghosted above roofs and trees until he came to the dead city. For a while he hovered in a sky like dark velvet, a faint breeze murmured around him, and he heard the remote noise of crickets and the sea. But stillness enveloped it all, there was no real sound.

Sol City, capital of the legendary First Empire, had been enormous. It must have sprawled over forty or fifty thousand square kilometers when it was in its prime, when it was the gay and wicked heart of human civilization and swollen with the lifeblood of the stars. And yet those who built it had been men of taste, they had sought out genius to create for them. The city was not a collection of buildings; it was a balanced whole, radiating from the mighty peaks of the central palace, through colonnades and parks and leaping skyways, out to the temple-like villas of the rulers. For all its monstrous size, it had been a fairy sight, a woven lace of polished metal and white, black, red stone, colored plastic, music and light—everywhere light.

Bombarded from space; sacked again and again by the barbarian hordes who swarmed maggot-like through the bones of the slain Empire; weathered, shaken by the slow sliding of Earth's crust; pried apart by patient, delicate roots; dug over by hundreds of generations of archeologists, treasure-seekers, the idly curious; made a quarry of metal and stone for the ignorant peasants who finally huddled about it—still its empty walls and blind windows, crumbling arches and toppled pillars held a ghost of beauty and magnificence which was like a half-remembered dream. A dream the whole race had once had.

And now we're waking up.

Jorun moved silently over the ruins. Trees growing between tumbled blocks dappled them with moonlight and shadow; the marble was very white and fair against darkness. He hovered by a broken caryatid, marveling at its exquisite leaping litheness; that girl had borne tons of stone like a flower in her hair. Further on, across a street that was a lane of woods, beyond a park that was thick with forest, lay the nearly complete outline of a house. Only its rain-blurred walls stood. But he could trace the separate rooms; here a noble had entertained his friends, robes that were fluid rainbows, jewels dripping fire, swift cynical interplay of wits like sharpened swords rising above music and the

clear sweet laughter of dancing girls; here people
whose flesh was now dust had slept and made love
and lain side-by-side in darkness to watch the moving pageant of the city; here the slaves had lived
and worked and sometimes wept; here the children had played their ageless games under wil-
lows, between banks of roses. Oh, it had been a
hard a cruel time; it was well gone but it had lived.
It had embodied man, all that was noble and splendid and evil and merely wistful in the race, and
now its late children had forgotten.

A cat sprang up on one of the walls and flowed
noiselessly along it, hunting. Jorun shook himself
and flew toward the center of the city, the imperial
palace. An owl hooted somewhere, and a bat fluttered out of his way like a small damned soul
blackened by hellfire. He didn't raise a windscreen, but let the air blow around him, the air of
Earth.

The palace was almost completely wrecked, a
mountain of heaped rocks, bare bones of "eternal"
metal gnawed thin by steady ages of wind and rain
and frost, but once it must have been gigantic. Men
rarely built that big nowadays, they didn't need to;
and the whole human spirit had changed, become
ever more abstract, finding its treasures within itself. But there had been an elemental magnificence
about early man and the works he raised to challenge the sky.

One tower still stood—a gutted shell, white under the stars, rising in a filigree of columns and
arches which seemed impossibly airy, as if it were
built of moonlight. Jorun settled on its broken upper balcony, dizzily high above the black-and-
white fantasy of the ruins. A hawk flew shrieking
from its nest, then there was silence.

No—wait—another yell, ringing down the star

ways, a dark streak across the moon's face. "Hai-ah!" Jorun recognized the joyful shout of young Cluthe, rushing through heaven like a demon on a broomstick, and scowled in annoyance. He didn't want to be bothered now. Jorun was little older than Cluthe—a few centuries at most—but he came of a melancholy folk; he had been born old.

Another form pursued the first. As they neared, Jorun recognized Taliuvenna's supple outline. Those two had been teamed up for one of the African districts, but—

They sensed him and came wildly out of the sky to perch on the balcony railing and swing their legs above the heights. "How're you?" asked Cluthe. His lean face laughed in the moonlight. "Whoo-oo, what a flight!"

"I'm all right," said Jorun. "You through in your sector?"

"Uh-huh. So we thought we'd just duck over and look in here. Last chance anyone'll ever have to do some sightseeing on Earth."

Taliuvenna's full lips drooped a bit as she looked over the ruins. She came from Yunith, one of the few planets where they still kept cities, and was as much a child of their soaring arrogance as Jorun of his hills and tundras and great empty seas. "I thought it would be bigger," she said.

"Well, they were building this fifty or sixty thousand years ago," said Cluthe. "Can't expect too much."

"There is good art left here," said Jorun. "Pieces which for one reason or another weren't carried off. But you have to look around for it."

"I've seen a lot of it already, in museums," said Taliuvenna. "Not bad."

"C'mon, Tally," cried Cluthe. He touched her

shoulder and sprang into the air. "Tag! You're it!"

She screamed with laughter and shot off after him. They rushed across the wilderness, weaving in and out of empty windows, and broken colonnades, and their shouts woke a clamor of echoes.

Jorun sighed. *I'd better go to bed*, he thought. *It's late.*

The spaceship was a steely pillar against a low gray sky. Now and then a fine rain would drizzle down, blurring it from sight; then that would end, and the ship's flanks would glisten as if they were polished. Clouds scudded overhead like flying smoke, and the wind was loud in the trees.

The line of Terrans moving slowly into the vessel seemed to go on forever. A couple of the ship's crew flew above them, throwing out a shield against the rain. They shuffled without much talk or expression, pushing carts filled with their little possessions. Jorun stood to one side, watching them go by, one face after another—scored and darkened by the sun of Earth, the winds of Earth, hands still grimy with the soil of Earth.

Well, he thought, *there they go. They aren't being as emotional about it as I thought they would. I wonder if they really do care.*

Julith went past with her parents. She saw him and darted from the line and curtsied before him.

"Good-by, good sir," she said. Looking up, she showed him a small and serious face. "Will I ever see you again?"

"Well," he lied, "I might look in on you sometime."

"Please do! In a few years, maybe, when you can."

It takes many generations to raise a people like this to our standard. In a few years—to me—she'll be in her grave.

"I'm sure you'll be very happy," he said.

She gulped. "Yes," she said, so low he could hardly hear her. "Yes, I know I will." She turned and ran back to her mother. The raindrops glistened in her hair.

Zarek came up behind Jorun. "I made a last-minute sweep of the whole area," he said. "Detected no sign of human life. So it's all taken care of, except your old man."

"Good," said Jorun tonelessly.

"I wish you could do something about him."

"So do I."

Zarek strolled off again.

A young man and woman, walking hand in hand, turned out of the line not far away and stood for a little while. A spaceman zoomed over to them. "Better get back," he warned. "You'll get rained on."

"That's what we wanted," said the young man.

The spaceman shrugged and resumed his hovering. Presently the couple re-entered the line.

The tail of the procession went by Jorun and the ship swallowed it fast. The rain fell harder, bouncing off his force-shield like silver spears. Lightning winked in the west, and he heard the distant exuberance of thunder.

Kormt came walking slowly toward him. Rain streamed off his clothes and matted his long gray hair and beard. His wooden shoes made a wet sound in the mud. Jorun extended the force-shield to cover him. "I hope you've changed your mind," said the Fulkhisian.

"No, I haven't," said Kormt. "I just stayed away till everybody was aboard. Don't like good-bys."

"You don't know what you're doing," said Jorun for the—thousandth?—time. "It's plain madness to stay here alone."

"I told you I don't like good-bys," said Kormt harshly.

"I have to go advise the captain of the ship," said Jorun. "You have maybe half an hour before she lifts. Nobody will laugh at you for changing your mind."

"I won't." Kormt smiled without warmth. "You people are the future, I guess. Why can't you leave the past alone? I'm the past." He looked toward the far hills, hidden by the noisy rain. "I like it here, Galactic. That should be enough for you."

"Well, then—" Jorun held out his hand in the archaic gesture of Earth. "Good-by."

"Good-by." Kormt took the hand with a brief, indifferent clasp. Then he turned and walked off toward the village. Jorun watched him till he was out of sight.

The technician paused in the air-lock door, looking over the gray landscape and the village from whose chimneys no smoke rose. *Farewell, my mother*, he thought. And then, surprising himself: *Maybe Kormt is doing the right thing after all.*

He entered the ship and the door closed behind him.

Toward evening, the clouds lifted and the sky showed a clear pale blue—as if it had been washed clean—and the grass and leaves glistened. Kormt came out of the house to watch the sunset. It was a good one, all flame and gold. A pity little Julith wasn't here to see it; she'd always liked sunsets. But Julith was so far away now that if she sent a call to him, calling with the speed of light, it would not come before he was dead.

Nothing would come to him. Not ever again.

He tamped his pipe with a horny thumb and lit it

and drew a deep cloud into his lungs. Hands in pockets, he strolled down the wet streets. The sound of his clogs was unexpectedly loud.

Well, son, he thought, *now you've got a whole world all to yourself, to do with just as you like. You're the richest man who ever lived.*

There was no problem in keeping alive. Enough food of all kinds was stored in the town's freeze-vault to support a hundred men for the ten or twenty years remaining to him. But he'd want to stay busy. He could maybe keep three farms from going to seed—watch over fields and orchards and livestock, repair the buildings, dust and wash and light up in the evening. A man ought to keep busy.

He came to the end of the street, where it turned into a graveled road winding up toward a high hill, and followed that. Dusk was creeping over the fields, the sea was a metal streak very far away and a few early stars blinked forth. A wind was springing up, a soft murmurous wind that talked in the trees. But how quiet things were!

On top of the hill stood the chapel, a small steepled building of ancient stone. He let himself in the gate and walked around to the graveyard behind. There were many of the demure white tombstones—thousands of years of Solis Township, men and women who had lived and worked and begotten, laughed and wept and died. Some-one had put a wreath on one grave only this morning; it brushed against his leg as he went by. To-morrow it would be withered, and weeds would start to grow. He'd have to tend the chapel yard, too. Only fitting.

He found his family plot and stood with feet spread apart, fists on hips, smoking and looking down at the markers, Gerlaug Kormt's son, Tarna Huwan's daughter; these hundred years had they lain in the earth. Hello, Dad, hello, Mother. His fingers reached out and stroked the headstone of his wife. And so many of his children were here, too; sometimes he found it hard to believe that tall Gerlaug and laughing Stamm and shy, gentle Huwan were gone. He'd outlived too many people.

I had to stay, he thought. *This is my land, I am of it and I couldn't go. Someone had to stay and keep the land, if only for a little while. I can give it ten more years before the forest comes and takes it.*

Darkness grew around him. The woods beyond the hill loomed like a wall. Once he started violently; he thought he heard a child crying. No, only a bird. He cursed himself for the senseless pounding of his heart.

Gloomy place here, he thought. *Better get back to the house.*

He groped slowly out of the yard, toward the road. The stars were out now. Kormt looked up and thought he had never seen them so bright. Too bright; he didn't like it.

Go away, stars, he thought. *You took my people, but I'm staying here. This is my land.* He reached down to touch it, but the grass was cold and wet under his palm.

The gravel scrunched loudly as he walked, and the wind mumbled in the hedges, but there was no other sound. Not a voice called; not an engine turned; not a dog barked. No, he hadn't thought it would be so quiet.

And dark. No lights. Have to tend the street lamps himself—it was no fun, not being able to see the town from here, not being able to see anything except the stars. Should have remembered to bring a flashlight, but he was old and absentminded, and there was no one to remind him. When he died, there would be no one to hold his hands; no one to close his eyes and lay him in the earth—and the forests would grown in over the land and wild beasts would nuzzle his bones.

But I knew that. What of it? I'm tough enough to take it.

The stars flashed and flashed above him. Looking up, against his own will, Kormt saw how bright they were, how bright and quiet. And how very far away! He was seeing light that had left its home before he was born.

He stopped, sucking in his breath between his teeth. "No," he whispered.

This was his land. This was Earth, the home of man; it was his and he was its. This was the *land*, and not a single dustmote, crazily reeling and spinning through an endlessness of dark and silence, cold and immensity. Earth could not be so alone!

The last man alive. The last man in all the world!

He screamed, then, and began to run. His feet clattered loud on the road; the small sound was quickly swallowed by silence, and he covered his face against the relentless blaze of the stars. But there was no place to run to, no place at all.

To Earth there's no returning. She vanished with the childhood of our race. Yet as a poet once said, "No matter how far we range, the salt and rhythm of her tides will always be in our blood." One chapter has ended. Humankind's saga flows on.

A CHRONOLOGY OF THE PSYCHOTECHNIC SERIES

volume	date	event
Volume I: Psychotechnic Leagues	1958	*World War III*
	1964	"Marius"
	1965	*First Conference of Rio makes U.N. world government*
	1975	*Psychotechnic Institute established Expeditions to Mars an d Venus, then colonization*
	2004	"The Un-Man"
	2009	"The Sensitive Man"
		Second Industrial Revolution
	2035	*Second Conference of Rio, Venusian break with U.N.*
	2051	"The Big Rain"
Volume II: Cold Victory	2055	*Planetary Engineering Corps founded*
	2070	*The New Enlightenment*
	2080	*Corps becomes Order of Planetary Engineers*
	2105	*Solar Union founded*
	2120	"Quixote and the Windmill"
	2125	*Humanist Manifesto published*
	2126	*First STL ship launched*
	2130	*Beginnings of Cosmic religion*
	2140	"Holmgang" (formerly "Out of the Iron Womb")
	2170	*Humanist Revolt, Psychotechnic Institute outlawed*
	2180	"Cold Victory"
	2200	"What Shall It Profit?"
	2205	"The Troublemakers"

volume	date	event
II:	2220	["The Snows of Ganymede"]
	2270	"Brake"
Volume III: *Star Ship*	2300	*The Second Dark Ages*
	2600	
	2784	*Hyperdrive invented*
	2815	"Gypsy"
		Nomad culture develops
	2875	"Star Ship"
	2900	*Stellar Union and Coordination Service founded*
	3000	["The Acolytes"
		["The Green Thumb"]
	3100	"The Virgen Planet"
	3110	"Teucan"
	3115	"The Pirate"
	3120	[*The Peregrine*] (formerly *Star Ways*)
	3200-	*The Third Dark Ages*
	post-4000	"The Chapter Ends"

Prepared by Sandra Miesel, based in part on the chronology published by Poul Anderson in *Startling Stories*, Winter, 1955. Many dates are approximate and the author is not bound by them. Stories not collected in these Tor editions are listed in brackets.